"I think it would be best if I left," Julia said.

Slamming his fist on the counter, Tony faced her. "*I* don't think it's best. *Rachel* doesn't think it's best. My daughter loves you. How can you stand there and tell me it's in her best interest if you leave?"

"Tony, please. Don't you understand? If Social Services comes here and questions our living arrangement, you could be denied your petition for adoption. Are you that much of a gambling man? To risk losing Rachel?"

His gut churned as her words sank in. Rachel. He looked at the baby, as much his daughter as if he'd had a part in creating her. The little girl sat quietly, her right hand in her mouth, her eyes wide.

Lose Rachel?

Reaching blindly, he hauled Julia to him. "I can't lose her," he muttered into her hair. "But I won't lose *you*, either."

Dear Reader,

Merry Christmas, Happy Holidays of all sorts and welcome to another fabulous month's worth of books here at Intimate Moments. And here's a wonderful holiday gift for you: *Captive Star,* the newest book from bestselling, award-winning and just plain incredibly talented author Nora Roberts. The next of THE STARS OF MITHRA miniseries, this book has Nora's signature sizzle and spark, all wrapped up in a compellingly suspenseful plot about a couple on the run—handcuffed together!

We've got another miniseries "jewel" for you, too: *The Taming of Reid Donovan,* the latest in Marilyn Pappano's SOUTHERN KNIGHTS series. There's a twist in this one that I think will really catch you by surprise. Susan Sizemore debuts at Silhouette with *Stranger by Her Side,* a book as hot and steamy as its setting.

And then there are our Christmas books, three tantalizing tales of holiday romance. *One Christmas Knight,* by Kathleen Creighton, features one of the most memorable casts of characters I've ever met. Take one gentlemanly Southern trucker, one about-to-deliver single mom, the biggest snowstorm in a generation, put them together and what do you get? How about a book you won't be able to put down? Rebecca Daniels is back with *Yuletide Bride,* a secret child story line with a Christmas motif. And finally, welcome brand-new author Rina Naiman, whose *A Family for Christmas* is a warm and wonderful holiday debut.

Enjoy—and the very happiest of holidays to you and yours.

Leslie J. Wainger
Senior Editor and Editorial Coordinator

Please address questions and book requests to:
Silhouette Reader Service
U.S.: 3010 Walden Ave., P.O. Box 1325, Buffalo, NY 14269
Canadian: P.O. Box 609, Fort Erie, Ont. L2A 5X3

A FAMILY FOR CHRISTMAS

RINA NAIMAN

Silhouette®

INTIMATE™MOMENTS®

Published by Silhouette Books

America's Publisher of Contemporary Romance

SILHOUETTE BOOKS

ISBN 0-373-07828-5

A FAMILY FOR CHRISTMAS

Copyright © 1997 by Rina Najman

This edition published by arrangement with Harlequin Books S.A.

® and TM are trademarks of Harlequin Books S.A., used under license. Trademarks indicated with ® are registered in the United States Patent and Trademark Office, the Canadian Trade Marks Office and in other countries.

Printed in U.S.A.

Dear Reader,

Welcome to my world.

In my first book for Silhouette Intimate Moments, my world centers around the fictional town of Silver Creek, Wyoming. Deep inside my city-born body beats the heart of a cowgirl.

I love everything I'm allergic to—horses, ranches and grassy plains. Thankfully, my list also includes things I'm not allergic to, such as handsome cowboys sitting high atop their magnificent steeds…mmm…. (I also like chocolate and "I Love Lucy," as will be discovered in future books, I'm sure.)

All of that is my inspiration for writing
A Family for Christmas. The recipe is simple: take one New York-born male—Antonio "Tony" Pellegrino, determined to remain single—put him on a ranch and give him an orphaned niece. Add one feisty schoolteacher who, after losing a child of her own, doesn't want anything to do with taking care of anyone's child, let alone the man she's had a crush on since school, and you've got the kind of love story that always makes me smile.

I hope that will apply to you, too.

A Family for Christmas comes out just in time for the holiday season—in fact, I consider it my gift to myself and a gift I would present to all my friends during this time of giving. People who celebrate any of the wonderful holidays in the upcoming days will embrace the love embodied in this story for many months to come.

Interested readers can write to me at: P.O. Box 271, Rochester, NY 14526-0271.

Happy Holidays!

This book is dedicated with love to:
Carol Backus, the founder of Lake County Romance
Writers and a friend, who wouldn't let me
"talk" my way out of a contrived motivation…

Kathy Schaefer and Patricia Ryan, my critique
partners and friends, whose eyes never glazed over…

Linda Van De Walle and Dianne Hegeman, lifelong
friends who always heard only the first three chapters
of my books, but haven't disowned me…yet…

And mostly to my newly-wed husband, Raymond,
who never let me forget I was a writer…
even on days I forgot I was a wife.

Prologue

She opened the door and listened.

Silence.

Julia Rourke expelled a sigh of relief as she swung open the door of her Chicago apartment. Four o'clock. She knew her husband Hank wasn't due for two more hours, but sometimes he was home before her, and already drunk. Thankfully, not today. She'd have some quiet time to study for her finals.

The Fates must be smiling on me...at least for right now.

Between teaching third grade, attending courses for her master's degree and coming home to their nightly arguments, she hadn't had much peace lately. Sometimes she wished, in vain, for a "designated arguer."

Entering the living room, she dropped her books on the couch and turned on the switch. Pure halogen light illuminated the room, and her attention was immediately drawn to her wall unit—or rather to the gaping hole in the middle where the television and stereo had been. *Had been.*

She'd been robbed!

Taking a quick inventory, Julia saw knickknacks still on the shelves, but spread out as though... As though trying to fill in gaps. Some of the doodads were missing: Hank's autographed Mets baseball, his model Cessna, but not her collection of thimbles.

Oh, great. A picky thief.

Wait a minute. What kind of thief locked a door behind him?

Slowly she entered the kitchen. The kitchen radio still sat on the counter nearest the sink. And the sewing machine was here, as was her collection of antique European letter openers.

She opened the cabinets. The plates were here, but the silverware was gone. Oddly enough, given the circumstances at the moment, she recalled the time she had purchased the plates, at the little Navajo reservation she'd visited while Hank—

Hank had purchased the silverware! Whirling around, she stared at the empty microwave stand. *She'd* bought the stand, and *he* the microwave.

Walking quickly into the bedroom, she spied the air purifier she'd purchased just two weeks ago, but not the framed picture Hank had surprised her with on their honeymoon.

The television and stereo also belonged to Hank. She walked to the closet they shared and, with shaking hands, slowly opened it. Her clothes were still there. His were gone.

Did she really need more proof?

Yes, you did. The same way you made them test you over and over, to make absolutely sure....

Dazed, she returned to the living room and saw a piece

of yellow legal paper folded neatly in half, her name boldly printed on it. It sat on the coffee table she'd bought.

Picking it up, she read the first two words: *Dear Julia.*

Crossing over to the chair, she sat and ran her hand over the cool black leather. Then she continued to read.

He loved her, he wrote, he just couldn't take it any longer. He accepted all the blame, and was sorry. He detailed how busy he was going to be as a new lawyer. He wouldn't be able to *be there* for her. He wrote how he had certain expectations, and that she'd be better off without him.

Julia knew that—she just never expected it to hurt like this. Her hand rested on her stomach, and she swallowed hard.

Crumpling the note, she got up, closed the front door and walked on rubbery legs to the bedroom. She lay down on the bed, and her gaze rested on the hideously large fluorescent-green-and-orange Aztec fertility god he'd bought on their trip to Mexico.

Why couldn't he have taken that?

He probably thought it would do her more good than him.

She closed her eyes. The floating sensation she'd had after losing their baby returned.

The doctors said the feeling would go away.

It had.

Snatching a last piece of strength before sleep overcame her, she reached a decision of her own.

It was time for her to go away, too.

Chapter 1

"A perfect evening, Maxine." Tony Pellegrino opened the door of his house, and ushered the willowy blonde in out of the cold Wyoming October night. Tossing his black suede Stetson on the hall table, he helped his date off with her mink coat.

Maxine Mallone walked over to the sofa, putting a little bit of a come-hither hitch in her step. Tony admired the way her red dress hugged every voluptuous curve. She sank gracefully onto the overstuffed beige cushions.

"It's only going to get better." Her husky voice practically purred, and she patted the spot next to her. Catlike green eyes reinforced her promise.

Tony took a step toward her, his body primed. The phone in his office, off the living room, rang. Damn. The only thing to keep him from a date would be something urgent having to do with his ranches, so while he continued in Maxine's direction, he kept one ear on the incoming message.

"Tony," Maxine said with a sigh of exasperation. "Go take care of whatever it is." Her glossy carmine lips settled into a complacent smile.

Maxine was anything but submissive, so he knew she wanted something, and that something was one uninterrupted evening, which he'd been promising her for months, ever since she returned home to Silver Creek. For that reason alone, he didn't take offense with her for telling him what to do—something most people who knew him wouldn't think of doing.

"Go on," she urged. "I know how important it is to you."

"I'll only be a minute, and then I'm all yours."

"And I'll keep you," she called out as he left the room.

Tony ignored her implication—being one of the most sought-after bachelors in his small town, he'd heard more than one eager woman hint at commitment—and he strode quickly into his den. He removed his black suit jacket, dropping it on a chair, and, just as the caller began leaving a message, he lifted the receiver.

"This is Tony Pellegrino." He loosened his tie.

After a momentary silence, a voice belonging to an older woman, spoke. "Mr. Pellegrino, this is highly irregular for me, but I felt you had to know, before it was too late."

Tony instantly recognized the accent, the faster-than-a-bullet speech pattern. The number displayed on his identification machine confirmed it. The call was from New York City.

His birthplace.

This couldn't be about his brothers. Matt was in Boston and Nick in Chicago. That meant... His heart raced. He willed its cadence to match the ticking of the clock on his oak desk before he spoke. "This is about Anne, isn't it?" A solid lead, after all these years?

"Yes. It's a long story, but the nuts and bolts of it is, I'm a nurse at City Hospital in Manhattan, and your sister was my patient."

"Was?" He gripped the receiver tighter. "What happened?"

"I'm sorry, Mr. Pellegrino." His spine stiffened at her tone. "Anne died six months ago."

"Six months ago? And you're just—"

"Please, Mr. Pellegrino, I know this is a shock, but if you'll let me finish…"

"Sorry, go on," he said.

"I can't talk too long, I'm at work, on my break, and I'm taking a big chance doing this, not knowing who you are and all, but I figured family should know. I found Anne's knapsack yesterday, in a storage room. It must have been tossed in there and forgotten. Anyway, there was a journal, and your name and number…"

Tony only half heard the nurse's recitation.

His search was over. Pain and sorrow spiraled through his body, and twisted around his heart. "How'd she die?" he asked.

She hesitated slightly. "Anne struggled with drugs for many years, Mr. Pellegrino."

"She died of an overdose?"

"Not exactly," the nurse began.

Maxine sauntered into the room, one perfectly tweezed eyebrow arched gently. The words *perfect evening* mocked him.

He held up his hand. She approached quietly.

"Go on, please," he said.

"Well, I figured since I was the one who found her knapsack—I mean, I never go into that storage closet—it was meant for me to call you. You see, time's running out. We kept her for four months—the poor little thing needed us, so there was no problem—and we even managed to extend it for another two, 'cause we fell in love with her, but we can't stall any longer.'' She stopped to take a breath. ''They're coming to take her away.''

''You mean to bury her? It's been six months—wouldn't that have been done already?''

''Oh, I'm going on again. Not *Anne*, Mr. Pellegrino. *Rachel*. You've got to do something before social services come and take *her* away.''

Rachel?

''This isn't making sense. I don't know a Rachel,'' Tony said, his lack of comprehension putting a noticeable edge in his voice.

''Oh, of course you don't. Not yet. Rachel's your niece.''

''My...my niece?''

''Yes, your niece. Your sister died in childbirth.''

''Tony, I don't know if I'm ready for this.'' Maxine shook her head.

Tony walked down the aisle of the grocery store, searching for the items Miss Irene said he'd need before the baby came.

''That's okay, neither do I. I'm not asking you to give up anything, Maxine. We can see each other like always, but at least Rachel will be with her family.''

''I still don't see why one of your brothers couldn't take her.''

''I'm sorry I haven't filled you in on all the details. It's been a busy two weeks. In New York, when we met to see Rachel for the first time, Matt, Nick and I discussed this. Matt's law career is just taking off, and Nick's police work involves him being gone for too many hours, so they can't do it. I'm in the best position to make sure she'll have a stable life.'' He took Maxine's hand. ''And anyway, she's just a baby. How much trouble can she be?''

''A family could handle her better. Kids grow up and change.''

Tony knew that better than most; he'd grown up with more changes in his life than any child should have to endure. After reading his sister's journal, and discovering that although she'd been adopted as a baby, she'd had a very hard life, he was damned if his niece would have to go through a repeat performance.

''She's not going to strangers,'' he said through clenched teeth, then took in a calming breath and smiled. ''Besides, when she grows up, you know, two or three years old, she'll be able to do practically everything on her own. You'll see.'' He patted her hand, confident he'd be able to maintain the status quo he'd worked hard to acquire, and reached for the Pampers. ''She's barely six months old. She'll spend most of her time at home, sleeping. Now, have you got any idea where the bottles are?''

''Are you serious?'' Maxine walked to the next aisle, looking at the shelves, muttering, ''Bottles. Bottles of Moët, yes. Baby bottles...''

Tony chuckled and continued down his aisle. Within a few minutes, he was surrounded by friendly neighbors who'd heard about his news.

''What's the story, boy?'' Mr. Milligan asked, patting him on the back good-naturedly. ''Are you a father, yet?''

''When's the young'n due to arrive?'' Mrs. Stover chimed in.

Tony shrugged. ''Well, I met with the judge in New York last week, and now John is there, putting the finishing touches on the paperwork.'' He trusted his lawyer and friend John Lewiston implicitly, and was waiting to hear from him any day now.

"Tony, you're gonna get her, aren't you?" Mrs. Winslow asked, her kind face looking at him in serious concern. "She's kin."

Tony's neighbors had loved him ever since he came back to this dying town ten years ago, bought the old Crowley Ranch—now called Pellegrino Ranch—expanded it to include the one next door, and hired only local workers to run it, reviving the economy. The town never failed to let him know how much they cared about him.

He put a hand on her arm. "I can only tell you what John told me. He believes the judge will make me her legal guardian." Tony felt an ache in his gut at the possibility that something might go wrong, that he might not get Rachel. He'd seen her only twice, and he couldn't have said anything about her other than she was indeed a baby—and that maybe her eyes *were* just like Annie's. He couldn't be sure about that, but he did know that losing her would be like losing Anne all over, and he didn't want to go through that again.

Mentally shaking himself, he looked up over the heads of his well-wishers and spotted a woman, about thirty-two or -three, with angular features, large red-rimmed glasses, and light brown hair pulled tightly into a bun, peering at him from the corner of an aisle. She wet her full lips, and he caught his breath.

"Once you get her, don't let her go, Tony," Mr. Milligan said, slapping him on the back.

"What?" Tony said, momentarily distracted by the woman's quiet allure. When he looked back at aisle four, the woman had disappeared.

When was the last time he'd been so affected by a woman? He didn't know, and the conversation around him didn't allow him any time to ponder it. Tony listened patiently to the advice of the women on child care, the bragging of the men on their grown children's accomplishments, and finally managed to extricate himself. He grabbed the diapers and headed for the cashier.

Maxine was waiting for him with some bottles of food and toys. "I guess she'll need these." She saw Tony's eyebrows go up, and sighed. "What's wrong?"

"That's solid food. She doesn't have any teeth."

"There, you see. I don't know babies, Tony."

"What's to know? Don't worry so much, Maxine. She's a quiet kid, and before we know it, she'll blend right in. Nothing much has to be different."

"Oh, are you kidding yourself. This is going to be a major upheaval, and I'm not all that sure I'm ready for another one, having just moved up here, and settling in and..."

Maxine continued talking, but a sudden flash of memory replaced her words in Tony's mind. As he went through the checkout line, the sounds around him blurred into background noise....

I just can't take it no more, Tony. It's best this way. Someone will come for you all soon. Make sure your brothers and sister is okay till then.

His mother had kissed him, and then she'd been gone, her two suitcases clanking against each rickety wooden step as she ran down the stairs and jumped into the waiting car. The man driving it hadn't even turned his head, but his mother had.

She'd waved goodbye....

"Well, I guess this doesn't have to be goodbye, either," Maxine said. "So maybe you're right. I think we're good together, so maybe we'll just work something out later."

"Yeah," he muttered, knowing she was blissfully unaware of the memory he'd just endured. Maxine wasn't interested in his past. Just his future. She never pretended to be more than she was—a woman who liked the good life, and all it could offer her. Just like all the women he'd dated over the past few years. There were no surprises, no bumps in the road emotionally, with Maxine. That was the way he liked it.

No more changes. No more surprises.

And that was good.

"You're hired. You can start on Monday. Welcome to Pellegrino Ranch, and welcome home, Julia."

"Thanks, Rose." Julia Rourke shook Rose Shepherd's hand and relaxed in her seat. She and Rose had been friends from their sophomore year in high school until Julia left Silver Creek to find her happiness in Chicago. It was great to see her again, and especially to know she'd be working with her. Rose was also thirty-four, and with her curly mop of honey-blond hair framing her pixielike face, she still looked like the girl Julia had left behind.

"Do you think you can be happy here again, Jules?"

Julia smiled at how easily her old nickname slipped from Rose's lips. In the past seventeen years, nothing had really changed. "After spending most of my time in high school hanging out with you and your cowboy brothers, I think I'll be able to settle here without much trouble. You know, once a cowgirl, always a cowgirl." She pushed back the glasses that constantly slipped down her nose. "Besides, it's a moot point, anyway. My mother needs me now that my father..." Blinking back the tears that still formed at the mere thought of her father, Julia smiled wistfully.

Rose's oval face softened, and her eyes clouded over. "I'm mighty sorry about your daddy, Jules. He was a good man."

She nodded. "I still miss him."

"Sugar, it's only been a little over a year. Give yourself

some time." The pretty woman patted Julia's hand. "But you're back home again, and now you've got yourself a great job. With me at the cattle ranch next door, and you here at the stud ranch, we'll see each other often. It was pure good luck that made you turn up the same day that Cindy had to leave."

Straightening the collar of her white blouse, Julia said, "Luck had nothing to do with it. While in town with my mother, I met Cindy's husband, and he told me about them relocating. My mother mentioned that Cindy had been the office manager here, so I hurried over." Julia knew it was more the hand of fate at play here than it was luck.

"Well, whatever you think it is, I think it's grand luck." She looked at the ground and whispered, "It's good to have you to talk to again, Jules." Rose rummaged in her purse, walked over to the pop machine in the hallway and plunked in her three quarters.

"What's wrong? Is everything all right between you and Tom?"

"Yes." Rose retrieved the can from the machine, snapped open the top and took a sip, before walking back to her desk and sitting on the chair near Julia. Her hands shook. "I hope I don't bring up old hurts. I know it was over a year ago that it happened to you...."

Bitterness found its way to Julia's mouth. "Oh, Rose. A miscarriage?"

Rose nodded. "Our third."

Julia swallowed the acid taste. "You must be devastated."

"We are."

"What can I do?"

"Just what you're doing. Just listening. Don't go on, like my other friends, telling me about how I should put it behind me, keep trying, that it wasn't meant to be, and so on.'' She paused. ''I hope it's not too hard for you, since you…you know.''

''It's okay. Like you said, it's been over a year, and time heals…some pains.'' Julia's voice hitched, but it went unnoticed. The town didn't have to know everything.

Rose smiled shakily. ''Well, we are still trying, and now we're talking about adoption.''

''Adoption? Are you sure that's what Tom really wants?''

Rose shrugged. ''He says so, and I believe him. He's great with kids.''

But they won't be his.

Julia was grateful that the door to the outer office opened at precisely that moment. She was spared having to think of something supportive to say, and she didn't want Rose asking any probing questions about her life.

They turned at the sound of a man's annoyed voice.

''For the last time, Maxine, I'm sorry we had to leave New York early, but I wanted to get home today.''

Rose sprang to her feet, wiped her eyes and hurried toward the voices. ''You got her!'' Rose stopped in front of Tony Pellegrino and reached for the bundle in his arms. ''Give me that little sugar-child.''

Julia watched as the baby girl eagerly kicked her feet and jerked her arms at the sound of Rose's voice. She happily went into her arms. Julia knew she would make a wonderful mother, and hoped she'd have another chance.

With her own kids…

She clenched her jaw, her attention drawn to the man who stood proudly looking on, then clutched the bag on her lap. Six-plus feet of raw masculinity leaned back against the desk in the outer office, his arms crossed over his chest, muscles stretching his expensive suit.

Tony Pellegrino, all grown up.

Julia recalled when he'd been the new kid at their small high school. After a rocky start—always in trouble, always testing everyone around him—he'd seemed to settle down a bit. And it hadn't been too long after that that he became captain of the football and baseball teams, and a track star. He had a drive, almost an inner ambition, to be the best at whatever he did, and sometimes it got him into trouble.

Julia smiled as she stared at Tony's chiseled features—dark skin, aquiline nose and square jaw, so well-defined, so different today than from the day she'd been in the school office helping the secretary with some filing when Tony was hauled in to answer for one of his transgressions. He'd quickly become one of the most popular boys at the high school, in his black jeans and T-shirts, dating a new girl almost every month. Julia had had a crush on him ever since she could remember, but because she was one year behind him, he'd never even given her a second glance.

And now she'd be working with him.

Good thing there was a statute of limitations on adolescent yearnings.

Julia slowly approached the group. Maxine Mallone stood by Tony's side, still as beautiful as she'd been in high school, looking smart in her own red designer suit, tailored to fit her body like a snake's skin. Julia felt dowdy in her gray tweed suit—especially because it hung on her body. She'd lost a lot of weight, and while she hadn't given her clothes much consideration lately, right now, as she tugged on the jacket, she wished she'd worn anything but this sensible outfit.

Rose spoke again as she neared the doorway. "Has she been across the yard to the house yet?"

"No, we came straight here from the airport. I needed to get the tickets for tonight's concert in Casper." He looked at Maxine. "Are you sure you don't mind going without me?" he asked tersely.

Julia could see the stress lines bracketing Tony's mouth.

"Oh, no," Maxine gushed, oblivious to his displeasure. "And besides, I'm sure I can find someone to go with me, darling. Maybe Jillian."

Darling. The word settled inside Julia like a heavy meal. Tony raked a hand through his hair. She watched his long fingers, and wondered what it would feel like to run hers through the straight brown strands. Then she fisted her hand. It was no use dreaming about something she would never experience.

And something I don't even want to experience anyway. Great. Tempt fate, why don't you?

Julia shoved aside the second voice and its warped sense of humor when Tony spoke again. "Good." He turned to Rose, whose eyebrows were raised. "The tickets were ordered weeks ago, and it's a sold-out show. I didn't want to leave Rachel with a baby-sitter on her first night here, and I didn't see a reason why Maxine should miss out on it."

"Uh-huh." Rose didn't break eye contact.

Maxine added, "And important people will be there, people good for my career." She hugged Tony's arm. "I'm so glad you understand."

He nodded, then glanced into the baby's eyes, and Julia remembered the eye contact she'd had with him at the grocery store earlier today. It had been great to see him surrounded by friends, and to overhear the mounds of unsolicited advice he had to endure.

She wondered if he'd remember her.

Julia caught her breath and refocused on the present, looking up and meeting his glance.

"Excuse me, I didn't know we had...company?" Tony asked, his eyes narrowed. "I know you, don't I?"

Apparently not as well as I'd hoped.

"I'm Julia Rourke. Your new office manager." So he didn't recall her from this morning. It was no big deal. It probably meant that he wouldn't remember her from high school, either. But why should he? He'd been surrounded by his bevy of beauties. He wouldn't recall the five times he'd spoken to her in the hallway. Only she would.

Not that she did.

"Julia Rourke? Frank Rourke's daughter?" She nodded, and awareness lit his eyes. "Maxine, this is Julia Rourke. Her father was foreman here."

"Oh. He died recently, didn't he?" Maxine asked.

"Last year," Julia said.

"Your father was a good man, and a great foreman," Tony said. "He had a wicked sense of humor," he added warmly. "He's missed around here."

"Thanks. It's nice hearing that."

"I know your father was buried elsewhere, but I don't remember seeing you here, at his memorial services."

"He's buried in Iowa, his birthplace. His lodge has a cemetery there." She ignored his first comment, not wanting to recall that time of her life, and why she hadn't been able to be here for the memorial service.

"So, now you're home again?"

"Yes. My mother's health started failing her recently, so I came home." That was all they had to know, she thought.

Rose chimed in. "Julia worked as an office manager in Chicago for twelve years. She supervised a staff of two hundred before she decided to go into—" Julia quickly shook her head, and Rose switched tracks "—before she came back home." She frowned at Julia.

Rachel held out her arms to Maxine, who took her reluctantly, smiling only when Tony looked her way. She made two quirky faces, in what Julia interpreted as a way of communicating with the baby.

"I'm sure she'll be fine, Rose." He looked at Julia again. "I'd like to speak with you, to make sure you understand your responsibilities here." Shaking the baby blanket, he added, "But I have some things I have to take care of right now, unless..."

He eyed Maxine speculatively. She still held the child slightly away from her, as though afraid to have her touch her clothes.

"Um, I don't know, Tony." Maxine tried to look at her watch, and couldn't with Rachel in her arms.

Fighting her instincts, Julia didn't reach for the child. Instead, she clasped her hands together, smiling weakly when she caught Tony watching.

"Here, let me." Rose stepped in and bounced Rachel on her hip.

"Thanks." Maxine's shoulders sloped downward in obvious relief. She studied her watch. "It's late, Tony. I have to check in on my boutique and then get back to my studio with the ideas I jotted down. Then I have to get ready for the concert. I don't think I'll have time to be with the sweet little thing today. Maybe tomorrow. I've got to dash. Nice to see you both." Kissing his cheek quickly, she waved goodbye in everyone else's general direction, and like the whirlwind she'd been in high school, she spun out of the room.

Tony sighed as the door closed, then turned at Rose's sharp intake of breath. "She'll get used to having Rachel around, Rose. You'll see. She's a cute baby. How can anyone help but fall in love with such a sweet-tempered child?"

And indeed, Julia felt herself drawn to the baby, but along with those wonderful, special feelings came the blackness of reality. She knew it would take some time for the hurt to lessen, she just wished it would happen soon. Biting her lower lip, she resisted the impulse to take the baby from Rose, kiss her neck and inhale her special scent of baby lotion, shampoo and milk.

"Didn't you get married?" Tony asked Julia.

"Married, and divorced."

"I hadn't heard about that." His brow furrowed. "Last I remember, your parents were visiting you because..." Tony rolled his eyes. "Hell. I'm sorry. Your father was killed in Chicago during their visit, right?"

"Yes, he was," Julia said. She'd been afraid he'd remember that her parents had come to visit her because she was pregnant and too sick to travel. Thank goodness he'd redirected his own thoughts, albeit in another tragic direction. At least he hadn't asked her about her child, making her have to explain it to him.

Few people knew about Julia's miscarriage, since, according to her mother, after she returned, no one had asked about Julia. Everyone in town had been more concerned about making sure her mother was okay.

And that had suited Julia just fine.

Tony looked at her closely, but she knew her real secret was safe. "Now I remember. You were at the store this morning. And didn't we know each other in school, too?"

So he *did* remember her from school, and *had* noticed her this morning. Big deal. "Well, we went to the same school, but I wouldn't say we knew each other."

"Ah. Well, why didn't you join in with everyone at the store?"

"I decided to take pity on you. Besides, with the crowd around you, I'm surprised you even noticed me."

"Oh, I noticed you," he murmured. After scrutinizing her for another long moment, during which she was sure her cheeks were flaming red, he smiled. "How could I miss those eyes?"

"That's what I always say when I put on mascara and get the stuff on my cheek instead." Self-conscious, she pushed her glasses up her nose.

He laughed. "I meant they're remarkably blue." He leaned in closer.

Rose watched, a broad smile of approval on her face.

"Is that a new color, like cobalt blue?" Julia said quickly, shifting uncomfortably under his intense scrutiny.

He laughed again. "More like sapphires," he corrected casually, then took Rachel from Rose's arms and lifted her over his head. Bringing her down to his lips, he bussed her cheek loudly. She giggled and squealed in delight. "She laughs like Annie did."

"Speaking of Anne, were there any medical complications?" Rose asked.

"You mean drugs? No, luckily. I met with Sylvia, the nurse who'd phoned me, and who'd been with Annie, and she said that Annie told her she'd been clean while she was pregnant. Rachel was a little underweight at birth, but nothing worse than that, at least nothing visible at this point."

"Tony...how did it happen?" Rose cocked her head.

Julia knew small-town living allowed a certain level of familiarity, and she just hoped she wouldn't be put to the test too soon. She wasn't ready to share her past with anyone yet.

But apparently Tony didn't share her caution.

"According to Annie's journal," he said, "the couple who adopted her were incredibly strict. They kept her corralled tight, didn't let her do normal things a kid wants to do."

"Could it be—" Julia cut herself off.

Tony bounced Rachel in his arms. "What?"

"I didn't mean to butt in."

"You're not. So, could it be, what?"

Julia hadn't wanted to participate in the personal conversation—distance was the best way to remain safe—but to not continue now would draw more attention to herself, so she said, "Well, sometimes kids have a hard time adjusting to the fact that they're adopted, that they weren't wanted by their birth mother."

"She did write several times how *she* didn't have the right to tell her what to do," Tony said contemplatively. "She wrote how *she* wasn't her *real* mother. The same about her adoptive father." Tony shrugged. "So anything's possible."

"I've read how that can happen even in the best of placements," Rose added, then touched Tony's arm. "I worry about it all the time now that we're thinking of adopting."

"You've got nothing to worry about," Tony said. "You and Tom will be great parents."

"Just like you'll be...Dad," Rose teased.

"Yeah, well, it's nice to have you here again, Julia," Tony said, changing the topic. He wrapped Rachel in her blanket again, then headed toward the door.

"Will you need help with Rachel?" Rose asked. "You haven't had any experience with a baby before."

"Piece of cake. She acts like she knows who I am. And Miss Irene will be there during the day. Anyway, how much trouble can a little, sweet baby be?" He kissed her nose and smiled at them, ignoring their raised eyebrows. "I'll see you both on Monday, then we can discuss the more intimate things you'll be privy to."

Julia gasped—inaudibly, she thought—but at the door he looked at her quizzically.

"Do you have a problem with handling personal information? You know, my social security number, where I stay when I travel, things like that?"

"No, no, of course not. I'll be here at..." She looked at

Rose who mouthed, "Eight-thirty". "Eight-thirty Monday morning."

He chuckled at their byplay, nodded at Julia, then left.

"You *still* have a crush on him, don't you?" Rose asked.

"What are you, part elephant?"

"Yup."

"Well, my *teenage* crush was over long ago."

"Uh-huh." Rose smiled cryptically. "Tony's in for a rude awakening, huh? About the baby, I mean."

Knowing all about rude awakenings, Julia simply agreed and reached for her coat. Shrugging into it, she buttoned it up to her throat. "I'll see you on Monday, unless you've got something else to show me."

"Nope, we're all set." Rose walked her to the top of the stairs. "But I'd like to know why you stopped me from telling him you were a teacher going for your master's."

Julia looked down the metal steps and gripped the cold iron railing. "Plans change." This was hardly the place she wanted to be while talking about those changes...or anything else.

"Okay, I get the message. I can wait until Monday." She squeezed Julia's arm. "You've got a place of your own, right?" Julia merely nodded. "Well, if you need help getting settled in, or just someone to talk to, call. You've got my number."

Julia nodded again. "You too. I know it's hard for you right now, so call me if you need to." She quickly turned toward the steps, anxious to leave.

Rose must have sensed her unease, even if she didn't know the true reason, because her friend simply let the subject drop. "Thanks, Jules. I'm glad you're back. Pretty soon it'll be like you never even left."

Julia closed her eyes. "I'm counting on it, Rose." Then, looking straight out in front of her, she began her descent.

One step at a time.

Chapter 2

"I didn't know what else to do, Tony. I had to call you." Irene Phillips took Tony's briefcase and coat, and led the way into the baby's room. "She hasn't stopped crying since she woke up an hour ago. And Maxine left."

Tony strode to her crib and scooped the infant into his arms. "Shh, Rachel. It'll be all right." He rocked his body as he'd seen mothers on television do, and walked around the room, hoping the steady movement would soothe the child.

Irene stood by the white couch. "I hope I didn't interrupt anything, Tony. I know how important your time at work is, but I have to leave soon."

"That's okay. The baby is more important."

"You're a good man, Tony." She put her hand on Tony's shoulder and squeezed. "And Rachel's one lucky little girl."

Tony smiled sadly at the plump housekeeper who'd worked for him over the past three years, and continued to pace. "Yeah, well. Let's hope she thinks so when she gets older."

"Don't you worry none, she will." Miss Irene folded a blanket. "Tony, I didn't ask this before, what with you bringing the baby home, then deciding to bring Annie's body back here for a proper burial, but what happened to Rachel's natural father?"

Tony sighed. "There's a Mitch Brown on her birth certificate. According to what John's dug up about him, he's a drug dealer, and up to this point has shown no interest in Rachel." He hugged the child tighter. "He'd been living with Annie, but now he's nowhere to be found." His insides hardened, and he couldn't fight the feeling that Mitch was responsible for Annie's death, even if not directly. "Because of his name on the birth certificate, I can't have total custody until the department of social services investigates me, pops in for a few surprise visits, and obtains his signature."

"Why would Anne have gotten messed up with someone like him?"

"City life is…cold, Miss Irene, and scary. Makes you hard, fast. In her journal, she wrote how she ran away from home, had to find a place to live, and met that son of a bi…bad seed—" he smiled sheepishly at Miss Irene "—and believed it when he said he'd take care of her."

"Hmph. Big-city living does no one any good. Do you think he'll make trouble for you?"

"He'd best not." He kissed Rachel's check.

He didn't think Mitch would give him problems about Rachel. From everything John had learned from Annie's neighbors, Mitch had never helped around their apartment after Rachel was born. So if Mitch suddenly decided that he wanted Rachel, he'd have to be found, first of all, and then he'd have to comply with the court's orders. They

stated should he ever be found, he'd have to undergo re-
habilitation, and that hardly seemed likely, given his exten-
sive police record.

"It was a fine funeral you made for Anne, Tony," Miss
Irene said. "And such a big turnout. Everyone knew how
much finding her meant to you, and they're all real sorry
with the way it turned out. Why couldn't your brothers stay
longer?"

"Matt's about to try his first court case, and Nick's in
the middle of a big sting, so they had to leave right after
the memorial services. I'm surprised they had time to fly
out in the first place." That knowledge didn't stop an uncomfortable feeling of anger from emerging. He'd wanted
them to stay longer, to get to know their niece better.

Tony knew his brothers had busy lives, as did he. Regardless of the fact that they'd been separated most of their
lives, though, they'd managed to become very close. He
just couldn't figure out why he was angry with them over
their lack of time.

Miss Irene crossed her plump arms across her ample
bosom and cocked her head. "Now, on to Rachel. What
are you going to do about this child? She needs full-time
care."

"I suppose I'll have to get a nanny. Part-time baby-sitters
just aren't reliable. In just two weeks we've gone through,
what, six? I just can't understand why they have so much
trouble with her. She's just a baby."

Miss Irene snorted. "So much for the nineties man and
his newfound empathy. The best thing for you," she continued, wagging her finger in his face, "would be to take
care of her yourself for a week or two, then you'll understand what kind of a special woman it takes to be able to
be around a baby for twenty-four hours."

Tony held his tongue with the older woman. From the

time he was fifteen, he'd lived in Wyoming. He'd had a difficult time adjusting to a cowboy existence—believing, at first, that "The Beverly Hillbillies" was a step *up* from life in Silver Creek—but he'd eventually come to accept that most of the people around were just simple folks with simple needs. And even if he still hated to be told what to do, or to listen to others tell him what was best for him, he wouldn't lambaste Miss Irene. With the help of his last foster parents, he'd learned how to take the advice of elders.

So, maybe Miss Irene was right.

He was used to delegating responsibilities to the competent employees around him on his ranches, and rested easy knowing that his orders were being followed to the letter. But he had experience with running a ranch, so he instinctively knew how much work to give out. He didn't know about babies. Maybe he did need to take care of her for a while. That way, he could find the right help, because it wasn't good enough just to know she was being taken care of; he wanted her to be cared for all day, the way he would care for her if he could.

And that bothered him. She was beginning to mean a lot to him. How was that possible? How could she have entered his life and made him want to change things so quickly? He knew firsthand that too many changes, too fast, weren't good, so...

Well, that wasn't entirely true. One change he kind of liked was that Rachel was on his mind most of the time. He wondered what she was up to, whether she was laughing or sleeping. While most of her days went along quietly, if she did get agitated, the tenacious child wouldn't settle down unless he was holding her.

Sure enough, as though he'd spoken the words aloud, Rachel began hiccuping, and finally calmed down. Her tiny fists opened and closed, and her head lay against his chest.

"Shh, baby. It's gonna be all right." Kicking off his shoes, he sat on the couch and leaned back, cradling her head. He looked at the swirl of dark brown hair, so like the family's. "What am I gonna do with you, Rachel Anne Pellegrino?" He'd added on his sister's name after the funeral. Now, as he murmured it out loud, he thought how appropriate it sounded.

Rachel settled down, breathing deeply, her little body shuddering slightly every once in a while. As if making sure he was still there, her left hand touched his face, patting his nose and sliding down to his lips.

He kissed her fisted hand and watched in amazement as it unfurled. A sharp pang of emotion shocked him—he, a confirmed bachelor and ersatz father, had the power to open her fist, and with nothing more than a mere kiss!

But would that be enough to guide her? Could he really be a father to her, when he had had such a difficult life himself? When his own mother had abandoned him?

"Maxine couldn't calm her down?" he asked, needing to change the track of his thoughts.

"Humph. She didn't even try. When Rachel started crying, she put down her sketchpad, walked over to the crib and told her there was nothing to cry about." Miss Irene shook her head, her dark brown hair waving softly about her plump cheeks. "I suggested she check her diaper. She did, told me it was wet, and stood there. I showed her how to change it...again. But when Rachel didn't calm down afterwards, Maxine said she couldn't concentrate with the noise and left."

Tony didn't want to deal with what Miss Irene was hinting at. It meant making more changes, and he didn't want to do that.

"Well, that makes sense. She wouldn't be able to work with distractions. And she did me a big favor, showing up this morning, after the sixth sitter reported in sick at the last minute.''

''Humph. Mark my words, Tony. Maxine's not capable of giving a little baby what she needs. She needs a mother, and Maxine's too selfish to be that mother. There're half a dozen girls around who would be more than willing to be with you. Stop flitting from woman to woman. Find yourself a nice girl and marry her, Tony.''

Tony bit the inside of his cheek. It was bad enough to have to listen to someone telling him what to do, but it was worse now that it was about the one subject that wasn't open for discussion in his life—marriage.

''You're wrong, Miss Irene. I don't need to go to any extremes to meet Rachel's needs. I'll rearrange my schedule and take care of her for the next week. I'll talk to Maxine, and we'll work out something between us. In the meantime, I'll advertise down in Casper, and hopefully we'll have someone by the end of a week.'' He nodded, his business acumen back on track, the thought of marriage dismissed. ''After all, it's just like any business—simply finding the right woman for the right job.''

A week later, Tony studied the dark circles beneath his eyes and chuckled. The terms *piece of cake, no problem,* and *simple,* flashed in his mind, and he shook his head. Boy, had he been naive. He tossed the shaving mirror on the desk and sighed.

Rachel was down for her late-afternoon nap. He sat in his office at the house, trying to get some work completed—actually, trying to keep his eyes open—when Miss Irene stuck her head in.

''It's almost time for dinner, Tony.'' She smiled, her hands on her hips. ''Any luck with the women you interviewed today?''

"Nope. I don't know what's wrong with me." He raked a hand through his hair. "I can't seem to find anyone, and I don't know why. I've hired and fired lots of people. The two women today—and the three from the past week—all had proper credentials, and looked fine, but..."

"But you're hiring with your heart, dear."

He glanced up sharply. "That's ridiculous. Emotions play no part in this. She's just a little girl, and this is just a job, like any other job."

"Then why *are* you having trouble finding someone?"

"That's simple. Everyone is incompetent."

"Hogwash." Miss Irene entered and sat down on the chair opposite the desk, unconsciously wiping her hands with her apron. "You just got through saying all the women had the proper credentials, and you hadn't had any trouble finding the right person for any job before. And as you've said time and time again, she's just a baby, how hard could the job be?"

"What did you do? Tape me?" Tony shifted in his chair. "Ranching's a breeze compared to taking care of a baby. I must have been out of my mind to think I could be her father. I can't even find her a baby-sitter."

Maxine was right. She'd be better off with a family.

"Now, Tony, don't give up so fast." Miss Irene interrupted his thoughts. "I was just having some fun with you. You're like any new father—scared of making a mistake, that's all. I've been watching you this past week. I really thought you'd have fallen on your face, but you didn't. You asked me questions, listened to me, *and—*" she stressed the next part "*—*actually did what I told you to do. You've done fine."

"Yeah, well, you were right. I can't believe a little baby could be this demanding. I'm exhausted. And that still doesn't explain why I can't find someone to help with Rachel.''

"It's because you're not hiring someone to brand your horses, or corral your steer. You're hiring someone to be a surrogate mother for a little baby that you've grown to love.''

Love? Was it possible? Did he love her? *Could* he love her?

"You don't want to leave her," Miss Irene added gently.

"But I have to get back to work."

"I didn't say you weren't going to leave, but you don't want to. You're actually having a good time with her, regardless of how much work is involved.''

The words penetrated, slowly at first, then with ever-increasing speed, until the small smile he'd felt beginning turned into a full-blown grin. "I'll be horn-swaggered! You might be right, Miss Irene. She may have crawled under my skin after all.''

She laughed at his exaggerated use of the cowboy language. "I know. So, what are you going to do?"

He expelled a fierce breath. "I want to spend some time with Rachel, so...I think I need to speak with Maxine. We'll just have to work out something between us so that Rachel won't have to be with a nanny full-time.''

"Oh, please," she responded. "And here I thought we made progress. It's time for you to settle down. Find a woman who wants a family.'' Shaking her head, she continued, wagging a finger in his direction. "You have Rachel to consider now. Mark my words, nothing good is going to come from this relationship. Maxine's too ambitious. She doesn't want any ties.''

Neither do I.

Tony bit back his retort. Her comments were the same ones everyone in town shared—and voiced at every possible chance. He had no plans to take the plunge into the abyss and marry, just to find a mother for Rachel. Maxine was fun and definitely uncomplicated. They'd be together for a while, then...

"Once Maxine sees that she won't have to give anything up, we'll be able to handle one more responsibility. She's as capable of caring for a child as any woman is." Or as any man was? In the short time he had had Rachel, she'd become very important in his life.

Maybe this child was a way for him to redeem himself for past wrongs.

"Suit yourself," Miss Irene said, breaking into his thoughts. "But as long as we're on the subject of responsibility, tell me I heard Chris wrong, that you didn't climb on a horse with that young'n in your arms yesterday after I left."

He stood and escorted Miss Irene down the hall. "Chris held her until I was settled." They entered the kitchen, and Tony sniffed the air appreciatively, the aroma of the sizzling steak making his mouth water. "Have the ranch hands eaten yet?" He sat down at the large oak table.

"Eaten and out again for evening chores, and don't you change the subject on me. A child her age shouldn't be on a horse. It might frighten her."

"Nah. You should've seen her laugh when Shadow snorted in her hand." He waved away her concerned look. "Shadow's as gentle as a babe himself. And I know a thing or two about riding."

"Yes, but *I* know a thing or two about raising children." She cocked an eyebrow at him, effectively silencing him. "Don't do anything else like that unless you talk it over with me, first." She dished out a large helping of fried potatoes and steak and placed it in front of Tony. "And don't get any on your clothes," she warned, then laughed when Tony put the napkin on his lap. He'd had a meeting this morning, and he hadn't changed out of his suit.

She scolded just like a mother. He held his fork and stared into space. Anger he'd thought he'd buried a long time ago suddenly surfaced. And along with it, another memory of his mother materialized....

Tony, try to understand. I know what's best for you. I can't give you what you need, but that's all going to change You'll see....

He gritted his teeth. Yes, it had changed, all right. For the worse. At least for Annie and him. Not for his two younger brothers, luckily.

"So, until you know what's best for that babe, don't go doing anything else that's foolish, or I'll find a hickory switch." Miss Irene's good-humored threat snapped Tony out of his past.

Suppressing the anger with a practiced hand, he chuckled, cutting a piece of tender meat. "I don't suppose you'd change your mind and do it?"

"You know I'd love to, but as we've already discussed, you need someone to be here all the time, and with George's ailing back, you know I can't do that." He nodded. "Find someone to care for your child." She was wagging her wooden ladle at him. She did that a lot, he thought fondly. "You hear me, Tony?"

"Yes, boss," he said, then ducked when she swatted his head affectionately. "I mean, ma'am."

Miss Irene wagged that ladle at him again. "Boss was just fine, Tony." She winked and crossed her arms.

Just like a mother.

"It's done." Julia wiped her brow and sat back on her heels, stretching her tired back. She placed the well-used rag in the bucket of murky water near the last drawer of the filing cabinet, and smiled triumphantly at Rose, who was spreading her lunch on Julia's desk. "Hi, Rose. What's on the menu today?"

The perky blonde picked up a closed container and attempted to peer through the opaque sides. "Either tuna salad or cold sesame noodles from last night. I don't know which one Tom packed for me." She raised her eyebrows at Julia's chuckle. "Just because he's a cowboy, doesn't mean he can't be domesticated. He gets up much earlier than I to do the chores on the ranch, so he makes my lunch." She indicated the file cabinet. "You've been cleaning this office for a week. Keep it up and you'll make us all look bad," she teased.

"Relax. It'll be six months before I'll do this again."

"Six months? Lord, Jules, you're so efficient…"

"Don't say it."

"You'll make some man a wonderful little ol' wife." Her hazel eyes twinkled, and she laughed as Julia walked into the bathroom to wash her hands. While Rose had really behaved herself—not asking her about her marriage—she had made it more than a little obvious that she wanted to hear all the details. She'd also made it clear that she wanted to see Julia married again, and as happy as she. If she only knew…

"Sesame noodles. Mmm, great!" Rose exclaimed joyously.

Julia emerged from the bathroom and grabbed her lunch from the small refrigerator behind her desk. "How can someone who eats like you maintain such a fabulous figure? I envy you."

Rose held up her fork. "I don't want to hear one word about your figure. It's probably sensational, beneath your baggy clothes. What gives?"

Julia looked down at what she'd chosen for today. The

green slacks and matching silk blouse comprised her favorite outfit. "I'd lost a lot of weight recently." Rose smiled at her sympathetically. "Are they really that bad?"

"Sugar, you and I could fit into those pants, and still have room to samba."

"I guess so." Julia chuckled. "I haven't gotten around to buying any new clothes."

Rose took another mouthful, swallowed, then smiled. "Idea time. Why don't we drive into Casper this weekend and go on a shopping spree?"

Almost about to agree, Julia suddenly felt apprehensive. When she tried to figure out why, she realized that new clothes would mean even more attention from the men around her. And she just wasn't ready for that yet.

"Great idea," she said, "but we're midseason. Let's wait till the spring fashions arrive, then we'll hit the stores, okay?"

"Sure. Better yet, we'll overdose on hot-fudge sundaes till your stuff fits again." Rose patted her stomach suggestively.

Julia forced a chuckle and bit into her extracrunchy-peanut-butter-and-grape-jam sandwich. Spring was still half a year away. She'd be ready by then, if nothing else happened before that to thwart her. She glanced up to heaven and mentally addressed the Fates.

Well? Got anything else in store for me?

No answer.

Rose leaned forward earnestly and interrupted Julia's mental tête-à-tête. "Now, why don't you give any of the men around here a chance to get to know you?" She put her empty container down. "I saw Jim Henessy waiting for you on Monday and Clark O'Neal on Wednesday. They're good men, and definitely not hard on the eyes, but you didn't give them the time of day."

Julia shrugged. "I don't want to get involved with anyone."

"You're divorced over six months now, right?" Julia nodded. A moment of silence passed, then another. Finally Rose spoke again, her voice low, an air of confidentiality enveloping the two of them. "Your mother filled me in on some of the details, like how after the miscarriage, he started staying out late, and stuff like that. Is there something else?"

Julia longed to unburden herself to someone, but knew she couldn't. It would mean having to face it; having to utter the words out loud, and hear their finality. And even though she liked Rose a lot, she had just moved home again and didn't feel comfortable sharing this with her yet.

"No." Rose's eyebrows raised in disbelief at Julia's response. "There's really no mystery. Hank and I weren't right for each other. Anyway, there are plenty of women who opt to remain single." Putting away her half-eaten sandwich, she sighed. "There are ways of being fulfilled without a man, you know."

"Uh-huh, but they all require batteries."

Julia's mouth dropped, and the two women laughed. When the moment passed, Julia added, "I have more than enough work to keep me busy, Rose."

Rose stood and wandered over to Julia's tidy desk. "Why aren't you teaching?"

Rose looked at her beseechingly, and Julia knew that she was asking her to open up a little. Settling in her chair, tucking a strand of hair back into its bun, Julia spoke. "Between my father's death, the...loss last year, and my divorce this year, it felt like the walls were closing in on me."

"But your mamma said you really loved teaching. Why not apply for a teaching job here?"

"I'm not certified in Wyoming. And I didn't even complete my master's degree. I have one year left."

"So, do what it takes to change that."

"But that wasn't all. Being around kids was too hard."

"I understand that." The two women shared a look. "I never heard the whole story about your father. Would you tell me?"

Julia sighed. "I was supposed to pick him up at my apartment for dinner, but my mother and I got tied up shopping. Hank was still at the office, so we told my dad to grab a cab." She swallowed hard, the guilt working its way back into the forefront of her mind. "The cab was sideswiped by a drunk driver. My father was killed instantly." She tamped down the feelings waiting to emerge, and smiled instead. "First my father, then…then the divorce. You can see why I came back home."

"I'd go running home, too, if all that'd happened to me."

Julia whirled at the soft tenor of Tony's voice from the doorway, and saw a man with sympathy etched on his face. For the past week, Julia had managed to avoid contact with him, which wasn't easy, since this office was on his stud ranch near the workers' quarters, right across from his house.

Julia looked up at Tony. His hair was windswept, and he radiated the smell of the cold Wyoming air.

"I didn't mean to eavesdrop," he said.

"You're not," Julia replied, returning the files to the cabinet. "We're just chatting." Had he heard about the miscarriage?

Tony narrowed his eyes slightly, then nodded. "A nice way to pass the time." He leaned against the door frame, the light from behind casting an ethereal glow around his milk-chocolate hair.

"How's Rachel?" she croaked, then grimaced inwardly. Julia had been trying not to ask about the baby, knowing that getting involved would be painful. But the habit of inquiring about a child's welfare was too deeply entrenched in her for her to merely wish it away. And, to make matters worse, she was glad she asked; Tony's eyes lit up.

"She's amazing, undaunted by anything." He waved his arms about. "She's even standing!" At their look of disbelief, he quickly amended, "With help, of course. This morning she reached for my cup of orange juice. You should've the seen the look on her face when the tart flavor hit her tongue." The three of them laughed as Tony imitated Rachel's screwed-up expression.

"I love watching babies discover things." Rose sighed, a hand resting on her abdomen.

Taking a step forward, Tony hugged her briefly. "Pretty soon you'll be telling your own stories, Rose. Don't think it won't happen."

"Thanks, Tony. In the meantime, there's all that practice, and you know what they say about practice making one perfect." Batting her eyes innocently, she shrugged. "And just in case it doesn't, just yesterday, we filled out some adoption papers."

"That's great," Tony said. "We're going to start a trend in Silver Creek." He smiled. "One way or another, your house will be crammed with kids."

But they won't be Tom's, Julia almost blurted out, but stopped herself in time. Her friend didn't need to deal with the doubts Hank had left her.

Unwinding the scarf from his neck, Tony hung it up on the coatrack behind the door in Julia's office. "Here's something for you to gnaw on, Rose. Rachel's with Maxine today." When Rose didn't respond to his lighthearted barb, he chuckled. "We've talked it over, and we're going to try rearranging our schedules. She'll do her clothes designing at my place during the day. Now, all I need is part-time help.''

"Is Miss Irene at the house, too?" Rose asked with false innocence.

"Sure," Tony answered, then grimaced. "Very funny. Maxine's just not used to kids, any more than I am. She *is* trying, Rose."

"Oh, she's trying, all right," Rose muttered, then raised her eyebrows at his look. "I'm just agreeing with you, boss."

Tony approached Julia's desk. "And what's your opinion?"

"I don't have one."

"That makes you a unique person. Everyone in town has an opinion about Maxine," he said. "Well, thanks for asking about Rachel, anyway." Pausing, he surveyed her desk. "If you're done with lunch, then I'd like to talk about your duties here."

"That's my cue to get back to work," Rose said. With a conspiratorial wink in Tony's direction as she exited the office, she proclaimed, "She's all yours."

He arched an eyebrow and chuckled at Julia's smirk. "You *do* work for me. It's about time I get to see what I'm paying for." If there were any double meanings, his broad grin hid them. "The office looks great, by the way."

Julia chided herself when she felt her cheeks heat up at the compliment. "It needed to be done, and I'm—"

"Someone who gets things done, right?"

"Right. After all, that's what you hired me for." As long as she stuck to topics about her work, she'd be safe. She sat back confidently.

Tony opened his dark blue corduroy jacket, revealing a gray shirt that fit his muscled contours snugly, and stuffed his gloves in his pockets. Walking behind her desk, he moved some papers and sat on the edge, near her chair, a long leg swinging back and forth. He crossed his arms.

"I looked you up in my yearbook last week, but you weren't there. Why's that?"

"I graduated a year behind you." She pushed her glasses up her nose. "Checking up on me, or is this your subtle way of trying to figure out how old I am?"

An impish grin broke out on his face. Her heart quickened. "Just curious." He shrugged off his coat and hung it up. "I only vaguely recall you from school. Talking to you in the halls, right? You weren't in any of my after-school clubs." Opening his office door, he indicated that she should accompany him.

"I'm surprised you remembered me at all. You led a busy life, and I didn't hang out with your crowd. But that's not what we're here for, is it? To reminisce?"

He looked at her a moment, and then, loosening his midnight blue silk tie, he leaned back against his black leather chair and swiveled gently from right to left. Ignoring her comment, he continued. "Rose has been filling me in on what you've been up to. I like the way you've reorganized the place, including the files in the computer. They're much more accessible now." He paused. "I haven't had much of a chance to be here last week."

"I know. I can't imagine how difficult it must be for you, to have found and then lost your sister." Rose had filled her in on how long Tony had been searching for Anne.

"You would have thought that she'd have had a better chance at life, being a baby when she was adopted, and being wanted and all. I guess it just proves the best-laid plans of mice and men..." He expelled a breath, and that seemed to shake off the touch of the doldrums.

"I'm really sorry," she said, knowing it wasn't enough. "I wanted to tell you this at the services, but I didn't want to intrude on you and your brothers. The service you held for Anne was touching."

"Yeah, well...she deserved it."

So he couldn't accept a compliment. It fit. In school, he used to be so arrogant, so sure of himself, walking the halls as if he owned them. How scared he must have really been all those years as a tough New Yorker, trying to find his place in a quiet community. She wondered how Tony had ended up in Silver Creek, but squelched the desire to ask. No use getting any more involved with him than she had to.

"At least Rachel will have a better life," Tony added.

"She's lucky to have you." He glanced at her, and she saw a need for encouragement in his eyes. "Any adjustment is tough for a child, but because she's so young, it shouldn't be too difficult." She sat back and crossed her legs, automatically warming up to the topic. "Most children need patience and understanding while they're coming to grips with the changes in their routines, and you appear to be a patient man."

"You pegged me right. Still, I worry about her."

"Is she sleeping through the night?"

"I guess so. I don't hear her crying. Should I be checking on her? She usually falls asleep around seven. I put her to bed, then I just peek in from the doorway. I don't want to wake her up by entering her room too often."

Julia instantly tried to reassure him. "You're very thoughtful, but a baby doesn't wake up that easily. Does she nap through the day?" Tony nodded. "Does Miss Irene stop her work when she does?"

"No. Oh, I get it," he said, his eyes bright. "So, I can walk in to check on her as often as I like?"

"Absolutely."

Tony leaned forward, his handsome face serious.
"Where'd you get this information? Are there books I
should be reading?"

She gave him the name of several books her professors
had suggested to her, but refrained from mentioning where
she'd heard about them. He didn't ask her.

After jotting down the last title, he sat back. "There's
so much more to this than I'd thought. I figured, give her
some food, make sure she had a stable existence, love her,
and she'd be fine."

His desire to do the right thing, despite his ignorance
where children were concerned, moved Julia. Without
thinking, she reached out and patted his hand. "Love is
ninety percent of the battle. If you read a few of these
books, you'll find you're doing everything right."

Tony looked down, and Julia followed his gaze, stopping
where her hand rested on his, her skin pale compared to
his. She could feel the heat from his fingers. She pulled her
hand off.

"I reorganized your files." She stood and walked over
to them quickly, pulling out the first one and showing him
what she'd done. "Since you have so many outside contracts, like the one with Canadian steer ranches, I've created
a subsection where those files can be found." She was rambling, but couldn't help herself.

"I see that. The plants are a nice touch, too."

Julia looked at the one by the front window, her favorite
plant. "It's called a mother-in-law's tongue."

He stood and walked over to the plant, taking one of its
long stalks in his hands and slowly stroking the length of
it, from base to tip. Julia watched his strong fingers, her
gaze traveling down to his muscled forearm, and she pulled
at the collar of her blouse, a futile attempt to cover her

body's traitorous response. Her blush rose from her chest up, as usual. His fingers traveled down the stalk again, then up another one, stopping at the tip, which he probed with his thumb. He jerked his hand away, looked at his finger, then at her.

Glancing at his bemused expression, she found her sense of humor again. "Beautiful to look at, but watch the edges—sharp and pointy." Suddenly she thought of Maxine and had to stifle a giggle.

"Want to share the joke?"

She couldn't resist teasing. "I was just thinking about how some people I know fit the description of the plant."

Rubbing his thumb with the palm of his other hand, he arched an eyebrow. "Are you speaking of someone in particular?"

"No, of course not." She took a step backward, the file drawer sliding shut with a sharp click. Tony stepped forward. Holding her breath, she watched as his hand reached toward her...and continued over her shoulder, straightening the papers on the top of the cabinet. She was trapped between his arm and the wall on her right.

"Are you sure?"

"Sure? Oh, yes." She commanded her mind to focus on the conversation, and not on silly high-school fantasies, or her desire to lean forward. Taking in a deep breath, she said, "Just making a general observation."

"I see." When he withdrew his hand, it brushed against her cheek, and her insides coiled tighter than a jack-in-the-box whose latch was one note away from opening. "Julia?"

She felt his hands on her upper arms. "I'm ready to get down to business anytime you are." Julia shrugged his hands off and moved toward his desk, her fingers grasping the back of the chair she'd been sitting in. She asked, "What are my other duties?"

He expelled a breath, then approached his chair. Sitting behind his desk, he assumed a businesslike attitude and outlined her more intricate responsibilities, explaining them in detail as she took notes.

Tony hadn't done anything wrong. She was the one who'd gone from being at ease with men to being afraid of their advances. Glancing up, she saw a look of concern on his face. He probably felt confused because she hadn't responded to his flirting the way countless other women had. There was no other reason for his concern. She hadn't overreacted, she'd just moved out of his reach.

"That's about it," Tony said. "Any questions?" He sat back in his chair, and waited for her answer.

"These responsibilities are well within my abilities." In control again, she read her notes and managed to smile. "There's nothing here I can't handle."

He chuckled, and she quickly looked up. There, on his face, was a look so masculine in its arrogance that she caught her breath. She didn't need anybody to interpret the look.

It said clearly, *Wanna bet?*

Chapter 3

Tony recalled the feel beneath his fingers when he'd had them clasped on Julia's arms.

Tension.

He didn't get it. At first she'd looked up at him with those crystal-blue eyes, but then she'd stiffened, and their mild flirtation vanished. Had he come on too strong, or had she suffered at some other man's hands?

Her ex-husband's?

His fists clenched.

He looked at her through his office door, left ajar on purpose. Her fingers glided across the keyboard of the computer. At least her color had returned to normal. Tony continued his perusal. She wore her hair up in a bun, and according to Rose, she called her color "mousy brown," but he thought it was actually more like warm caramel.

Rose also said Julia had lost a lot of weight recently, and that was why her clothes hung on her. Tony thought Julia looked great, and hadn't noticed any problem with her clothes. When he told Rose that, she'd clucked her tongue and muttered something about men living in outer space.

As Tony watched, Julia reached above her to retrieve a book from the shelf against the wall. Her green silk blouse stretched tight against her, and he caught his breath, his chest and groin tightening with desire. Her breasts were full and high-tipped. If this was how she looked in clothes that were too *big*... The sound of the phone ringing on her desk drew him from his musings, and he exhaled sharply.

The women Tony dated were usually city women, from Casper or other metropolitan areas. They were sophisticated, more citified than country, all eager to enjoy an exciting nightlife. Julia was the kind of woman he'd always avoided, the stay-at-home, want-a-commitment type.

No, she wasn't at all like the women he'd always dated.

So what was it about her that stirred his interest? She was pretty, in a wholesome way, and intelligent, too. He looked up to find her in his doorway talking to him.

"Maxine and Rachel are on their way over from the house. I thought you'd want to know."

She didn't say his name. Now that he thought about it, he couldn't recall her ever using it. "Thanks."

She walked back to her desk, her hips swaying gently. There was something about her...about her demure manner...

"Darling." Maxine gushed into the room, the cool air still swirling around her. Tony stood and reached out his arms, glad for the distraction. Before he could take the carrier with Rachel in it, Maxine placed it on his desk and slid into his embrace. Her lips were cold beneath his, and her breath was minty.

"How're my two favorite girls?" After disentagling himself from Maxine's arms, Tony removed Rachel's snowsuit, then hugged her.

"We're just peachy, darling."

Tony looked into the outer office, and his eyes locked with Julia's. She hurriedly returned to work, a rush of color blossoming in her cheeks. So, she'd been caught snooping. He chuckled. Small-town living; everyone knowing everyone's business.

"Darling, a new client called an hour ago and is very eager to see my line. She may want some things on consignment."

"That's great, Maxine. This could be your big chance."

"Oh, I knew you'd understand." Maxine walked to the door. "I have to rush. Mrs. Sheridan is expecting me in about an hour."

"Now? What about tonight? I have a meeting, and you were going to stay with Rachel."

Her eyes darted left and right. "Oh, Tony. I don't know how long this meeting will be, and it's in Casper. With last night's snowfall, I don't want to drive too fast. I guess you'll have to get another baby-sitter."

"On short notice, not likely." She raised an eyebrow, and he held up a hand. "Okay, I'll try and find someone," Tony said. "Maybe the Chase girl is free."

"Oh, good. You know, if Mrs. Sheridan wants my clothes, then I'm going to be *very* busy the next few months," she said, glancing at the baby pointedly. "Oh, well, I'll manage."

"I'm sure you will," Tony said, trying to keep the edge out of his voice. Maxine's obvious disregard for Rachel bothered him.

"Then, when things have settled, you and I can get reacquainted. You want that, too, don't you?" He watched her as she sidled up to him, batting her eyelashes.

Were they real or fake? "Yeah. You expect to be *very* busy?"

"Yes, I imagine I will be. You sound angry."

"Well, I guess I am. I'd counted on you being around more—especially now that Rachel's here. I thought you'd like to get to know her."

"I think you're asking a lot for two people who are only dating," she said, throwing his words back at him. "Or are you implying something else?"

"No, it's not that," he said quickly. How was he supposed to get out of this?

The answer appeared in the form of Julia poking her head into his office. "Why don't I take Rachel and occupy her for a while?" She took a step in, then stopped, looking at the baby.

Tony looked at Rachel. Her arms and legs were jerking, and she was blinking rapidly. He hadn't realized they were getting that loud. "Thanks," he said.

Julia faced the baby and, after another momentary hesitation, reached for her. Rachel went into Julia's arms quietly and looked up at her face. Julia smiled, and Tony was transfixed. Her face glowed.

He'd thought she wasn't comfortable around children. Boy, had he been wrong. She obviously loved children. Why had she resisted so much?

He glanced at Maxine, then back to Julia. Julia, with her full lips and slightly upturned nose, wasn't as strikingly beautiful as Maxine, but there was a genuine quality about her that Maxine seemed to lack.

"I'll just take her out here so the two of you can talk freely." Julia cooed at Rachel, and walked out. She sat on her desk and held Rachel facing her. Leaning forward, she spoke softly. Rachel grabbed her glasses, sucked on a lens, then waved them around in triumphant glee.

Maxine turned her attention to Tony, pressing her body against his, and Tony glanced at the door to see whether

Julia was watching. She wasn't, and he was glad, but damned if he knew why.

"Tony, I was afraid of this. You don't want to make a commitment to me, but you expect me to juggle my schedule to meet her needs, and she needs more time than I have to give."

"Have to, or want to?"

"That's not fair."

"Sorry. You're right. I didn't mean to dump on you."

"That's okay." She sniffed. "I still think your initial idea was the best—hire a full-time nanny. You'll be rested, and we can have more time for ourselves."

Ourselves. The two of us. Stepping back, he held her at arm's length. That was what he'd *wanted*—past tense— time for the two of them. Time to go to premieres and night clubs and dance.

Maxine was waiting for him to say something. But what? He'd liked her independence and ambition. He knew she wouldn't cling to him as others had, but he didn't just want to spend time with her alone anymore. The baby laughed, and Tony spied Julia snuggling into Rachel's neck. He wanted to spend time with Rachel *and* Julia.

Julia? His mind scrambled. Maxine. He meant Maxine.

"Things have changed, Maxine," Tony said, annoyance egging him on as he spoke the words aloud. He'd never liked change.

Maxine's eyebrows rose. "I know, but I thought you liked things the way they were between us."

"I did." Tony faltered. "I *do*." He was in control. "I'll find a nanny." When he realized he still called the shots, his near panic receded.

He didn't need to get married, didn't need to find another woman right now.

"Good, I don't want another letdown."

"Another letdown? What are you talking about?"

"Oh, nothing, really," she said quickly, then sighed when she saw he didn't believe that. "In Cheyenne, I dated a man. But his attention turned to…other things, and I got ignored." She pouted. "I won't be slighted again."

Ah, finally, a hint. He'd heard the rumors in town, and they indicated it had been more than what she had just made it sound like.

Laughter from the outer office caused them both to turn their heads. They spied Julia lifting the squealing baby and bussing her cheek. Rachel shrieked, her arms and legs flailing in joy. Tony's heart seemed to expand, and as his eyes traveled to the woman who brought such happiness to her, he felt gratitude that she was giving Rachel all this attention.

Glancing at her designer watch, Maxine muttered, "I really have to go, Tony. Why don't you offer Julia the job? She seems to get along with the child so well." And then she was gone, leaving her expensive perfume hanging in the air.

Tony sighed. The child. Didn't she remember Rachel's name?

"She's right, you know."

Tony jumped. "Stop sneaking in on me, Rose." He joined her at the desk. "You make me sorry I put in that back door."

"Don't con me. It was a federal law that made you put it in, and you know it. I just happen to use it because—"

He waved a hand through the air. "I know, I know. Because it saves you sixty-four steps." He took the sheaf of papers she held out for his signature. "What did you mean, 'She's right'?"

"What Maxine said." Rose smiled like the cat that swallowed the canary. Tony laughed. No apology for eavesdropping. "Julia *would* be perfect for the job, and since she didn't actually tell me *not* to say anything…'' She went on to blithely tell him about Julia's training in early childhood education.

At first he couldn't believe it. Then he recalled the way she'd spoken to him about Rachel. So, Julia was full of surprises. And possibly fear. Tony wanted to ask Rose about Julia's marriage, but he figured it'd have to remain a mystery a bit longer. He wasn't about to snoop behind her back.

He glanced at Rose and was surprised to see her smiling at him. "What's up?" he asked.

"Up? Nothing, why?" she asked, innocently—too innocently.

"You look like the proverbial canary."

She laughed and looked through the doorway, then back at him. "I just think that people deserve happiness, even if they don't think they do."

"People? You mean Julia, right?" Tony closed the door as Rose shrugged.

"Her, too. Now, about the job. I think you should ask her."

"You really think so?"

"Absolutely. Ask her." Rose walked to the back door. "And keep on asking her." She stared at him. "Sometimes people need a push to do what's best for them." Then, smiling again, she left.

Tony pondered her words. Hiring Julia as a nanny would be the answer to his problem. Rachel had taken to her immediately. And maybe, as he got to know her better, maybe he could figure out why he wanted to know more about her.

Besides, it *felt* right to have Julia with Rachel. In fact, the more he thought about it, the more right it felt. Keeping that in mind, he entered the outer office.

Just at that moment, Rachel grasped the tie around the collar of Julia's blouse and pulled, revealing her collarbones, and the slight indentation at the base of her long neck. Clearing his throat, he remembered what he'd come out for. "I have a proposition for you."

Julia's eyes widened, and scarlet spots appeared on her cheeks, accentuating her classic cheekbones. His eyes quickly darted back to the exposed part of her neck. Her skin looked creamy-white, an easterner's color.

Now that she was back home, would she tan rosy, or golden?

Shrugging off the errant thought, he stuffed his hands into his front pockets. "Uh, what I mean is, I would like you to take care of Rachel."

Her eyebrows rose. "You want me to baby-sit Rachel?"

"Yes."

"Tonight?"

"Well, yes, for starters."

"For starters?" She bounced Rachel on her knees, her eyebrows drawn together.

"I want to hire you."

She looked around the office. "You already have."

"No, what I mean is…" he began, licking his suddenly dry lips and wondering what had happened to the man who could negotiate multimillion-dollar deals without blinking. "I want you to take care of her—be her nanny—full-time."

Slowly, Julia rose, her mouth agape, and blinked twice, her lush lashes framing her slowly widening eyes. "A nanny?" He nodded. "Full-time?" He nodded again. "For Rachel?"

"Yes."

She looked at the ceiling, then back at him. "This is a joke, right?"

"No. Rose seemed to think…" He let the sentence go,

deciding it wouldn't be wise to mention that Rose believed Julia wouldn't know what was best for her. "She told me about your teaching background." He shrugged at the look of consternation that flitted on her face. "In a small town, nothing is sacred."

"Apparently," she muttered. Julia walked around her desk and held out Rachel, who promptly reached for Tony. He enveloped her in his arms and the little girl immediately grabbed his nose.

He gingerly eased Rachel's strong grip off his nose, kissing her palm gently. "Rachel likes you, and you certainly have the skills. She deserves someone who can give her the attention she ne—"

"No." She backed away slowly, shaking her head rapidly.

And keep on asking her.

"The salary will be more than enough, and you'll have free room and board. You'll have to live here at the ranch." Her eyes widened even more. "It's necessary. Rachel gets up very early, and with foaling season almost on us, I'll have to be available to help with the numerous births. We've got champion mares who'll—"

"No." Grabbing her coat and bag, Julia walked stiffly to the stairs. "She's great, but I don't want the job."

And with that, Julia was gone, her heels clanking on the metal steps. Tony stood in the middle of the office. Had he pushed too hard? Had she thought he was asking for more when he told her she'd have to live on the ranch with him?

He chased after her. Rachel giggled in delight at being jostled against his chest. "Julia!"

She paused at the front door, her back rigid.

"I didn't mean anything else." Reaching her, he lowered his voice. "My home is huge, and Miss Irene is there from eleven until five, three days a week. I could have a lock put on your door, if you want.''

She turned slowly, bewilderment on her face. ''A lock? This isn't about a lock. If you want a nanny, then advertise. I'll even help you select one.'' There were tears shimmering in her eyes, and she blinked them back. ''But, for the last time, I...don't...want...that...job.'' Opening the door, she stepped out into the chilled late-afternoon air. ''If I still have this one, I'll see you Monday morning.''

Rachel's hands shot out, her tiny fists pumping open and shut, reaching for Julia. The door closed with a bang. Rachel stuck her fist into her mouth and looked at Tony, her eyes fluttering rapidly, her furrowed brow showing her confusion. Tony chucked her under the chin. ''Me too, sweetness. Me too.''

''A lock!'' Julia slammed shut her apartment door. ''Don't you get 'I Love Lucy' up there?'' she asked, her eyes glancing upward. ''Why do I feel like I'm your *only* source of entertainment? Pick on someone else.'' Setting the groceries she'd bought for her mother down, she dropped her coat on the one chair she had. Striding into the bedroom, and unbuttoning her blouse, Julia replayed the events of the past few hours in her head.

What absurdity! Imagine, her taking a job watching his child, watching *any* child. She'd kill Rose.

She removed her blouse and threw it on the bed. Dropping her slacks, she slowly faced the mirror. Today she had turned down a job she would have loved at any other time in her life. She needed to remind herself why.

There it was—the scar that screamed her pain....

I'm sorry, Julia. We'll have to do exploratory surgery....

It lay horizontally across her lower abdomen, the outer

corners tilting upward ever so slightly, like a cruel smile at a private joke.

Of course we'll adopt, honey. Now, sleep some more....

Looking away, she brutally closed her heart. "I *won't* feel bad about refusing the job. I won't do that to myself."

Her image nodded in agreement.

Changing into jeans and a blue cable-knit sweater, Julia concentrated on what she needed to do next. She put on her coat, lifted the parcels of food, and headed over to her mother's house.

The following evening, Tony, fresh from the shower, stood wrapped only in a towel, shaving while Rachel slept. She was in the center of his king-size bed, secure in her carrier.

He smiled, remembering how excited Rachel had been on his lap atop Shadow, his favorite steed. At almost seven months, she was really adventurous. Just as her mother had been. Wiping the remaining shaving cream from his jaw, he stared at his face, but saw Anne's image in his reflection.

There had been one photo of Anne in her journal, taken, as the note was written on the back indicated, on the day she found out she was pregnant. Her smile was weary, but hopeful. Tony looked at it, blown up, framed and sitting on his nightstand. Rachel looked exactly as Anne had when she was Rachel's age. He recalled the day Anne had been taken from him, twenty-four years ago....

There's a couple interested in Annie. You want her to have a good life, don't you, Tony? Of course you do. Now, if the adoption goes through, you won't be able to see her again. You do understand, don't you?

No, he hadn't, he recalled angrily. He'd thought he could keep the family together, without outside help, but all the adults wouldn't listen to him. So, he'd let them take her, not that he had any choice. And for reasons unknown to him, Anne had rejected—or had been rejected by—her family. Piecing together what he'd read so far, he was beginning to believe the former. He shuddered to think that Rachel might have suffered the same existence. With him, at least she'd have a stable life, full of happiness.

But would he be a good father? That was a constant question lately, but on the heels of that thought he heard Julia telling him he was doing everything right, and his insecurities subsided.

Julia. Although at first she'd seemed hesitant to even acknowledge the baby, she never failed to ask about Rachel. On the other hand, Maxine seemed interested only when he reminded her of Rachel's existence. And once Julia held Rachel, she'd only reluctantly given her back to him. No such problem with Maxine. Still, on the other hand, he was being unfair to Maxine; she needed time to adjust to the change. On the other hand, Julia didn't. On the other hand.

Flustered, Tony stopped his vicious circle of thoughts and found his mind settling on an image of Julia.

Stay-at-home, rent-a-movie-on-Saturday-night Julia.

Julia, who told him over and over what a good job he was doing with Rachel. The memory of Rachel splashing water on him and giggling almost nonstop when he'd bathed her earlier popped into his head. He'd laughed at her delight.

How did Julia sound when she was delighted? How would her wet skin feel next to his in the shower?

Flinging his damp towel over the shower door, he banished that thought from his head. He was being fanciful, merely toying with an idea, acting like a randy teenager. That decided, he nodded at his reflection, then sniffed the air. Dinner!

Sure that Rachel was safe, he ran through the house and into the kitchen, opening the oven door. Reaching in with his right hand, he grabbed the handle of the casserole dish. Even before the pain began its ascent to his brain, Tony realized what he'd done, and he released his hold immediately. Stifling the yelp that sought immediate escape, he grabbed a towel from the counter, wrapped it around the dish of smoking tuna and noodles and hefted it into the sink, careful not to splatter any onto his nude body.

Turning on the water, he plunged his hand under the icy stream. His toes curled as the water tickled his pain.

"Am I overdressed?"

Tony rolled his eyes heavenward. "Hi, Maxine." He turned off the water. Wiping his hands with the dish towel, he chuckled at the absurdity of the situation. "Dinner is incinerated, as usual." He walked to the doorway. "I'd just finished my shower when I smelled the smoke. If you'll excuse me—"

"What's to excuse?" Maxine dropped her coat on the floor and approached slowly, like a hungry lioness, her eyes roaming over his body. For the first time ever, Tony felt unbelievably uncomfortable. She must have sensed something was wrong, because she stopped in front of him and raised an eyebrow.

"Rachel's alone," he offered as an excuse. He slid out of the kitchen, moving to his room where he hurriedly threw on his favorite black jeans and worn red-checked flannel shirt. Grabbing Rachel's carrier, he entered the living room again. Maxine sat on the sofa, thumbing through a fashion magazine she'd brought along.

He placed Rachel on the floor near him, then joined Maxine. She looked impeccable in an electric-blue sheath, the kind that hugged her every curve. An image of Julia in the dress, the material clinging to her body, flashed in his mind. He hoped she was okay. When she left yesterday, she'd been so upset—

"Tony? Are you okay? I said your name twice."

"Oh, sorry. I was thinking of some last-minute business. Tell me about Mrs. Sheridan and your meeting yesterday."

"Well, we went to a chic little bistro...."

Leave it to Maxine. In the middle of Wyoming, she managed to find a "chic little bistro." He was impressed. She went after, and got, whatever she set her sights on. Including him?

"Tony, you're *not* listening." She sighed. "I don't mean to be petulant, but...you've changed since—" She stopped short.

"Since Rachel's arrived?" Tony walked to the silent fireplace. Usually, a roaring fire would be burning by now, and the two of them would have forgotten all about dinner. In front of the blaze, they'd talk about their dreams.

His, to make sure his business succeeded so he could enjoy the kind of life he'd never had before. And then maybe a family...

Maxine, though, wanted to design clothes, make even more money than her already rich daddy had left her. Their dreams had never intermingled. How was it that he'd never noticed it before tonight? And what were Julia's dreams?

Maxine stood and approached him. "Tony, what's wrong?"

What *was* wrong? Why wasn't he satisfied any longer with the status quo? And why did he keep thinking about Julia?

Before Tony could figure that out, the doorbell rang. It was Saturday, and sometimes his friend and ranch foreman Chris Chambers would show up with some friends, or Rose and Tom would drop in. They'd take midnight rides, or rent a movie and order pizza.

Rent-a-movie-on-Saturday-night?

Naahh, he thought. Just a coincidence.

He went to the door and opened it. Julia stood there, shivering from the unexpected cold front that had dropped in on them, white puffs of breath coming from her parted lips.

"Julia? Come in, come in." He ushered her into the foyer. She clapped her mittened hands together and stamped her feet, chasing the cold from her long limbs. Her glasses fogged up, and she removed them to wipe them clear.

"I'm sorry for interrupting your date." She gestured with her glasses to Maxine, who sat in the living room. Then she replaced the big frames, pushing them up her nose when they slid down. "I need your signature on some papers so I can fax them to Houston tonight. I spoke with the president of Woodbriar yesterday, and he wanted the contract right away. I forgot to make sure you signed them before I..." She paused, and color slowly seeped into her cheeks.

"Left work," Tony said, and she smiled her thanks. "Why don't you sit while I check this?" He guided her into the living room. She and Maxine nodded at each other.

Julia surveyed her surroundings and honed in directly on Rachel. Just as she was about to head toward the carrier, she stopped, then walked around and looked at his paintings. The fact that she purposely avoided going to the baby hurt him. He didn't like the idea that he might have changed the nature of their relationship by making the offer he had yesterday.

"Would you like some coffee?" he asked.

"No, thanks." Julia sniffed the air, her nose crinkling slightly.

"Dinner," he explained.

Julia grinned. "No, thanks. I've already eaten."

He chuckled. "I mean, I burn it sometimes."

"Sometimes?" Maxine chided. "In the kitchen, he's a flop." Sauntering to his side, she patted his rear end. "But he does have some of the cutest kitchen outfits I've ever seen."

Julia's eyes volleyed between them, as though she sensed the private joke. Rachel came to Tony's rescue when she blinked her eyes open and gurgled. Julia's head instantly turned, and she stepped forward, but then held herself in check. He saw an inner struggle going on. Why was she fighting her natural desire?

Rachel took the decision out of Julia's hands. Spotting her, she began pumping her limbs, and an excited grin broke out on her face. A look of defeat appeared briefly on Julia's face. She dropped her handbag and knelt before the baby.

"Hello, sweetness," she mumbled.

The expression on Rachel's face was so full of joy that Tony's heart swelled.

"Tony," Maxine said, "shouldn't you sign the papers so Julia can get on with her Saturday night, and we can get on with ours? Even though it's late, she *may* have a date waiting." Her sarcasm was evident.

Julia rose slowly and spoke to Maxine. "Only thing waiting for me is a book, but I do so appreciate your looking out for me." Maxine acknowledged Julia's comeback with a slight nod. "But don't let me keep you from getting on with it. I'll just wait in the hall." Julia exited, tendrils of hair flowing as she walked past him.

Tony bit back his laughter. Maxine's eyes flashed, but she held her tongue. He moved to the dining room table, sat down and chuckled. When he'd checked over the contracts and signed them, he headed to the hallway. He spied

Maxine on the couch. A practiced pout pursed her lips, something he was finding less attractive lately. As he approached Julia, she held out her hand.

Instead of giving her the papers, he clasped her hand in his and shook it firmly, twice. It was warm and pliant, and her skin was soft. Would her skin feel that way all over? "It's a pleasure meeting you outside the ring, slugger."

Her eyes twinkled. "Was I too hard on her?" she whispered, and Tony sensed that she didn't really care if she had been.

"No, but you will be the talk of the town by tomorrow. Not having a date and all, you know." He released her hand reluctantly, enjoying their newfound friendliness.

"Of course." She put her mittens on again, took the papers and reached for the doorknob. "Good night."

"Tony." He leaned forward and spoke softly but firmly. "Say it."

Their eyes locked, and her scent spiraled gently upward—spicy, like its owner. Finally, she nodded. "Tony." Opening the door, she paused before exiting and added, "Enjoy your night."

"I already have, Julia Rourke. Thanks."

She pulled her red scarf up and headed out into the cold night. The wind howled. A threat of more snow hung in the air; the temperature was dropping rapidly. Tony shut the door and sighed. He had a feeling it would be even colder in his living room.

"No, Mom," Julia said, placing the casserole in the oven, "I can't imagine working with children now. I want the life I have."

"What life? You came over here last night—a Saturday night, I might add—instead of going out on a date, and today, instead of doing things for yourself, you're spending the day preparing my weekly meals. This isn't a life, it's a life sentence.''

''Well, you're not such a bad warden,'' Julia joked. She had shown up last night after faxing the papers to Texas, and decided to spend the night. ''I hear you, but I'm not ready to jump into taking care of children.''

''Rachel's *one* cute baby, not *children*. This might be the best thing for you.'' Marion Rourke carried the plates to the table and set them on the handmade placemats she'd embroidered. ''It'll give you something besides me to focus your attention on.''

''I need to be away from kids right now.''

Marion cocked her head. ''I said it when you were a little girl, and I'll say it now that you're a grown woman—what you *need*, when something bad happens, is to get back on the horse that threw you.''

''That doesn't work for everything, Mom.''

Marion pursed her lips. ''Julia, sit down.''

They'd always been very close, and Julia knew she was in for a lecture. She brought the teapot to the table and joined her mother.

''Listen.'' Marion took Julia's hand. ''We both lost a lot recently. Me, a husband of forty-two years, and a grandchild. You, a father, a child and a husband. And while the divorce may have been a blessing in disguise, it's still a loss.''

''Mom, please...''

''Hush, now.'' Her mother's voice softened. ''Julia, I know the greatest loss of all is that you can't have any more children. It's *terrible*. It's *unimaginable*.'' She squeezed Julia's hand. ''And it's *survivable*. You have a lot to offer a man.''

Julia felt her throat constrict. ''Can't you understand that I just need some time to heal?''

"Yes, I can, but it's been over six months, and you're still not dating." She smiled gently. "Look at me. No one will ever replace your father, but Josiah is here now. I'd be a blamed fool to pass him over." Marion shook her head, her more-pepper-than-salt hair gently brushing her ears. "Take the job, Julia."

"I'm just not ready."

"You have your father's stubbornness."

"Mom, I've *got* a job I like—"

"That isn't the thing you love—teaching."

"An apartment—"

"You aren't even trying to decorate."

Julia sighed. "Just *whose* stubbornness did I inherit?"

Marion laughed gently. "Okay. I'll stop…for now."

Julia nodded. She would accept even a temporary cease-fire. She studied her mother's haggard face. "You're still doing chores, even though the doctor told you not to."

"Doctors don't know everything. I can take care of myself, dear." Taking a sip of her tea, she chuckled. "And I have help."

On cue, Julia asked, "Have you seen Mr. Grayson lately?"

"Yesterday." Marion smiled shyly. "Your father would have liked him. I can't thank Tony enough for introducing us."

Her mother had met Josiah Grayson at an annual picnic Pellegrino Mills held every July. Since then, Josiah had been seen coming around frequently. Julia knew her mother had loved her father very much, but she wasn't the type to be without a man for long; she loved taking care of someone.

Just like you, huh?

Her mother broke into her thoughts. "Is Tony nice to work for? Your father used to speak so highly of him."

"Stop fishing, Mother. Tony is like any other boss." Any other boss with drop-dead looks and...a new woman every month.

It would do her good to remember that.

"Did you know he started a program at the ranch for high school kids to work after school?" Marion said. "It seems he loves helping people."

Maybe her mother was right. Maybe he—or actually the job with Rachel—would help her, too. No. Julia had to keep her distance from her charismatic boss to keep herself safe.

"The lasagna is baking," she said, ignoring her mother's bait. "I'm going to run to town and pick up some more cleaning supplies." She put on her coat and walked to the back door. "While I'm gone, I don't expect you to do anything, okay?"

Mrs. Rourke placed her empty teacup in the sink. "I'll pretend I'm the queen mother and I won't lift a finger—except to call Josiah and invite him for dinner."

"Good." Once outside, Julia got into her car and drove the four miles into town. Letting the scenery soothe her mind, she enjoyed the sight of the bare trees reaching up to the blue sky, and the hills in the distance covered with white.

Arriving in town, she parked on Main Street, the most crowded street in town, and walked to the local grocery store. Her shopping did not take long. Holding the full bag, she exited the store and turned left, heading back to the car.

The sight of the familiar red car passing caught her eye. She watched Tony's sedan pull up to Cicero's, the diner across the street. He opened the door and let Maxine out, then handed her Rachel's carrier. Giving Maxine a quick peck on the cheek, he got back into the car and drove towards the parking lot.

Julia stared, her curiosity piqued. Instead of going inside, Maxine looked around, then placed the carrier on the top step of the diner. She then took out a compact from her purse and checked her face. Julia looked at the glass door of the diner and saw that there were people about to leave.

She yelled. The heavy traffic drowned her out. One of the diner's patrons put his hand on the door handle. Dropping her bag, Julia darted across the street. Brakes screeched, horns blared. She reached the diner just as the door opened.

Leaping forward, she grabbed the carrier, pulling it off the top step, and got clipped by the rapidly opening door. She staggered backward, her left hand going to her forehead, her hold tightening on the carrier, which was steadily getting heavier.

''What happened?''

Tony's voice registered, and his hand closed around the handle of Rachel's carrier, thankfully removing it from her. His face was blurry.

She shook her head, trying to clear her vision, but that only made matters worse. Light-headed, she blurted out, ''Rachel was going to be knocked off the top step.'' She pointed to the three people who had just exited the diner. ''They were leaving. She would've been hurt.''

''Look, she's bleeding.''

A voice from her right caused her to turn her head quickly. Another mistake. As if she were a leaf slowly fluttering to the ground, she felt herself sway, first right, then left. An arm supported her back, clasping her upper right shoulder in a firm grip.

Blood tickled down her face from her forehead. Touching it, she vaguely made out the scarlet color. Her head fell forward. "I think I'm going to…"

And, true to her unsaid words, she did.

Julia drifted in and out of consciousness. She could hear voices as if coming from a great distance.

"She'll be all right, Tony. Let her rest for a while."

"Thanks, Doc. Anything else?"

The two voices, one belonging to an older woman and the other to Tony, continued talking, but they moved away from her. Slowly Julia opened her eyes, and tried to lift her head. Pain exploded inside her skull, colors blinding her with their intensity. Instantly, she remembered what had happened, and settled back down on the soft pillow under her head.

How nice. Someone carried a pillow with them in case of emergencies.

Just as that thought coalesced, Julia realized she was no longer on Main Street, and someone hadn't magically pulled out a pillow. She was lying on a bed in someone's house.

"I don't understand, Tony. Why'd you bring her here?"

The voice came closer. Blinking her eyes, she made out some figures standing in the doorway, lit from behind. The effort hurt her head, so she closed her eyes again and simply listened.

"Julia's got a mild concussion. I'm not going to leave her with a mother who needs looking after herself. And that's not the point. None of this would have happened had you been more responsible. Why on earth would you leave a baby…"

The voices grew louder, but receded, so she couldn't hear Maxine's response. Taking in a deep breath, Julia propped her elbows behind her and forced herself upright. When the rolling sensation ended, she looked around. The room was a plainly furnished bedroom—most likely a guest room—and she was lying on a large bed in the middle of it.

She was in Tony's house, and she needed to get home. She had obligations—had to make sure her mother was okay—and she didn't want to be in the middle of Tony and Maxine's squabble. There was a throbbing in her left temple, and when she placed her hand on it, she felt a bandage.

Julia slid her legs over the side of the bed. She was a bit wobbly, but after closing her eyes, she managed to stand unaided. Placing her hands on either side of her head, she made her way slowly toward the door.

Once there, she leaned her forehead against the wall, the cool surface relieving her heated brow. She could see out into the living room from the doorway. Maxine was pacing in front of the fireplace, and Tony stood with his back to Julia, watching her, his arms crossed. Rachel was on the floor, on a blanket, a few toys scattered around her.

"I know you're not used to having a baby around, but just use some common sense." Tony's voice was low. The whistle from a teapot sounded. Rachel's arms waved. "I'll make the tea for Julia." He left the room.

Maxine glanced down at Rachel. "I've got to go…you know, powder my nose." She stared at the baby, then lifted her and placed her in her carrier. "You'll be safer in here." She placed the carrier on the couch and hurried from the room.

Julia's eyes widened. She hadn't strapped Rachel in, and she'd placed the carrier by the edge of the sofa. Rachel squirmed. The carrier teetered. Her arms and legs kicked out. The carrier tottered.

Julia's legs engaged before her mind did, and she raced into the living room just as the carrier tilted dangerously toward the floor. She grabbed the handle, got dizzy, and sank to the floor with the carrier.

"What the— Where's Maxine?" Tony said, entering the room.

"She had to go to the bathroom," Julia said, resting her head in her left hand. "She put Rachel in, but didn't strap her, and then she put her on the couch. But, she really thought—"

"I know what she thought." Tony put the steaming mug of tea down. He took Rachel from the carrier, then removed it from Julia's hand. "Can you stand?"

"I think so." With help, she made it to her feet, and sat on the couch. "Wow. It's like living inside a kaleido-scope."

Maxine walked in, humming. As soon as she saw the two of them, she stopped. "What's wrong?"

"Even if you're only going to be gone a moment, you have to strap a baby in," Tony said, his voice tight. "And you don't perch her on a rounded surface. If Julia hadn't come out when she did..."

Maxine sighed. "Not again."

Tony glared at her. "Yes, again. This tops the time you left her on the floor near the open basement door. Or the time you gave her marbles to play with because they were pretty." He handed Rachel to Julia, and stood.

Julia smiled at the baby. Rachel grabbed her nose and tugged. She kissed her cheek and, despite all the warnings to the contrary, inhaled. Oh, yes. She smelled sweet.

"Maxine, not counting today's two near disasters, I'd say you were batting a thousand."

Maxine's lips compressed, and she darted her eyes in Julia's direction.

Julia's urge to rescue anyone in distress overwhelmed her. "Tony, I know you're upset, but Maxine—"

Maxine shot a look at her. "I don't need your help."

Julia's head ached, and her stomach roiled. She closed her eyes, and laughed to herself humorlessly. Only *her* guardian angel would set her up like this. It knew her weakness—rescuing people, injured animals and defenseless babies, not necessarily in that order.

"You're right," she said to Maxine. "You don't need my help. But Rachel does." She looked at Tony. "I'll take the job."

Chapter 4

Slowly, very slowly, consciousness crept into Tony's sleep-laden mind. He resisted it, or at least attempted to, but along with the sentient trickle of perception—the ticking of the clock, and the whooshing of the wind outside his windows—there was another sound nudging his awareness. Singing.

A soft, lulling song, about mockingbirds and diamond rings, meandered through his brain, tying into his dream. Familiar, it stirred a sensation deep within him of being cradled in his mother's arms. The soft pillow and bed cushioned his tired body, and Tony fought back every instinct to awaken; he wanted to bask in this rare memory, of a time when he was loved and cherished, when he was a baby.

A baby.

"Rachel!" He bolted upright. It was Tuesday morning. He glanced at the clock. It read 8:46. "Damn." He'd overslept. He had to get to Rachel.

Tony grabbed his green terry robe, rushed from his room and slipped along the hallway until he reached her room. Pushing open the door, he skidded to a stop.

Rachel was eating breakfast…in Julia's arms.

"She's eating," he said lamely. "I forgot you were here."

Julia, smiling and cooing at Rachel, slowly looked up at him…then down, then up again. Her eyes widened, and she turned brilliantly scarlet before she averted her eyes.

Tony looked down at his nude body. "Damn." He stepped back into the hall, and leaned against the wall, chuckling.

"Is the first act over?" Julia called out.

He slipped on his robe, tied the sash and chuckled some more. Sticking his head in, he said, "Yup, curtain's down." He stepped into the room. "And I didn't even get a standing ovation."

She smiled. "No, but I almost did."

Julia's humor was quick, and a good way to defuse what might have been an awkward situation. "I thought I overslept."

Her eyes twinkled. "You did. But as you can see, Rachel's fine."

"She sure is." He walked to the sofa. "Sorry about my dramatic entrance. I've never slept this late before—"

"Don't worry. You're exhausted. Anyone can see that."

"Yeah, well…" Tony saw she'd exchanged the bulky white gauze on her forehead for a Band-Aid. He felt gratitude swell in his chest again. "Does it still hurt?"

She touched her injury. "No, not after two days."

"What you did for Rachel… I can't thank you enough—"

"Sure you can…and already did." Julia turned Rachel around to face Tony.

He sat down. Rachel climbed over Julia to get to him. It gave Tony an excuse to admire Julia's early-morning attire. She was dressed in a mauve quilted flannel bathrobe, with little roses splattered around, and tufts of lace at the collar and cuffs. She wore it buttoned to the neck, and Tony was surprised that he found it alluring; it was so unlike the more revealing lingerie to which he was accustomed.

"I like Rachel's room," she said. "Was this your idea?"

"No. It used to be my office. Maxine helped me redesign it." He looked around at the white walls, white carpeting and cream-colored furniture: crib, sofa and changing table. The only item of color in the room was the rocking chair. It was of old mahogany, darkened with age. He pointed to it. "I bought it at an auction three years ago. I like the color."

"Mmm..." She nodded. "I love auctions."

"We have some great ones around here. When was the last time you were at one?" he asked.

"A few years ago. I bought this great old leather chair," she said, smiling sadly. "The kind you sink into, you know?" Shifting on the couch, she pulled the collar of her robe tighter around her neck. "Did you ever think about adding a splash of color in here...for Rachel?" she asked, changing the subject.

She seemed so sad suddenly. What had happened to that chair?

"No. I thought quiet colors would be calming." Rachel climbed over his lap toward the arm of the couch.

"Quiet colors *are* good, but..." Standing, she walked toward the crib. "Here." She pointed at the wall behind the baby's bed. "Wouldn't a colorful poster be nice on this wall? One that she could look at?" She moved to the opposite wall, the one with the large bay window. "And here, a nice picture of clowns, or butterflies? And maybe a plant for the window, one that purifies the air.'' She smiled brightly. ''A butterfly plant.''

He bristled, despite Julia's excitement. ''No. It's too many changes too soon in her life. It's unsettling. It would upset her.'' Made sense to him. ''Things should stay the way they are.''

She looked at him contemplatively for a moment, then nodded. There was a glint in her eyes that sort of said, *Okay, for now.*

Before he could comment on it, Rachel started babbling, and for a second, Tony wondered whether she'd start talking soon, and then, whether she'd call him Daddy. He pulled her back into his arms and stared at her.

''What's wrong?'' Julia inquired.

''I was just wondering what to do when she started talking.''

''Well, you could take out a full-page ad, but most parents just talk back.'' Julia tilted her head.

He chuckled. ''I meant, what should I do if she calls me Daddy? I don't know if I should allow that.'' Lifting Rachel into the air, he rocked her from right to left.

''You *are* her father now.'' She looked directly at him. ''Make no mistake about that. You're the one who's going to be here when she needs you the most.'' Her face showed compassion. ''You'll be a wonderful father. You're doing so well already.''

''Yeah, well...'' For the first time, Tony couldn't just shrug it off. ''Thanks.''

''You're welcome. Was that as bad as you thought it'd be?''

''What?''

''Accepting a compliment.''

He shrugged it off. ''I guess not.''

''I'm surprised you're not used to it. Everyone appreciates all you've done for the town. You must know that, and now you're bound to get a lot more compliments, with what you did for your sister, and what you're doing for Rachel."

"It's hard to think I did enough for Anne. I mean, I'd searched for years, and found my younger twin brothers Matt and Nick, but no sign of Annie."

"That must have been hard, to be partially reunited."

"You can say that again. Finally, after more years went by, the detective I'd hired called and suggested I stop looking in New York, that she obviously didn't want to be found. But—and here's the part that gnaws me—I had had a feeling he wasn't telling me the whole truth, and sure enough, after reading Anne's journal, it seems I was right."

"You mean he'd found her?"

"Yeah. Apparently he had. She wrote how she'd bluffed him, but copied down my address and phone number." He wondered how ashamed Anne must have felt. "And I think the detective knew it was her, and decided not to tell me. And I didn't press him. I don't know why."

Tony stopped. No woman he'd ever known before had ever stayed quiet this long when he talked about his past. Like Maxine, they'd always said, "Why dwell on it?"

"Did you end the search?" she asked.

"No," he said. "I told him to broaden it to include other major cities and keep me informed." He balled his fists. "And now I read how she'd been shacking up with a 'wonderful man who had to deal drugs 'cause no one would give him a job. A drug dealer who couldn't have cared less for her in life, and now that she's dead has faded into the woodwork, like Anne'd been nothing more than a minor diversion in his life."

His jaw clenched, and he fought to keep his anger contained.

"How did you end up here?" Julia asked after a minute of tense silence. "You're from New York, too."

"It's a long story," he said, not wanting to go into it. He looked at Rachel, and his anger turned into determination. "At least Rachel will know her *family*."

"That's important to you, isn't it? Family, and keeping them together." Julia looked sad for a quick second, then smiled.

"Absolutely." Tony buried his face in Rachel's chest. She latched on to his hair and tugged. "I messed up the first time."

"The first time?" Julia leaned back against the crib railing. "You have other children?"

"No. I was talking about..." He took in a deep breath. How'd he gotten back to talking about himself? "Nothing relevant. It happened a long time ago. It's not important any longer."

"You don't have to belittle its significance. You just don't have to talk about it. And maybe it's better if you don't."

Tony looked up. There had been an abrupt shift in Julia's attitude, and it irked him. "Sorry. I had the feeling you didn't mind me talking. Obviously I was wrong. It won't happen again."

"No...it's not that." She bit her lower lip.

He watched her inner battle and, in a flash of insight, understood what had happened; they were having an intimate discussion, and Julia didn't want it to continue because she was scared he'd want her to reciprocate. And he did.

But not now. Now, Tony wanted to know how she would react to the rest of his story. It was crazy, but he felt drawn to open up to her. "It's...okay...." he said slowly, exaggerating a sigh, waiting for her compassion to kick in.

And it did. "Please, I didn't mean to stop you. Go on."
Stinker.

A twinge of guilt tugged at him, but he promised himself he'd confess later. Right now, his need to see her reaction compelled him to go on, almost as much as his need to unburden himself. "My mother walked out on us when I was twelve."

Her eyes widened. "That's terrible."

"You said it. One day she told me to take care of my two younger brothers and my six-month-old sister until someone came for us." He kissed Rachel's palm. "She left us in this broken-down tenement in New York City."

Julia's brow knit, and she shook her head slowly. "How sad." Her right arm reached for him, but then, as if catching herself, she drew it back.

"Yeah, well, my brothers were lucky. They had a relatively stable existence in their foster placement. But not Anne or me. I wanted to keep us together. I would have gotten a job, but…"

"You were twelve, and it wasn't possible."

"No, it wasn't." He looked at Rachel. "I just wish I knew the whole story about why Anne's life turned out so bad."

"What about contacting her adoptive parents?"

"The only identification they found was in Anne's journal, and it was under our original family name. I don't have any clue what her adoptive name was, and I'm not sure I really want to know what did happen. It wouldn't change anything now."

Tony took little comfort in that knowledge, but his conscience eased a bit when Julia agreed with his reasoning.

"That's the story," he said. "That's what I meant by failing the first time, you know, keeping the family together."

"You were only—" She inhaled sharply and looked as though she were struggling to keep from saying anything more. After a few seconds, she composed herself, and spoke softly. "You felt they were your responsibility. I understand that. But, how awful for you—a young boy forced into being a man. I see why you might have a hard time forgiving yourself."

Tony was stunned. He expected typical comments: "Well, it's over now," or, "You think that's bad? When I was little…" And a competition of suffering would begin. He never participated. He didn't understand why anyone would want to win that contest.

Maxine knew bits and pieces of his life, but she always told him he shouldn't linger on bad memories, should just be grateful he made it out of that kind of life. And she always said, "That kind of life" with just the right amount of disdain.

But he'd told Julia more, and she'd listened, with no judgments. He was dumbfounded. And annoyed. Why did it matter to him what her reaction had been? Why had he bothered to test her at all? And why trick her into it? This was getting out of hand. "Thanks for listening. You didn't have to."

"After that performance you gave a few minutes ago?" She pressed a hand to her heart. "It's…okay…." She paused and sighed as dramatically as he had.

"How'd you know?"

"I was a third-grade teacher."

He grinned. "Angry?"

"I guess not, if you don't make that a habit."

"Agreed," he finally said, backing toward the door slowly, wanting to leave…wanting to linger.

"Are you okay?" Julia asked.

"I'm tired. Hope I don't start sleepwalking again." He

chuckled at her look of surprise. "Relax. I haven't done it in a long time. I don't even know why I mentioned it." But he did. Other than Rose, Julia was the first woman in a long, long time he had enjoyed talking to.

Stay-at-home, plant-flowers-in-the-garden-out-back Julia.

"Well, whatever the reason, thanks for the warning," she said. "Do any strange things occur during these midnight excursions?"

"No," he said. "I usually just grab a drink. Sometimes…"

"You might as well finish. You know, in for a penny…"

He laughed. "And sometimes I wake up halfway through it, sitting at my desk, signing papers. It's only been whenever I had a lot on my mind. I guess I get up because I believe I'm accomplishing something." He picked up Rachel's bunny from the floor, putting it back in the crib.

"Or searching for something," Julia suggested, then ran a hand over the crown of her head. What would she do if he reached around her and removed the pins she'd painstakingly used to secure her bun in place? "Considering how you sleep, it would probably be awkward—if not downright amusing—if we bumped into each other at night."

Those were not the words that popped into Tony's head at the picture of bumping into Julia late at night, their bodies touching. He felt a stirring as the image blossomed, and he had to turn away from her.

He couldn't understand his body's reaction to her. Julia was hardly dressed for seduction, in a sedate bathrobe, her nightgown's purple ruffle peeking out from beneath the hemline. There was something wholesome about her clean, makeup-free face. And her hair smelled mildly of shampoo, fresh and slightly fruity.

Get a grip on yourself.

Instantly his overly aroused imagination pictured another grip he'd enjoy even more. Glancing into the hall, he cleared his throat. "Do you walk in your sleep, too?"

"In my sleep, no. On a treadmill at the health club, yes."

"You should try it my way—no yearly dues."

Julia chuckled. "And think of what I'd save on leotards." She sat down. "I check on Rachel at night." She cleared her throat. "To avoid any embarrassing midnight crashes, maybe you should wear—"

"Pajamas?"

"I was going to say a bell around your neck, but I suppose pajamas would work just as well." She grinned impishly, but couldn't stop a blush from spreading up her neck and covering her face.

They laughed, and Tony was beginning to think she used her humor as armor.

Armor to protect herself. The way he protected himself from changes. Or at least he used to. It was time to leave, put some distance between Julia and him, and think about what was happening here. He glanced at the clock on the wall. "I have to get ready for work," he said somberly.

Tony knew he should say something more to her, to try and explain the sudden change in his attitude, but he couldn't find the right words. Rachel reached out her arms. Julia stood and, taking her, turned toward the couch. Without thinking, Tony touched Julia's arm. Looking down, he watched his fingers rub the flannel. He liked the feel of it, all soft and worn, indicating this was probably a favorite robe of hers. But it wasn't as soft as he remembered her skin to be.

Julia coughed, nervously.

Tony snapped his head up, releasing his hold on her arm at the same time. "Sorry." He recalled his manners. "Thanks for listening."

She averted her glance. "You're right about getting ready for work. You're going to be late."

"Tonight, too, but I'll be just across the yard at the office. You won't have anything to worry about, though. Miss Irene will be here soon, and she'll do the cooking. The ranch hands will eat whenever they get a chance, so they'll be in and out of the house all day." He was going on and on, and couldn't figure out why. It was obvious she wanted him to leave, and he should want to, too, but he hesitated. It might have been her wide, expression-filled eyes that stopped him.

Julia nodded, a bewildered expression on her face—in response to his rambling, probably. "I know the routine. Miss Irene was here yesterday, too." She paused and cocked her head, pushing her glasses up her nose. Rachel grabbed the frames and pulled them down again.

"Well, I'll see you tonight, I guess."

"Not if I see you first," she quipped as he left Rachel's room. He chuckled ruefully, then stared at his foot, wondering how he could have gotten anything that big into his mouth.

The ranch hands had long since eaten, and Miss Irene was gone. Determined to put her free time to good use, Julia pulled out the ingredients for a stew she'd purchased earlier. She'd make her mother's meals here and deliver them on Saturday, her day off. Her mother complained she was doing too much for her, but Julia didn't mind the work. Her mother needed her help.

She reached for the leeks. It would be a slightly different taste from standard onions, but she liked to experiment with new flavors. She'd inherited that from her mother's adventurous meals. There had been many times she didn't quite know what she was eating as a child, and she fondly remembered occasions when she and her father had been loath to ask, casting conspiratorial looks at one another. They had been afraid her mother wouldn't know, either.

So Julia was used to changes, even welcomed them—unlike Tony. She continued cutting the other vegetables, recalling the uneasy look on his face when she'd suggested a poster for Rachel's room. His discomfort hadn't really surprised her, considering how he'd grown up. He probably longed for stability, having had none as a child, being shuffled from one home to another. So many of the children in her student-teaching class had lived that very life. No wonder Tony displayed a penchant for orderliness—his house and business were very organized.

But there was one area in his life where change was the prevailing theme—with women. According to Rose, he dated a lot, and always short-term. Just like in high school, he never stayed with one woman long enough to form a lasting relationship.

She wondered how much longer his current affair with Maxine would last. Rose had said it had been going on longer than most. With the changes happening in his life concerning Rachel, he might not want to deal with another new woman.

After all, it's better to dance with the devil you know…

She wondered how Tony would react to the colorful addition in Rachel's room. Rachel had become so excited when she first hung the new poster she'd bought today. Even after Julia put her down for her afternoon nap, she'd seen Rachel looking at the picture through the rails of her crib, babbling while falling asleep.

Hope I don't get fired for insubordination.

Filling the pot with water, Julia dumped in the sliced vegetables and started cubing the meat. She put the pot on the stove, and turned on the burner with a sharp flick of her wrist.

If anyone had told her a week ago that she'd be working with a child again, and listening to Tony talk about his turbulent past, she would have laughed aloud. She hadn't wanted to get this close to him, to be privy to information he hadn't shared with anyone else. At least she was pretty sure he hadn't shared this with anyone else.

But here she was, thanks to fate, not only working with a child, but in Tony's house, and caring how he'd react to a poster. Julia reminded herself that she was the one who'd made the choice to be here, and she would also be the one who would have to maintain their distance. There was no way she could allow any harm to come to the child she was beginning to love, but she didn't need to become intimate with Tony. That decided, she left the stew to check on her charge.

Rachel was sleeping quietly, her little fist curled near her mouth. She knew Anne had been drug-free while pregnant, and while Rachel didn't show any indications of having any birth defects, Julia wasn't too sure she was qualified to tell what they would be. She'd just watch her closely for any signs.

Julia closed Rachel's door and walked back to the kitchen. She checked on the simmering stew, closing her eyes and inhaling the mouthwatering aroma. Glancing at the clock on the wall, she decided it was a perfect time to take a quick shower. Rachel would sleep until dinner. She walked to the kitchen door, then stopped in her tracks when the front door burst open.

Tony strode in, looking haggard, and Julia figured the look was from more than a hard day. Maxine followed him, her lips drawn in a crimson slash. Julia backed into the kitchen, unseen, and looked around for another way out. There was none.

"Tony, you're overwrought. Don't make any rash decisions." Maxine's harried voice carried through the house. "And telling me over the phone isn't right."

"It's not rash. We talked about it Sunday night," Tony said. "When you called me today, I had no choice but to repeat it."

Julia looked over her shoulder, in the direction of Rachel's room, and crossed her fingers, hoping the baby wouldn't awaken. Julia thought about telling them she was within earshot, and moved to the doorway, then stopped. Though she was uncomfortable about eavesdropping, Julia was more uncomfortable announcing her presence in the middle of a private conversation. She remembered Maxine's expression the night Tony had criticized her in front of Julia.

If Julia were Maxine, she'd be humiliated to know someone had been witness to her being rejected, and even if she didn't like Maxine much, she didn't wish that on her. She knew humiliation too well, and how it hurt. She decided to remain quiet.

"I apologize again," Maxine said. "I never meant to put Rachel in danger. But Julia's here now. You and I can resume our relationship." Tony didn't respond. She continued, "I'll tell you what. I won't even go near the baby."

"Not go near the baby?" Tony said.

Julia rolled her eyes.

"That's not the answer," Tony said. "Things have cha—are different now. I want more, Maxine. I tried telling you this, but you didn't want to hear."

"So tell me again. I'll listen."

Julia looked up at the ceiling.

Please keep them out of the kitchen.

Maxine continued. "Let's go get some coffee. We can discuss this calmly."

Julia closed her eyes. She mentally chided fate and looked frantically around the kitchen. The only place to go would be into the pantry, and she wasn't about to share a hiding place with canned beans.

Quickly moving to the kitchen table, she sat, wishing vainly for a mug of coffee, a newspaper…or, at the very least, a dry martini—stirred, not shaken.

"Maxine, wait," Tony said just outside the kitchen. "I don't want coffee. What I want is to see my…Rachel, so I'll be brief. We were only dating. I never made any promises, and you knew that. I like you, but I don't want someone who avoids Rachel."

"So I'll—"

"No. It wouldn't be fair to you. Your goals are different than mine. Your career is just starting. And that's great. But I want to spend time with Rachel. I want…"

"What?" Maxine's voice rose.

"A family. It's real important to me. I just didn't know how important until recently."

Julia stiffened, that same feeling of sadness she'd felt the first time he said how important a family was to him coming over her again. He would make a wonderful father, and a good husband, once he finally settled down.

But not for you.

She'd known that, but that hadn't stopped her from fantasizing. When she was ready, she would love to date a man like Tony. He was kind and funny, and incredibly easy on the eyes.

Maybe an affair with Tony *would* be perfect. No strings, no attachments, and he'd tire of her soon, so no need for further explanations. No pity, no obligations.

No way.

He'd want a whole woman. Now she knew why she was trapped in here—she'd needed a dose of reality, a reminder of why she had to leave eventually. Julia swallowed the bitter taste of disappointment.

Tony's voice roused her. "And I don't think you want any kids, do you? Well, I do. Lots of them. I want my house filled to the ceiling with noisy, lively children."

"But not a wife, right?"

"What's that suppose to mean?"

"You're so transparent, yet you can't even see it. We were dating about three weeks, and now Julia's here and I'm getting dumped. Do you get it yet?"

"Julia has nothing to do with this. If you really want to know why I broke up with you, besides the problem with Rachel, it's because I found out why you left Cheyenne so suddenly."

"You...you snooped behind my back?" Maxine asked, sounding outraged.

"You didn't leave me any choice. Whenever I asked, you wouldn't tell me anything."

"What did you do?" Maxine demanded.

"For starters, I spoke with some people you worked with."

"And what lies did they tell you?"

"They explained why you left."

"And you believed them!" she shouted.

"Yes," Tony said softly. "Then I spoke with Jason Rollingston. Calling the IRS with false information could've ruined him."

Maxine raged, her anger boiling over. "How dare you! *He* cheated on *me*. Whatever I did was justified, but you don't care about that, do you? Of course not," she said, answering her own question.

"Regardless of the validity, you did something behind

his back. To me, that's unconscionable,'' Tony said. "I would never be able to trust that you wouldn't do it to me." His voice dropped. "And the facts were corroborated by enough people who have nothing to gain by lying."

"*Everyone* has something to gain by lying. Even you."

"Don't be ridiculous," Tony said, and they moved back to the front door. "And lower your voice."

"Ridiculous?" she hissed, following him. "How much more ridiculous can it be than watching you play daddy to your niece?" she growled. "You're lying to yourself if you believe you're any more of a parent than me."

"Maxine..." he began in a warning tone.

"Don't 'Maxine' me. You were lying to yourself when you believed you could have rescued Anne. You're lying to yourself if you believe Rachel belongs here—instead of with a *real* family." She lowered her voice to a snarl. "And you're lying to yourself if you don't admit you want Julia."

Julia caught her breath at her last comment, but she didn't care to deal with that lie now. She'd heard enough of Maxine lambasting Tony's efforts with Rachel. Her fists curled, and she hurried forward, but she paused when she reached the doorway.

How would she explain her presence now? Tony might be placed in an awkward position if she started hurling her own insults at that woman. She might substantiate Maxine's ridiculous claim that Tony wanted her. Julia couldn't do that to him. She respected him too much.

Suddenly she felt a cold draft waft in.

"Fine, I'm going," Maxine said. "Have fun living in your *honest* world."

Julia cringed, expecting to hear the door slam, but it didn't. She heard a soft click, and then blessed silence.

"You can come out now."

Julia jumped, then took a step into the hall.

Tony leaned against the front door, his overcoat open, revealing a gray suit. "She's gone." He nodded in Rachel's direction. "Still sleeping?"

"Thankfully, yes." Julia took in a breath and released the anger, stepping out farther. "I didn't mean to eavesdrop—"

"I know. You were being discreet. I appreciate that."

"How'd you know I was—"

"Your perfume."

She touched her throat, shaken that he should be aware of her in so intimate a manner. "Don't believe her about Rachel, Tony," Julia said. "She's wrong. She was angry and talking nonsense."

He sniffed the air appreciatively. "That smell's making my mouth water," he said, ignoring her remark. Removing his coat, he hung it on the wooden peg by the door. "Is that for dinner?"

Julia's heart went out to the man who approached. The muted lighting in the hallway cast shadows on his face, making his already handsome features even more breathtaking. She swallowed, and forced her dry mouth to work. "I—I made it for my mother, but if you want some, there's plenty."

He stopped before her. "You cook for your mother?"

Tilting her head up, she took a step back. "Yes. You know she's ill." He nodded, his eyes briefly flitting down, then up again. "I usually spend Sundays cooking meals for her," she continued, crossing her arms in front of her chest. "I figured I could do that here, then bring them to her, since I'll be working on Sundays." His scent reached her, full of spice and musk, and she stopped herself from leaning forward to inhale more.

Sliding his hand through his hair, Tony nodded. "Why

not think about inviting her here for Thanksgiving and Christmas so you won't have to do double duty?"

"That's...that's very nice of you," she said softly. "I'll ask them."

"Them?"

"Oh, I'm sorry, she's dating Josiah Grayson, and I just—"

"Relax, it's okay. I forgot about Josiah. Of course he's welcome. Maybe we'll invite a slew of people and make it a real hoedown."

Her heart expanded at his generosity. "There are lots of lonely people around the holidays. If you give me a list of who you'd like invited, I'll start spreading the word."

He studied her closely. "You're a good person."

He must have read the concern she knew was on her face. At least she *hoped* it was the worry he'd read, not the desire she felt. Stepping back, she shrugged her shoulders and tried to breath normally. "Thanks." She began moving down the hall. "It's in the genes," she said, hoping the tension would lighten.

"You don't have to do that, Julia."

"Do what?" she asked casually, concentrating on placing one foot in front of the other.

"Make jokes to distract me." They stopped at Rachel's door. He touched her shoulder lightly. She turned and looked into his dark brown eyes. "You don't have to hide your feelings behind comedy all the time."

Julia didn't know he'd read her so easily. Nonplussed, she opened the door and looked in. "Rachel's awake," she said, and moved out of the way, but not fast enough.

Tony started past her, forcing her back against the door jamb, then stopped and looked down at her. He was standing so close she could feel his warm breath stir the hairs on her head. She saw the pulse in his neck throb, noticed the stubble on his firm jaw.

If he grew a beard, would it be dark brown, like his hair, or reddish?

"Babababababababababa…"

At the sound of Rachel's voice, they both turned their heads. She'd pulled herself upright, and her legs were pumping her up and down.

"She's standing…on her own!" Tony grinned from ear to ear and walked over to Rachel. "Is this the first time?"

"Yes." Julia heard the unspoken implication. It was important to Tony that he be around for Rachel's "firsts."

He beamed and fastened his gaze on the poster she tried to gesture at. Julia held her breath.

Tony picked Rachel up and walked over to the poster. "So, you want to see the pretty picture, do you?" He stopped in front of it, close enough for Rachel to slap the paper. "Pretty colors, red, yellow…"

"Come to the kitchen when you're ready," Julia said.

Tony looked back and nodded. "Thanks." He paused and took in a deep breath. "For everything."

"You're welcome," she whispered, then backed out of the room and made her way to the kitchen. So far, so good. He hadn't fired her for getting Rachel the poster, even if she had done so behind his back. Maybe he was really learning to accept changes, and with a little time she could make some more.…

She thumped herself on the forehead, wincing at the twinge of pain. What was she thinking? She was getting too involved, imagining herself staying long enough to affect many changes.

You're lying if you don't admit you want Julia.

Now that the fracas was over, Julia recalled Maxine's words. Were they true? Or merely a way for Maxine to rationalize Tony's ending of their relationship? Either way, Julia knew she had to get out of here soon. According to what Tony had said, he wanted a family, complete with kids.

Lots of them. I want my house filled to the ceiling with noisy, lively children.

She could never be what he wanted, and despite the appeal, she knew she would never settle for a fling.

After dinner, she'd tell Tony that he had to start looking for another nanny. Entering the kitchen, she inhaled the fragrant spices as she stirred the stew, and recalled the scent of Tony's cologne, and how close she'd been to him. Her breasts had grown heavy and achy. Controlling her desires wouldn't be easy.

She was tempting fate a little too much, being under the same roof with him, and hoping that she was strong enough that nothing would happen between them. She felt the sparks already igniting within her.

Suddenly Hank's voice danced in her mind, reminding her of his parting words—thrown in anger, yet painful nonetheless.

A man wants his own children. And you can't—

"Is dinner ready?"

Tony's voice caused her to drop the spoon into the stew, splattering herself. She whirled around, drops of stew on her face. Glancing at the clock, she was amazed to see that twenty minutes had passed. Tony had changed into jeans and a sweatshirt. Rachel was in his arms, giggling and patting his cheek. He put her in her high chair. Julia reached for the dish towel.

"Wait." He stopped before her and reached out a finger, wiping a drop from her right cheek. His eyes locked on hers, and he slowly brought his finger to his lips. "Tastes great."

Her heart slammed against her ribs, and a stab of desire spiraled upward from her lower abdomen. She wiped the rest of the stew off before he could do it again—before she melted to the floor. "It'll taste even better in a bowl, with a spoon."

"I doubt it," he said softly, his eyes roaming over her face.

"I have to leave."

His eyebrows rose. "Okay, I'll use a bowl and spoon."

She couldn't help smiling. "I'm not joking. Please hear me out." He nodded. "Rachel's wonderful." She paused and looked at the beautiful face of the baby.

A face that will never belong to you.

Renewed strength flowed through her. She took a bowl from the cabinet, filled it with stew and placed it on the table, indicating that Tony should sit and eat. "I had a good job at the ranch office. That's what I wanted. I took this because Rachel needed me. But I'm getting too attached to her."

"What's wrong with that?" Tony asked, picking up a hunk of bread and ripping off a piece. He dipped it into the rich stew. "She's an easy kid to love. And she adores you."

"But this isn't what I need right now."

"Are you sure?" he asked, eyeing her intently. "Anyway, I need to know she's in good hands while I'm at work."

"I understand that, but there are plenty of other caring people in the world. It doesn't have to be me." She shook her head, her mind made up. "And it's better that I leave now, before she becomes too attached to me. I'll help you find someone. Okay?"

"Why don't you tell me why? The *real* reason," he added when she started to open her mouth.

"You mean the stuff Rose hasn't told you?" she answered glibly, then sighed. "Sorry. I didn't mean to..."

He took her hand in his. "I know it isn't easy for you to open up. Believe it or not, I share things with my friends, but I don't usually share my past experiences with anyone. With you, it seemed to be easy. And after a few minutes, it got easier." Tony squeezed her hand and smiled. "Try me."

Julia pondered his words for a full minute. She'd seen his caring side exposed when he was with Rachel, and his depth of feeling when he was telling her about his life. Maybe he *would* understand her pain. Maybe he would see why she couldn't remain here. *Maybe it was time.*

Julia took in a deep breath. "Do you remember why my parents came out to visit me?"

Tony furrowed his brow. "Your dad asked for time off.... He was excited...." He shrugged. "I don't remember why."

"They were coming to see me because I was pregnant. I suffered with morning sickness." She laughed bitterly. "Now there's a misnomer. *Morning* sickness. I was sick all day long for the five months of my pregnancy. It was so bad, I couldn't travel." Her eyes closed, and she pictured her parents' happy faces. "So they came to see me."

She heard the scrape of a chair on the floor. When she opened her eyes, she saw that he'd moved closer. Rachel gurgled, happily playing with the toys that were connected to the table of her high chair.

"My baby would have been ten months old." Julia's eyes filled with tears. She stood, needing to pace.

She heard Tony behind her, then felt his hands on her shoulders. How she longed to lean back and let him comfort her.

"A week after my father's death, I had an…ac—an accident."

Had he heard the hitch in her voice? For a second, there was no sound, no movement, and then she was hauled back against Tony's chest. His arms banded around her. "What kind of accident?"

"I…fell, and had a miscarriage."

"Oh, honey. How awful." He turned her around and hugged her, smoothing his hands over her back. "I remember what Rose was like after hers, and I know you both love children."

She calmed down, but knew the worst wasn't over. There was one more fact involving how she'd lost the baby that her mother didn't even knew about—a fact she was never going to be completely sure of. Still, it ate away at her, night and day. She only had temporary respite from the thought when her mind was occupied.

Tony held her upper arms, and looked at her. She saw the sorrow in his eyes. "First your father dies in an accident, then you lose your baby in one. I can't tell you how sorry I am."

The compassion Tony was showing her urged Julia to tell him her suspicions. The words pushed at her, needing release. She swallowed, then shut off the warning bell inside her and made a decision. Tony looked at her with such understanding, such caring, that the words found release. "Mine was no accident," she said softly, out loud, for the first time.

Tony's eyes hardened.

Chapter 5

"Son of a bitch!"

Tony's epithet burst from his lips. Quickly he glanced over his shoulder, but Rachel was still playing contentedly with her toys.

When he looked back at Julia, he saw that the color had drained from her face, and as he watched, a stray tear streaked down her cheek. "Julia, what's wrong?" He attempted to reach for her again, but she shrugged his hands off.

She pushed her glasses up her nose. "Nothing. I'm okay."

"Bull. You look like a ghost. What happened?"

"I'm not comfortable with...shouting."

Tony studied her colorless face. "Not just shouting. Men shouting, right?"

Her eyes darted away from his.

"Hank yelled at you, didn't he?"

Meeting his glance, she nodded.

"And more?"

"No," she said, hugging herself. "Just verbally controlling, not physical, at least not until the end, and even then, I'm not entirely sure."

Tony cupped her chin. "Aw, honey, I'm sorry I yelled." He wiped away the tear that rested on her jaw, "But my anger wasn't directed at you." He exhaled. "Sit down, and tell me what happened." When he moved to the table, she resisted. "Please?"

"Why are you so interested?"

"I guess because you're so good with Rachel, I don't want to lose you."

Her color had returned to normal, so he took another risk.

"And it's also because I like you. And you listened to me, so I'd like to return the favor." He shrugged. "Are those good enough reasons?"

Color blossomed high on her cheekbones. "I'm sorry, I didn't mean to sound like I was interviewing you for the job as my friend, it's just..."

You're lying if you don't admit you want Julia.

Maxine's words came back to Tony's mind, and he wondered if that was what she was hearing too. He took a step forward, and held her hand. "Trust me, Julia."

She searched his face, then nodded. "Let me get Rachel her bottle and some cereal before I start. She's hungry."

Tony's heart, which had hardened a minute ago against the man who'd hurt Julia, softened with Julia's concern for Rachel.

Once Rachel was settled, Tony moved his chair close to Julia.

"Okay. First off, I have to qualify the statement I made. I'd been keeping it inside for over a year, so it sort of came out in a rush. I don't have definite proof that it wasn't an accident, but I have a gut instinct." She sighed deeply. "It's not enough to hang a man over."

"*I* trust your instinct. Hell, I trust you with Rachel."

She smiled briefly. "Thanks." Inhaling deeply, she continued. "Hank was a great catch, tall, with classic good looks—so when he pursued me so earnestly, I was very flattered. I'd dated other men, but he was so romantic, so cavalier, I was swept off my feet. We married shortly after we began dating, and for a while things were okay. Hank was intimidating, but I thought that was part of his charm—and necessary in someone who was struggling to become a top-notch lawyer."

Julia stood, walked to the sink and filled a glass with water. "Our marriage wasn't...easy. Hank liked having things his way. But when things *were* smooth, he was the nicest, most generous man I knew." Sitting down again, she took a sip, then continued, her voice calmer now. "I thought our problems were simply those that came from learning how to adjust to each other, and I made every attempt to compromise." She laughed bitterly. "But I felt that something wasn't right. Like, my actions and thoughts were being directed, controlled." Her lips compressed.

"I think it's wonderful that you recognized that. Lots of women wouldn't have."

"Thanks. Counseling helped. Anyway, I stayed with him for another two years. My parents hinted that maybe I should leave, but I stood by Hank steadfastly. His stories were always so convincing—he was dealing with a lot as a third year law student, clerking in a prestigious firm. The pressure on him was enormous. He always promised things would get easier, and besides, he'd never physically abused me once." She looked directly at Tony. "Sometimes I wish...not that I wanted him to hurt me, but if he had, I would have been able to leave him."

"I think I understand."

She smiled gratefully. "After he was hired by the firm, things did begin to get better. Then, I got pregnant. I thought Hank wanted that, since he always talked about having a large family. I didn't know, at the time, that that was one of the things he'd said just to keep me under control—keep me placated."

Rachel cried, and Julia instantly stood and took her from the high chair. "So, there I was, pregnant, teaching full-time plus in school at night for my master's, and thinking things would work out. But they didn't." She walked to the cabinet, took some large plastic bowls and lids and spread them on the floor near them. On her stomach, Rachel grabbed the items. "Hank started staying late…at the office. He said he was sorry, but as an up-and-coming lawyer, he had to make the sacrifices." Julia laughed bitterly. "He was fooling around. With his secretary, another clerk, anyone who made him feel like a man. It was so obvious. He flaunted it."

"What a bastard. I'd love to get my hands on him."

She glanced up at him. "It wouldn't change what happened, but thanks anyway." Sitting back down, she continued. "So I was five months pregnant, my parents had arrived three days prior, and my father had just been… killed." Her voice lowered. "The day before they were to fly his body to Iowa for the funeral, Hank and I were on the top of our third-floor walk-up, arguing. I wanted to go with my mother, and Hank refused to let me. He said it was because of how sick I was. He didn't think I should risk the baby's health." A shuddery breath escaped her lips, and she closed her eyes. "I think he felt if I wasn't around him, I'd see what he was doing to me, and never come back."

"You may be right."

"That's a small consolation—being right," she muttered, and when she opened her eyes, tears shimmered in them. "Boy, could I use a joke right about now."

Tony moved his chair closer, his knees touching hers. He stroked her cheek. "You're safe here, Julia."

She smiled weakly, but it faded as she spoke. "Hank always got loud and very animated when he was angry. I turned my back on him, and he said not to turn away—he wasn't done talking. I told him I wasn't turning away, and I was about to tell him I was just going to walk down the stairs, when—"

"Were you pushed?" Tony ground out the question. He had to control himself, for Julia's sake, but he'd never wanted to crush a man the way he did now. He'd wanted to kill Mitch Brown, for his apparent disregard of Annie, but the feeling now was somehow different, much more primitive.

"That's what I don't know. I turned back around, and remember seeing his hand come forward. Maybe he was trying to grab me, or maybe he tried to tap my shoulder, or maybe I bumped into him...."

Julia's eyes closed. She removed her glasses and pinched the bridge of her nose.

"In any case," she said, her voice deceptively calm again, "I lost my footing, and fell down the metal stairs."

Rachel whined, and Julia picked her up, hugging the baby to her chest.

"How did it end, between you and Hank?"

She kissed Rachel. "Like most bullies, once you stand up to them, they shrivel. After everything happened, I told him exactly what I thought about him, and that we were through. He tried some tricks, but none of them had any more power over me. I came home one day, and he'd moved his things out."

Tony nodded. He was glad she'd stood up to that jerk. He was about to tell her that when she spoke again.

"You must have a lot to do, Tony. Why don't you take care of whatever while I look after Rachel? Or you could rest until dinner. Or you can go to the office and work."

"Why are you telling me what—" he began automatically, immediately stopping at the look of shock on Julia's face. He expelled a sharp breath. "Sorry. It's a knee-jerk reaction. I don't like to be told what to do."

"I got that." She rocked Rachel in her arms.

Tony grimaced inwardly. Their closeness of a few minutes ago was shattered. Damn!

A sudden insight plowed into his brain. "You want time alone."

She shrugged. "Not if you don't want—"

Placing a finger across her lips, Tony said, "Just ask."

She hesitated slightly. "I could use some time alone."

"That wasn't so bad, was it?"

"As bad for me as accepting a compliment is for you."

"Touché. All right, you've had enough talking for one night, I got it. I'll be in my office. Call me when Rachel's ready to go to sleep, and I'll come to say good-night."

Rachel grabbed Julia's nose. "You're something else, Tony Pellegrino." She eased the baby's hand away, and looked at her. "And she's one lucky child to have you in her life."

Tony's chest swelled. "Thanks," he said. "Tomorrow we'll talk more, and over time you'll see how right I am."

"Right? About what?"

"About staying." Her eyes widened, but Tony didn't give her a chance to balk. He marched to her, and cupped her chin. "Now that you're here, we're not letting you go, right, Rachel?" He chucked the baby under her pudgy chin.

She giggled in delight. "Besides, there's something between us, and I want to discover what it is."

Julia's mouth opened, and her eyes sparkled with determination, but he cut her off.

"Don't deny it. You feel it, too," Tony said.

She slammed her lips together and didn't say anything,
but Tony would settle for that now. "In any event, Rachel
needs you, and you need Rachel. Fate brought you to
me—uh, to us, I mean."

"Don't go talking about the *Fates* to me. We're close
and personal friends, and trust me, they don't do things for
my benefit. If I *was* meant to be here, it was solely for their
entertainment purposes, and has nothing to do with you,
either."

"In that case, let's give them something to talk about."
He covered her mouth with his, swallowing her gasp of
surprise. Tony counted on Julia not struggling with Rachel
in her arms. Otherwise, he might have had to duck. She
probably had a mean right hook.

Rachel grabbed hold of his sweatshirt, but Tony didn't
break away from Julia. He simply put his arms around both
of them. Rachel giggled, and when he opened his eyes a
slit, he saw Julia's eyes darting from side to side, desire
mingled with indecision deep within them. She didn't know
how to stop the kiss, or even if she really *wanted* to.

You're lying if you don't admit you want Julia.

Yes, Tony did want Julia. He was physically attracted to
her—hell, he'd have to be dead not to be—but he wanted
more. He wanted to hear about her life, tell her about his.
He wanted to hold her, comfort her, protect her.

Delicately he kissed her. When she leaned forward, his
ego soared. He murmured against her mouth, "You'll
stay."

Slowly he let her end their kiss. Her sapphire eyes glowed. "Tony, don't press your luck—"

"Wrong." He smiled and walked to the doorway. "This time, I'm gonna press it for all it's worth." He left her standing in the kitchen, holding Rachel. This *was* happening fast, and he couldn't discount the warning sounding in his head, but for the first time ever, he wanted to actively disengage the alarm.

Fools rush in...

Yeah.

Fool, he thought, and entered his office, whistling.

Tony was still whistling the next day as he stripped the tack from Shadow's back following their ride. Placing the saddle on the rack, he hung up the bridle and reached for a towel. Steam rose from the stallion's glistening black coat as he rubbed down the overheated animal. He recalled Julia's equally overheated face earlier this morning. Last night, before Julia could mount a counterattack on his plan to keep her here, he had kissed Rachel good-night, and slipped into his room. She hadn't had a chance to argue with him, and this morning she'd still been steaming. He couldn't help but smile. She sparkled when she got angry.

Shadow twisted his head back and nudged Tony's leg with his nose. "I know you're thirsty, boy, but you'll have to wait a little longer." He knew it would harm the magnificent beast if he drank right away. He returned his attention to his task and put Shadow in his antisweat blanket, then covered him with a blue cooler, walking him around while he dried.

Chris Chambers, Tony's ranch foreman, entered the barn about forty minutes later. He brought in Planter's Pride, stopping the stallion two stalls down to give both horses enough kicking room, should the need arise.

"Afternoon," Chris said, and began currying his horse, his practiced hands moving the round comb in small circular motions. "Where's Rachel? Miss Irene's not here, so I expected to see her with you again."

Chuckling, Tony felt Shadow's drier flank. "Left her with Julia. Rachel has a soothing effect on her." He reached for a bucket of water and let Shadow take a few gulps. Glancing sideways, he saw Chris's eyebrows rise.

"So Julia's all riled up? What'd you do to her?" he asked.

"Nothing, yet."

"So, it's like that."

"Like what?"

"She's under your skin."

"Yeah, I guess so. The hell of it is, she argues all the time, she's ornery, opinionated, and likes changes. And I'm as attracted to her as mustard is to a tie at a county fair."

"Never heard you talk about a woman like that before."

"Never *felt* this way before. Hell, I'm ignoring all the warnings. She's definitely a stay-at-home-and-plant-a-garden woman, but she's also warm, and sharp—got a sense of humor that would leave you hurtin'," Tony said, pushing back his black suede cowboy hat. "And she's not bad on the eyes, either."

"She's got you hog-tied. Do I hear wedding bells?"

Tony jerked the water bucket and sidestepped splashing water. "Hey, I didn't say anything about marriage. In fact, I don't remember even *mentioning* marriage."

Chris laughed. "Not yet you didn't, but I never met a man who talked like that about a woman and didn't end up marrying her."

"Well, you've just met that man."

"Whatever you say." He brushed the other side of the chestnut horse. "So things are over with Maxine?"

Glad they'd dropped the uncomfortable subject of marriage, Tony said, "Yeah. We had too many differences. Why?"

"Just wondering."

"Uh-huh."

"Okay, I've a hankering to speak my mind with her."

"You never said anything."

"I know. She had to get you out of her system."

"Well, she's done that for sure. Pissed as hell at me. Careful. She'd probably bite you, thinking she'd hurt me."

"Could be interesting."

The two men shared a look. Tony was glad they wouldn't come to blows over Maxine. "Good luck, buddy."

"She'll need it." Chris smiled and went back to his horse.

In school, Maxine had said Chris was too tall and lanky for her taste. Tony looked at the dark-haired man. He was about as muscular as Tony; they both took their chores seriously, and participated in all sorts of sports in the summer. Chris was a good man, and his best employee.

And he would be a handful for Maxine.

Tony looked out the window in Shadow's stall and saw Julia on the porch, carrying in some logs for the fireplace. "Uh, Chris, finish Shadow for me, would you?" He hardly heard Chris's reply as he grabbed his parka and headed out to meet his own handful.

She was garbed in *his* large beige overcoat, and he couldn't wait to put it on himself and inhale her scent. God, that woman's body should be draped in white silk togas, not bogged down by his nondescript shroud.

As he approached the porch, a great view greeted him, and he had to admire it. Bent over, the wind whipping the hem of her coat up, Julia displayed her jean-clad, totally feminine and most enticing fanny. He imagined long, lean legs and, not having seen otherwise, encouraged his imagination in that direction.

"Too tempting."

Julia dropped her logs and whirled around. She held up a hand to ward off the buffeting wind. Her cheeks glowed rosy, and Tony wished he knew whether it was because of the cold, or because of him. She wasn't wearing her glasses.

"I beg your pardon?"

"I said, 'too tempting.'" He nodded at her. "When I was a kid, anyone bent over with their...uh, rear guard unprotected was fair game for all sorts of...potshots." Her eyebrows rose as he walked up the steps and smiled down at her. "An upturned butt got whacked, kicked, goosed or, at the very least, laughed at." He pointed to the logs. "How many more you need?"

"Just a few more. I've already brought in three loads."

"I'll get them." Tony picked up the four logs she'd dropped and added five more before he felt the first blow sting his butt. "What the hell?"

Spinning around, he stared at Julia. She stood, legs spread, tossing a snowball from one ungloved hand to another, a sinister smile on her radiant face. "You're right. It's really tempting."

Before he could utter a sound, she hurled the second snowball. He tried to duck, but wasn't fast enough, and it struck his right shoulder. He sputtered as flying snow entered his open mouth.

"It was *your* bright idea, cowboy. Just like *thinking* I'm going to stay."

Tony laughed. "Oh, I see. Going to change my mind?"

She packed the snow tighter, and hurled the next sphere at her target. She missed, and hoisted another ball. "You betcha."

Tony dropped the logs on the pile and grinned. He took the first step down. She backed up slowly. Bending, she scooped more snow, rolled it into another ball and shot them both at him.

Tony sidestepped them, laughing. He knew she wouldn't retreat without a fight—about staying. He removed his cowboy hat and threw it on the porch, out of danger's way, then grabbed a handful of snow and packed it together.

"Well, Tony, are you man enough?" she teased, forming another cold missile.

He threw the ball, and she yelped, turning and sprinting away. It hit her squarely in the back.

And the war was on.

She gathered more snow, forming the balls and throwing them blindly, kicking snow in his direction as he approached. Tony lunged for her, throwing the two of them into the white sea, tumbling around, grabbing fistfuls of snow and mashing it into her face.

Julia giggled, gasping for air, and struggled to free herself. At one point, she managed to wrest away and turned around for another attack, covering him with mounds of snow. Eyes closed, Tony found her foot and yanked. Julia fell back into a two-foot pile of shoveled snow near the porch steps.

"Say it!" Tony shouted, sitting astride her in the snow, digging his fingers into her sides, attempting to tickle her.

"Say what?" she yelled back, squirming around, throwing handfuls of snow haphazardly up at him.

"Uncle. Cry uncle."

"No!" Tears mingled with snow on her flushed face. But, after a few more feeble attempts to get him off her, she caved in. "Okay. You win! You win!" she called out.

"Not good enough!" He picked up a handful of snow and threatened to drop it on her. "Now, cry uncle."

"Only to the fight here—not the one from last night. I'm leaving, and you'd better get used to it." She laughed nervously, squirming beneath him.

Tony sat back on his haunches and stared at her. Her nose was red. She bit her lower lip, and it turned pink and swollen, beckoning him. Her hair had gotten loose from the perpetual bun—wisps of light mahogany tendrils covered with white crystals. Removing his right glove, he reached down, brushed snow off her forehead and touched her fevered cheek.

He felt, more than heard, her sharp intake of air. Looking into her eyes, he saw the lighthearted expression disappear, and apprehension take root.

"I know you're afraid to get close, honey, but—"

Tony stopped abruptly. Julia had paled, and he suddenly got the feeling that he'd better not push her right now. He got off her supine figure and held his hand out.

Julia shook her head and stood up on her own, brushing the snow off her back and legs. She stamped her feet and glanced up.

Tony decided to try another track. "As to whether I'm *man* enough...didn't you get a good impression of that the other morning?" he teased. He was rewarded with a smile.

"I did," she said, then added, "And that's why I had to ask." She batted her eyes, and darted into the house.

Humor. Her armor. He'd gotten close, and that scared her. Tony gathered the logs and entered the house, determined to learn why she kept bolting from him. When he'd deposited them and removed his coat, he checked on Rachel. Dressed in yellow flannel, she slept peacefully, her fist near her mouth. He glanced at the two newest colorful additions to the room—a stuffed toucan and a large gorilla.

Back in the hall, he noticed Julia's door ajar, and walked over. She was sitting on the bed, leaning back against the pillows, staring out into space, a book open on her lap. Her hair was neatly back in its bun.

Just because I like her doesn't mean we have to get serious.

Keeping that thought in mind, he leaned against the door jamb and asked, "How long has Rachel been asleep?" .

"Not long. About twenty minutes. She was outside with me all morning, so she'll sleep a while longer." She closed the book, and pushed her glasses up her nose. "By the way, Miss Irene can't come in tomorrow. Her husband George's back went out again. She asked if I wouldn't mind helping, so I took the liberty of telling her I wouldn't mind at all."

"I appreciate that. We'll all chip in, though. You won't have to do much."

"Oh, I don't mind. I like keeping busy."

"I know," Tony said, wondering if that was how she kept her sadness at bay. He glanced down at her reddened fingers. "You shouldn't play in the snow without gloves."

She looked at her hands, rubbing one over the other. "They'll be fine. I slathered them with lotion." Throwing him a mildly scathing look, she added, "I hadn't expected to be out there that long."

"Hey, you were the one looking for trouble, and you got away without calling uncle." She grinned. "Feel better now?"

She nodded, and averted her gaze. Her profile held his interest, the high cheekbones outlined by the light over her shoulder, her nose slightly upturned, aristocratically.

"You don't like changes," she said suddenly, "or people doing things behind your back, yet you approved of the ones I did at the office, and in Rachel's room. Why?"

"Those weren't behind my back. That indicates doing something underhanded—evasive. You were hired to make things more efficient. Besides, those changes didn't affect me personally.''

"I see.'' She looked at him. "Are you against all changes that affect you personally?''

"I would have said yes to that before I met you. And as far as Rachel's concerned, I'd already decided to trust you. She likes the colorful additions to her room. I guess she needed more stimulation than she had.''

"Believe me, you're very stimulating,'' she muttered quickly.

He chuckled.

A blush crept up her neck. "Well, it's true. Regardless of the fact that I'd be feeding your ego, you do provide a lot of interaction with Rachel. The room just needed more of a personal touch.'' She leaned forward. "Did you have a room of your own in your foster placement?''

Julia didn't say foster *home,* or foster *parents,* two terms so inappropriate for what he'd lived through. Tony's appreciation rose. He sat on the edge of the bed. "It depends on which placement you're talking about—number one, two, three...or four.''

Her eyes widened. "I had a few students who had similar experiences. One little girl had been in three homes, and she was only seven.''

Tony laughed bitterly. "Yeah. My first home was with a woman who thought it was her duty to teach me respect. I was twelve, and thought I knew it all, but...'' He shook his head, remembering Susan Markham's painted face, and the belt she'd hung on the dish rack by the sink. "After a beating, she'd escape in alcohol. The money she got for taking care of us—there were four others—paid for it.''

"How long were you with her?''

"Only for about six months. They found out about her, and removed me. After Susan, I got placed with Mike and

Chelsea Brewster. They tried, but they were so messed up, they couldn't handle it. Mike was always out of work. Then he'd heard about a new car factory opening in Chicago, so we moved."

"That's illegal, to take you out of the state."

"Yeah, but that didn't stop them." Tony stared at Julia, seeing instead a scared young boy, afraid of telling anyone he needed help. "I didn't have anyone to turn to. I tried to tell the teacher of the fifth school I was shipped to, but by the time she got around to investigating, we'd moved again."

Julia crossed her legs. "Number three."

He nodded. "Exactly. It was Chelsea's brother. He worked at a factory as a foreman, had a decent wife and three kids of his own. He was a churchgoing man, and figured I needed him—and some God-fearing lessons, in the form of more beatings."

"Oh, Tony," she sighed.

Turning toward her, he rested his hand on his thigh, containing the urge to undo her hair and remove her large glasses, then kiss her soft, parted lips.

He cleared his throat and continued, longing to tell her all. "Then the plant closed down. Bill Clarkson, that's his name, found another job opportunity here, on the Crowley Ranch."

She pulled off her glasses and bit on the tip of the earpiece. Her blue eyes captured him.

He refocused. "I was fourteen by then."

"But you weren't with a large family when I knew you. Not that I particularly remember you," she added hastily.

He grinned. "By the time you and I met in high school, I was with my last, and best, family. The Jansons were terrific people, even if it took me a few years to stop being an ass so's I could tell them that. After Bill left me in the bus terminal with money to get back to New York City, I met Claire and Jonathan. They just returned from a trip and found me sitting, alone, with my one brown leather satchel at my feet."

"They had no children of their own?"

"No." He slid closer. She didn't move. "Their only child, a boy, had died at birth, and Mrs. Janson couldn't have any more kids." Julia shifted uncomfortably. "Sorry, honey. I'm so blasé about it. I didn't think how you would feel hearing that after losing your baby."

Julia shook her head. "I'm fine. I just felt sorry for Mrs. Janson."

"Don't be. She never did." Tony laughed. "I remember when they approached me, I was just fourteen, eating a candy bar. She sat next to me, ignored my grumbled warning about keeping her distance, and before I knew it, we started talking. By the time we'd finished, she knew my whole story, and was wiping the chocolate from around my lips with a tissue."

"So, you have a secret passion for chocolate." Julia's voice sounded throaty as she teased him.

"Yeah, among others." She blushed anew, but Tony didn't press his advantage. "Anyway, they brought me to their home, across town, a house surrounded by some of the prettiest flowers and friendliest neighbors I'd ever met. You know the place, right?" She nodded. "I had a chip on my shoulder—Lordy, more like a boulder—but that didn't stop them from trying to reach me." Julia's hand was rubbing his arm. He felt her fingers flex against his flesh. "Or love me."

"Obviously, they succeeded on both counts." She looked at her hand. Frowning slightly, she removed it and pushed her glasses up her delicate nose, then slid back on the bed. "No wonder you're so against change."

"Not anymore, and not all change. Sometimes it's for the best, don't you think?"

"Some changes," she agreed slowly. "Others should be learned from."

"We could learn from each other," he suggested, heedless of the warning implicit in her words...and the one flashing in his head.

"Some lessons exact too high a price," she said, then switched topics. "What happened to your mother? Is she still alive?"

"Haven't the vaguest idea," he said. "Couldn't care less."

"You don't *want* to know?"

"Nope."

"But—" She cut herself off.

"What?" he asked, pushing down a spark of anger.

"Well, don't you think Rachel deserves to know her?"

Tony recoiled. "No way. My mother gave up her rights the day she walked out on us." He stood and paced away, over to the picture of the flowers. "What's to stop her from seeing Rachel, letting her believe she cares, and then leaving? I'm going to protect my daughter from people like her."

"But..."

He faced her down, and damned his curiosity for needing to know. "Again but? But *what?*"

She spoke softly. "You're doing the same thing. You've gone out with different women over the years, never staying with them very long, never getting serious. Either you leave them, or..."

"Or what?" He practically shouted it, but contained himself at the last minute. "Go on."

"Or you create situations in which they have to leave you, like when they discover you weren't going to commit to them." She cocked her head. "Aren't you abandoning them before they can do it to you?"

"No. You're twisting things. It's not like that at all. I never promise any woman anything. It's not my fault if they think I promised more than I did." Tony felt a burst of anger coupled with a smidgen of self-doubt. He let anger dominate. "I can too form relationships. Look at me and Rachel. I love her, and only want the best for her. Are you saying I'm going to abandon her?"

"Of course not, but... Nothing. It's not my place to say—"

"It is now." He leaned toward her. "You started this. Don't have the guts to finish it?"

Her blue eyes flashed. "Fine. I'll finish it. Of course you can form a relationship with Rachel, and Rose, and even Miss Irene. They're not all threats to you." She took in a calming breath. "Look, I'm not a psychologist, and I don't play one on TV, but I don't need a degree to see what's obvious."

Tony slapped his thigh, ignoring her joke. "If it's so obvious, why can't I see it?"

"How should I know? Maybe you haven't seen it, or maybe you have and—" her voice dropped "—you've refused to face it. Look at how you've recently dropped Maxine and are suddenly interested in me."

"It's not sudden."

"Really? We've only known each other a short while, and in that time, you were involved with Maxine. Now—"

"Now, nothing. You know what happened between Maxine and me. Hell, you heard most of it. We didn't have anything in common."

"Did you have anything in common with all the other women you dated?"

"Sometimes. Most of the time. And there weren't that many."

She arched an eyebrow.

"There weren't!" he shouted, hands raised.

She shrank back on the bed.

"Don't," he said, the thought that she was scared of him irking him more than the topic of conversation. "I'm just frustrated. We were talking about Rachel, and her needs, and now we're discussing my active social life."

Julia stood, clutching her book to her chest. "We were talking about forming relationships."

"Don't you mean my inability to do that?"

Julia let out a long breath. The tension in the air was palpable.

"Besides, everything we're talking about has nothing to do with Rachel," he added. "She needs stability, and I'm going to give it to her. In that respect, I've changed from when I was a kid."

"Yes, you have, and maybe your mother has, too, if she's alive," Julia whispered.

"My mother?" he asked incredulously. "Again with my mother?"

"Yes, again. You just told me all about your turbulent childhood as though you were reciting something that had happened to another little boy. It didn't seem to faze you at all."

"So now I'm maladjusted 'cause I came out of this mess well-adjusted?"

"No, but you've got to admit it's odd that you can discuss it so casually. And look at how you reacted to the mere mention of your mother. There's obviously some unresolved issues—"

"Cut the psychobabble," Tony said tightly, angry at her for bringing up old wounds. "It's not gonna hurt Rachel.

She's happy, and well fed, and…adjusting, and…" Julia's words began to sink in. "Is it?" he asked quickly. "Is she gonna be hurt?"

"I don't know," Julia said softly. "I don't think it's healthy for you to harbor such hatred. It's bound to affect her somehow."

"I've got it under control," he said automatically, but was pushed to add, "but just for argument's sake, what do you think I should do?"

"Try and understand your mother."

"Are you serious?"

"Yes. What your mother did was horrible, unimaginable, but what if she thought what she was doing was in your best interest?" Tony opened his mouth, but her hand silenced him. "Did she look happy about leaving? I know this may be painful, but try and recall all the circumstances, not from a twelve-year-old's perspective, but as an adult." She paused. "Was she pleased?"

If he gritted his teeth any tighter, Tony knew he'd crack his jaw. His immediate response was to run, but something deeper warned him to listen to Julia.

He forced his thoughts back to that time period. Closing his eyes, he pictured the scene, Nick and Matt playing in the corner of their apartment, Annie in her makeshift crib—an old dresser drawer—and…and his mother's tears…her sad eyes.

"No, she wasn't happy." His voice sounded alien to him, echoing as the images took on substance….

I have to leave you now, it's for the best, but I promise, someone will be by in a little while to take care of you, and you'll have no more problems—none of you.

Tony jerked back.

Always remember that I love you.

He told Julia what he recalled, and when he finished, she

spoke softly. "It sounds like she was miserable. For some reason, she thought by leaving you, you'd all have a better chance at life. Her intentions may have been good."

"Her intentions?" Tony's voice rose. "Julia, there's no reason on earth for a mother to abandon her children."

"Not even if she knew that by staying, she was condemning them to a life of poverty?"

Tony's guts twisted. He stared at Julia. She was asking him to throw out everything he believed. "You didn't see her leave. You didn't—" His anger lifted its black head and roared. "You make my mother sound like a saint! She wasn't—"

"Of course she wasn't a saint—just a woman, overwhelmed by her responsibilities. What happened to your father?"

Tony raked a hand through his hair and strode to the door. How did Julia get to him so easily? "He died when I was eleven, right before she left us." Spearing her a look, he growled, "God, woman, you do wear on a man."

"I don't think I'm saying anything you haven't asked yourself over the years." She paused. "Did I overstep my bounds?"

"Yes."

She raised her eyebrows.

He expelled a breath. "No. I don't know. My mind's twisted around."

Standing, she laid the book down at the edge of the bed, and approached him. "I'll just say one more thing, then I'll shut up, okay?"

"I know I'm gonna hate myself for this, but go ahead."

"I'd want to know if she was still alive. I'd want to have answers to the questions I carried. And I think that one day Rachel will want to know the story, too."

She moved past him and left her room, leaving Tony and

his ghosts standing in the doorway. He leaned against the door and shook his head, his anger finally winding down. Julia's words replayed themselves, and he wondered if she was right.

He pictured Rachel in seven years. *Daddy, all the kids at school have grandparents. Where are mine?*

He shuddered. What would he tell her? Did she have the right to know her grandmother? Tony unconsciously glanced at the book Julia had been reading, his eyebrows rising. *A Price Worth Paying—A Study of Inner-city Adoptions.*

He looked at her door. She's been right about most things so far. But that didn't make her right about this, did it?

He didn't know, but one thing was for sure.

Now he'd have to find out.

After dropping off some food for her mother, Julia returned home. Luckily, she didn't have to listen to any lectures today. Josiah Grayson had been there. The most she'd had to endure were smiles—ones they wouldn't explain.

Tony was playing with Rachel in the sunroom. Chris and Ray were in the kitchen finishing the dishes. From the aroma in the air, she knew they'd had some of Miss Irene's chili for dinner.

Fighting her impulse to join Tony, Julia decided to relax in her room instead. Their discussion earlier had rattled her—she'd seen a man who was fixed on believing the worst about his mother open his mind to the possibilities she expressed. And all because of his love of Rachel. It was an appealing side of him, and she knew it just helped fan the fire within her.

"Julia, can I talk to you for a minute?" Tony called. Rachel was playing with plastic shapes, mouthing them and tossing them in the air, waving her arms around in glee.

Sighing, she entered the room, determined to keep her distance emotionally. "What's up?"

"I wanted to ask a favor." He smiled guiltily. "I'd like to run to the office for an hour and get some work done. Would you mind watching Rachel tonight—if you're not busy, I mean? I know it's your day off—"

"I don't mind at all." She loved doing the bedtime rituals she and the child had begun. "I was just planning on relaxing tonight, anyway."

"No date?" he asked casually, standing.

Julia took in his long legs, encased in tight-fitting jeans. His dark blue shirt was opened at the collar. She stared for a minute, and pictured being on a date with him. Dinner, dancing, being held close.

"Julia?"

"Huh?" She blinked and remembered. "Oh, no date." She moved to the doorway. "I'll get some toys—"

"Why?"

She stopped walking. "Because you asked me to watch Rachel."

He smiled indulgently. "That's not what I meant."

She turned and stared at him, willing her rapidly beating heart to slow down. It wouldn't obey, not when he looked so handsome, his dark eyes piercing into her soul.

"Tony, I'm not another of your women."

His eyebrows rose. "I'm curious. Just how many *women* do you think I have?" He rubbed his chin, his lips spreading in a slight grin. "A harem?"

"At least," she replied. "And in this day and age, it's not *chic* to do that anymore."

He laughed openly at her play on the word *sheik*. "You're good at diverting my attention, honey, but not good enough." He moved one step closer. "Why don't you date?"

"I don't want to."

"Hiding won't heal you any faster."

Neither will getting involved with you.

"Everyone heals in their own way," she said softly.

"Tony," he said in a taunting tone, daring her to speak his name.

But she couldn't. She was afraid he'd hear the longing in her voice. He stood close, towering above her. She could smell his cologne. She took a step back.

"It's really a simple name. Tony, short for Antonio." He smiled gently, but with determination in his eyes. "If you say it enough times, it should roll trippingly off your tongue. Try it."

Grasping the last strains of sanity, Julia shook her head. "I can't play this game."

"Who says it's a game?" Before she could counter with an attack, Tony continued. "I don't buy a lot of what you said before, about my inability to form lasting relationships." He moved closer to Julia. "So, I'm not saying you're right, and I'm not saying you're wrong, but if you were to be on the side of right—that's *if*, mind you—then I don't want to pass that trait on to Rachel."

"That's admirable, Tony, but that has nothing to do with us."

"It could, if you'd give *us* a chance. Come on, let's see if this old leopard could change his spots. Let's see if we could maybe have a lasting relationship. You know I'm attracted to you, honey—"

"I...I...I'll be right back." Quickly she left the room, not looking behind her, not trusting herself. He was too tempting.

In her bathroom, she splashed cool water on her reddened face. This was getting too hard.

So, tell him the whole story.

That would solve the problem. He'd avoid her.

And pity you.

Julia recalled all the pitying looks she'd received, from the day she found out to the night her husband lied to her for the final time. Even her own mother had looked at her in that "Isn't it too bad?" way at first. She wouldn't take the chance of seeing pity in Tony's eyes. Besides, this wasn't something she wanted to talk about yet. Maybe, eventually, she'd be ready.

Ah, foolish, foolish pride.

Yes, it was pride, but until she was completely ready to tell him, it was all she had left. Wiping the dripping water from her face, she buried the pain and went back to doing her job.

Chapter 6

"Hi, Nick. It's Tony. How're things in Chicago?"

"Tony! Things are hectic. You caught me running out the door. I've got midnight surveillance." Nick's voice took on a serious tone. "I wished I could have stayed longer after the funeral, but I had to get back on this case." He paused, just long enough to take in a breath. "It's great to hear from you. Have you spoken with Matt lately? He won his first case. What's happening out your way? How's Rachel? Any trouble from the natural, ahem, father?"

"Whoa, little brother." Tony sat down behind his desk, cradling the phone on his shoulder. Nick tended to rattle on if he didn't interrupt, his thick New York accent making Tony homesick to see him again. "One thing at a time. I spoke with Matt last week. No one's heard from Mitch, yet, but I don't think he'll be any trouble. He didn't want Rachel from the start."

"That's good to hear—for her sake and yours, that is."

"Yeah. Listen, I've got some stuff going on. I know

you're in a hurry, but I could use an ear. Got half a minute?''

"For you, sure. What's up?''

Tony filled him in on the things going on in his life, especially about Julia. Then he broached the subject that had driven him out of his warm house on a stormy night like this. "We don't speak about her, but could Julia be right? About our mother?''

Tony heard the pause. It stretched for a few seconds.

"She could be,'' Nick finally answered.

"Have you and Matt ever talked about her? I mean, have you ever wondered what happened to her? Like where she is, if she's even alive any longer?''

"I'm really surprised to hear you asking about her. Now I'm sorry I didn't stay longer and meet Julia. She's having an eye-opening effect on you." He paused. "As to your questions, yeah, I've wondered about her. Matt has, too.''

"So now that I've brought it out on the table, do you think we should do something about it?''

"Well, big brother, that's a very interesting question....''

Chocolate.

Streaming chocolate, sweet, sugary, syrupy.

Inhaling deeply, her mouth watering, Julia slowly opened her eyes and stretched, lifting her nose up to trap the scent. Focusing, she saw Tony standing at the side of the living room couch, holding a mug in his extended hand. She could see wisps of steam swirling upward.

She glanced up and caught him looking down at her, a teasing smile on his face. "Definitely a passion." He held it out to her. "Want to share it?''

She didn't wonder whether he was hiding any double meanings this time. "The hot chocolate? Sure." She took the mug and smiled as innocently as she could.

He chuckled, then crossed over and sat down next to her. "Sorry I'm so late. I got caught up in my work."

Julia looked at the mantel clock. It was a few minutes after midnight.

"What have you been up to?" He indicated the opened photo albums on the coffee table. "Snooping?"

She took a sip of the hot liquid. "Rachel went to sleep, and I wandered in here to read. I saw the albums, and since the warning on the cover only mentioned *removing* them from these premises..." she said teasingly, then pointed to the photo displayed. "I remember that game."

Tony nodded, looking at the picture of himself dressed in his high school football jersey. The football was in his hands, which were raised high above his head, and a triumphant grin was stretched across his handsome face.

"I'd just made the winning touchdown. It was a great feeling." He sat back and crossed his leg over his knee.

He'd removed his shoes, and that made Julia recall that she'd gotten undressed and was wearing her nightgown and robe. The flickering light from the dying fire cast a warm glow around the room, an intimate glow, and she suddenly felt very self-conscious. "Well, it's late. I'd better—"

"After I realized the Jansons weren't going to dump me as soon as things got too rough for them, I remember starting to dream about my future." He closed his eyes and leaned back. "I was going to conquer the world."

"You haven't done so badly, you know."

He sighed. "I know, but back then..." He trailed off, then, as if catching himself, opened his eyes and laughed, somewhat self-effacingly. "You don't want to hear this."

Julia knew he was giving her a way out, if she wanted it, but for reasons she didn't stop to analyze, she didn't take advantage of the opportunity to escape. She sat down.

Sitting back, his smile clearly indicating he was pleased,

he began. "I remember thinking that I was going to start my own business." His voice softened. "I couldn't wait to get back here after I graduated MIT. Massachusetts was fine, but I no longer enjoyed the fast-paced life of a big city. If the Jansons hadn't left me some money in their will, God bless them, I wouldn't have been able to buy this ranch, and start a second one."

Julia closed her eyes, and let the cadence of his voice move her. He wove a story about a young man, working hard, letting his neighbors help whenever they could. Tony had started the ranch and, with his business acumen, made it a success. She could picture the whole thing.

A young Tony, his body newly muscled from hard work, the tanned skin gleaming under sweat, danced before her eyes. She melted into the overstuffed cushions, her mug of warm chocolate all but forgotten.

"I knew cattle was a good investment, so I started the ranch next door, but my heart was with my horses."

Julia saw him astride Shadow, controlling the noble beast by squeezing his muscular thighs against his body. She shivered as she pictured those thighs lying near her, bare, with short dark hairs that would tickle her. Heat climbed up her body, and her head fell against the back of the sofa.

"Then there were the dreams of a family. Vague images, nothing specific...lots of noise, lots of kids... I could see it."

So could Julia. Dark-haired imps, running around, climbing the nearest trees, fishing in the pond, surrounding him when he came home from work. And although Tony had failed to mention a wife, Julia saw herself coming from the house, and the brown-haired cherubs parting, letting her hug him.

She vaguely heard a sound, like a moan escaping. Half opening her slumberous lids, she smiled as Tony leaned closer, his hand curling around her neck, pulling her toward him. Her breasts grew heavy, and she felt her nipples pebble against the flannel material of her nightgown. She wished she was freed of the restraining garments, and her aching breasts could be pressed against his chest.

She angled her head and sighed her lips apart. Tony growled, a sound from deep within his broad chest, and she felt their breath intermingle. Her eyes drifted shut, and an image of his child materialized in her mind.

Softness touched her mouth seconds before reality crashed around her. Sons and daughters that she could never give him. Coldness settled in her limbs, chasing the heat from her. Startled, she jerked back, spilling the tepid liquid from her mug all over her nightclothes.

She jumped off the sofa and turned to examine the material. "Thank goodness I didn't get any on the couch," she said, then tried to wipe off the spreading wetness from herself, putting the empty mug on the end table nearest her. "I don't have anything else to wear," she mumbled, needing time to frame her thoughts into some cohesive semblance of intelligence. "Everything's in the wash."

From the corner of her eye, she saw Tony. He sat upright, an annoyed look on his face. She averted her glance. He stood up silently, and left the room.

Closing her eyes, she cursed herself. How could she have allowed herself to fall under the spell of the wonderful story he'd been weaving? How could she have led him on so?

Yeah, a vamp in flannel.

"Here." She gasped, and whirled around. Tony held out a pair of deep green pajamas.

"It's not necessary. I'll find something—"

"Take them," he ordered, and her hands shot out, grasping the silk with her trembling fingers. "You said it yourself. You don't have anything else to wear." A lopsided grin appeared on his face. "And with my penchant to wander at night..."

An image flashed through her mind, and suddenly the room grew even hotter than before. "I guess I'll wear these after all."

Tony chuckled. "Sleep well." He stared at her for a moment, then left.

"Yeah, right," she muttered, and watched his long, muscular legs carry him to his room. She pictured him lying on his bed, wearing nothing but a grin. Her mouth dried, and she took a step in his direction, then stopped as another image materialized in her head—even more powerful than the first.

She saw his happy children running through this house.

Crumpling the pajamas to her chest, she walked to her room and closed the door.

The incessant ringing pierced Tony's brain. Grumbling, he looked over to Rachel, who was still sleeping quietly at his side. He squinted at the clock—8:25.

Who on earth would ring his doorbell at this hour of the morning, especially on a Sunday? He put pillows on either side of the baby, and grabbed his jeans from the foot of the bed. Pulling them on, he wished he'd gotten more than three hours of sleep.

Rushing from his room, he glanced behind him, thinking about the reason he'd been awake all night, and he became aroused again.

Julia's door was closed, but as he started forward to the front door, he spied her coming from Rachel's room, her hair flying around her ashen face. He reached her side. She grabbed his upper arms.

"Tony. Rachel's gone!" Tears shimmered in her eyes.

Tony was shocked momentarily, then spoke quickly. "She's in my room. She's okay."

Julia looked dazed, and then her stiff shoulders slumped. "Oh, God. I had a dream, and then she wasn't there...."

She bit her lip and fell against him. He wrapped his arms around her, relishing the feel of her slender body, but his concern over her superseded his lust, for the moment.

"I'm sorry, honey. She was restless when I went to check on her, and I brought her to my room. She's slept there all night." He cupped her head against his chest and rocked her. "I'm sorry," he murmured into her hair, inhaling its fruity fragrance.

She stepped back, wiping her eyes with the sleeve of the pajamas. "Don't be. I dreamt she was gone, and someone came to the house to tell me where she was. The doorbell rang, and I probably incorporated it into my nightmare." She dried her eyes. "I'll see if she's okay."

Her concern over Rachel had obviously distracted her, and she'd forgotten to put on her flannel bathrobe. She hurried to his room, the hem of the green pajama top tapping the backs of her firm thighs, which were, indeed, at the top of long, shapely legs—but, his imagination hadn't done them justice.

His body surged as the doorbell rang again, the sound this time followed by banging. If not for the noise at the door, he would have followed her, thrown her on his bed caveman-style and buried himself in her until... He adjusted his jeans and strode to the door, unlocking it.

"Who is it?" he bellowed at the same time as he swung it open, his frustration acute.

"Me." Maxine stood in the doorway, the fur collar of her coat turned up to ward off the early-morning wind. She brushed past him into the foyer, bringing in the cold air. "I come bearing a peace offering." She waved a bag in the air. "Hot, fresh-from-the-oven bagels, cold cream cheese, and even a half a pound of smoked salmon." She smiled brightly. "You know, lox. Like you had in New York."

"I never had lox as a kid, Maxine. It cost over twelve dollars a half a pound." He approached, knowing she would continue in if he didn't stop her. After spending a restless night wanting Julia in his bed, he didn't want to deal with Maxine.

"Oh, I'm sorry. Well, I brought the Sunday newspaper." Moving closer to Tony, she whispered, "We can cuddle in front of the fireplace, like we used to, and read the comics together."

"Maxine, no—"

She held up the hand with the newspaper in it. "Tony, please. I realize we both said things we didn't mean. Can't we talk about it?"

Tony raked a hand through his hair, but before he could answer, she spoke again.

"Why don't you wake up Rachel? She can join us, can't she?" She looked at him, her face a study in sincerity.

"Maxine, it's over—"

"It doesn't have to be." She moved to the kitchen. "I'll explain all about Jason and what happened. Once you hear—"

"It won't make a difference, Maxine. I'm sorry about what happened with you and Rollingston, but nothing you say is going to change the situation between us."

"I'll just spread this food out, and we can talk," she continued as though he hadn't spoken. At the door of the kitchen, she glanced back over her shoulder. "You poor baby. You look positively exhausted. Didn't you sleep well last night?"

A noise from Tony's room caught their attention. Maxine

turned her head just as Julia stepped out, Rachel in her arms. The baby's head rested against her shoulder, her little hand rubbing Julia's cheek.

Julia stopped outside his door. Her pajamas—his pajamas—were rumpled, and her hair fell around her shoulders. From crying earlier, her nose was slightly red. Her eyes glowed, and her lower lip was russet-red and swollen from being bitten. To him, she looked like a woman who'd been thoroughly loved.

To Maxine, she obviously did, too.

"So *that's* why you're so tired." She spun on her heel and flung the bag of bagels at him. He caught them. "And here I was, coming back to try and work things out, thinking how we both may have overreacted." Her voice rising, she pivoted and walked quickly down the hall.

Tony dropped the bag on the foyer table and followed.

Stopping in front of Julia, Maxine laughed bitterly. "Doesn't it bother you that he's rebounding from me? Don't you have any pride at all?" She pointed at Julia. "Look at you. Trying to pry your way into his life by playing the devoted mother, dressed in his pajamas."

Tony hauled her back a step. "Maxine, stop it. This isn't what it seems."

"Oh, how original," she spit out, casting a venomous look back at Julia. "I wonder what the department of social services will have to say about this? Let's see if they'll okay your adoption when they learn how 'nurturing' your environment's become."

Rachel looked at Maxine. The baby screwed up her face, and her arms and legs started to pump. Julia moved back, murmuring comforting words. Tony placed his body between the two women. "Maxine, you're upsetting my daughter—"

"*Your* daughter? Ha." Maxine's eyes narrowed. "She's

your sister's bas—" She inhaled sharply. "I won't say it in front of the kid, but you know what she is." She glared at Tony. "I guess it runs in the family."

"Now just a minute—" Julia started, but was cut off when the front door opened and Chris, Ray and a few other men walked in.

Tony expelled a sharp breath. They were here to get an early-morning breakfast before starting on chores. He grimaced. He'd forgotten to set the clock on the coffeemaker last night, so there wasn't even any fresh coffee brewing.

Chris tipped his hat, taking in the scene before him.

Tony greeted them. "Morning, Chris, fellas. Sorry, I didn't start breakfast yet, but Maxine's generously brought over some warm bagels." Maxine's expression darkened. Tony put his arm around Julia. "They're on the front table. Help yourself." He faced Maxine. "Maxine's a little upset. She was just leaving."

"Morning, all," Chris said, motioning the other men into the kitchen. Maxine opened her mouth, but Chris walked calmly over, stopping in front of her and tilting her chin up to him. "Morning, Maxine."

She jerked her head back and glared at him, her hair slipping from under the fur hat. "*Good* morning, *Christopher*," she said, enunciating her words slowly.

Chris chuckled. "I see the morning doesn't dull the spitfire in you, little filly."

Maxine's jaw muscles tensed. "Don't call me little filly, you Neanderthal." She poked him in the chest. "And I am *not* a spitfire."

He captured her hand and bent down, whispering something into her ear. Maxine turned beet-red and sputtered.

Chris smiled down at her. "I understand you're leaving. Allow me." Placing his hand on the small of her back, Chris nudged Maxine to the door, and out, tipping his hat in Tony's direction before closing the door behind him. The other men, seeing breakfast was far from ready, followed.

"What was that about?" Julia stepped out of Tony's hold. She rocked Rachel in her arms and smiled sweetly at her, but when she faced Tony, her expression said she expected an answer.

He raised an eyebrow.

"And don't explain what conclusion Maxine jumped to," she continued. "I'm well aware of *that*. I want to know what was going on between Chris and her."

Lord, did she look kissable in the early-morning sunshine.

"Ah, you want gossip," Tony said. Julia nodded, a grin on her face. "Chris wants Maxine."

"Oh," she said, somewhat crestfallen.

"You're disappointed." Jealousy sprang up. He clasped her upper arms and drew her to him. "Why?"

"I was hoping you knew what Chris had whispered. Must have been something juicy, to shut her up." Her eyes twinkled.

Tony's body sagged against the wall. Jealousy.

Imagine that.

"Dadadadadadadadada..."

"You want to go to your daddy, do you?" Rachel reached out her hands, and Tony lifted her to his body, cradling her bottom on his arm.

"Do you think she knows she's calling me daddy?" Tony asked, a warm spot in his heart expanding.

"Not yet, but soon she'll make the connection."

"Oh. Speaking about connections, I'm sorry about this morning," he said.

"Maxine was very upset. I can understand how she felt."

"You can?" he asked.

"Well, sure. You're a good man. Any woman in her right mind would fight to keep you."

"Would you?"

"If I was in my right mind," she quipped, then held up a hand. "No jokes. Under different circumstances, I would. But we have a bigger problem." She smoothed down her—his—pajama top, then stopped, but too late.

Tony had seen her beaded nipples pushing against the silk. He knew she'd seen him glance down, because she blushed at the look of desire he was sure still lingered in his eyes. His body responded again.

"Um, I'll get dressed and meet you in the kitchen. I'd like to talk with you."

"Julia." She raised her face to his. "I have seen scantily dressed women before, you know."

"Me too," she said, and quickly slipped into her room.

A few minutes later, Julia entered the kitchen fully dressed. Today, her jeans were topped by a metallic-gray sweater. Her hair was up, and her glasses were perched on her nose. Tony admired the glow of her freshly scrubbed skin.

The other men had come in again, grabbed a quick snack, and left. Rachel sat in her high chair, munching on some mashed bananas. Actually, she was wearing more bananas than she was eating, but she was happy.

When Julia entered, Rachel squealed and started babbling, her legs kicking out vigorously. "Mamamamama-mamama…"

Julia stopped dead in her tracks, and her eyes darted quickly in Tony's direction. He grinned at her, but she didn't return the smile. Instead, she grabbed a bagel and furiously bit into it, turning away from him.

Tony continued scrambling eggs, squelching the feeling that the bottom was about to drop out. "Would you mind getting me a can of mushrooms from the pantry?" he asked. "I'm making omelets, and we've run out of fresh ones."

"Sure."

When she didn't return quickly, Tony removed the frying pan from the heat and walked over to see if she was okay.

She stood at the top of the stairs, the can in her hand. Squaring her shoulders, she turned around and gasped when she saw Tony standing in the doorway. She took a step backward, and he reached out to grab her. Crying out, she flinched, dropped the can and grabbed the air.

"Julia!" Tony hauled her to him firmly, feeling her coiled muscles. Her fingers latched on to his chest, gently tugging at the hair. Tony glanced at the steps. Damn. She looked at him and his heart broke at the sadness in her eyes.

"Don't, Tony. It's getting better."

"I'm glad. I don't think my chest hairs could tolerate another attack like that," he teased gently.

She smiled and moved away, sitting in a chair at the table.

Tony hunkered down in front of her and took her hands in his. At that moment, Rachel threw some of her banana mélange and hit Tony's face and chest.

Julia chuckled. "Bull's-eye." With her index finger, she smeared the banana on his chest. "Does that soothe the hurt?"

He captured her hand, lifted it, and—his eyes never leaving her face—licked the banana from her finger. "What do you think?"

Her breathing increased. Her pupils dilated. Her lips parted. When things couldn't get any more tense, she broke the eye contact.

He let her off the hook, reluctantly.

"Actually, strained pears really take the sting out." He stood and grabbed a towel by the sink. "Are you okay now?"

"Yes." She retrieved the can from the closet and handed it to Tony. "I want to talk to you about finding a replacement."

Here it comes. "You can talk all you want."

"But you've got to listen, Tony. This is serious."

Tony's spine stiffened. "You just won't learn, will you? I don't want a replacement, and neither does Rachel. You're stuck with us."

"Tony, I've heard enough horror stories of women losing their children because someone phoned in a possible child-abuse situation. Social services can remove the child while an investigation is conducted. Rachel's not even yours legally. If there's the slightest possibility that your adoption could be jeopardized because of my presence here, then I've got to go."

His frustration level rose, and he tried to push it down by concentrating on finishing breakfast. Sliding the first omelet onto the plate, he placed it in the oven so that it would remain warm.

"Tony, Maxine could cause you trouble."

He broke two more eggs into the sizzling pan. "It's under control. I'll take care of it."

"That's not the answer." She handed him the salt and pepper.

His jaw tightened. "I said I'll take care of it."

"I still think it would be best if I left," she said.

Best if I left best if I left best if...

He slammed down the metal spatula and faced her. "*I* don't think it's best. *Rachel* doesn't think it's best. You're the only one who thinks it's best. Rachel loves you. How can you stand there and tell me it's in her best interest if you leave?'' Once again, he was going to have no say over actions that affected him personally. And once again, it was all under the guise of knowing what was best for him. His mind fostered an attack. ''You'd abandon Rachel? *You* could do that? After everything we talked about, *you* could be like my mother?''

''Tony, please. Don't you understand? Maxine has threatened to tell social services about me. If they believe, in the *slightest* degree, that Rachel's living in a bad environment, you could be denied your petition.''

Tony wouldn't let her sway him, regardless of the nagging feelings of doubt. ''No. She was just spouting off, but she's not vindic—'' He stopped short.

''Rollingston.'' Julia said, confirming his thoughts. ''I don't know the whole story, but if she exacted revenge on him—a man who rejected her—she could do it to you, too. Rachel will be sacrificed. I can't allow that.''

''Don't I have a say in this?''

She touched his arm. ''Are *you* that much of a gambling man? To risk Rachel on a chance?''

Caught in a whirlwind of powerful emotions, Tony moved away from the stove. The bacon started to burn, and he watched Julia lift the griddle from the flame and place it on the nearby trivet.

She approached warily. ''Tony, listen to me,'' she said, her voice low and steady. ''I know you don't like to be told what to do, but you can lose Rachel. It's best if I leave.''

His guts churned as her words sank in. Rachel. He looked at the little girl, as much his daughter as if he'd had a part in creating her. She sat quietly, her right hand in her mouth, her eyes wide. Lose Rachel?

Reaching blindly, he hauled Julia to him. He couldn't risk losing Rachel to keep a woman he was growing to care about. But did it have to be one over the other? "I can't lose her," he muttered into her hair. "But I won't lose you, either."

"Then find someone else to take care of her."

"No," he moaned, and crushed her lips with his. For a long moment, she did nothing. Then she kissed him back.

"Julia," he murmured against her mouth, then plundered her again. Her arms wrapped around his waist, and she formed her body along his. She groaned, and her lips parted. His tongue surged inside, drinking in her soft sounds of pleasure.

It's best if I leave it's best if I leave...

He was going to lose one for the other.

Not if you make her yours. Now.

Tony pushed her up against the refrigerator and kissed her face all over. She threaded her fingers through his hair.

Make her yours.

He was about to kiss her again when a noise hammered at his consciousness.

"Tony...Tony..." Julia's voice was insistent. Her hands were on his shoulders, her fingers digging into his muscles. "Rachel..."

Rachel. The baby. His baby.

He slowly focused and heard Rachel whining, on the verge of crying. Instantly contrite, he took a step back and followed Julia to Rachel's side.

Julia spoke first, her voice husky, breathless. "Shh, Rachel, it's all right, baby."

Tony lifted Rachel into his arms and kissed her banana-covered face. "Sweetheart, it's okay."

Rachel studied his face for a minute, then pointed to Julia. Tony handed the baby to her, then looked at the beautiful picture they made together. Julia took a napkin from the kitchen table and wiped Rachel's face, all the while speaking softly to her.

"I didn't even hear her," he said.

"Neither did I...at first," she admitted reluctantly, avoiding his glance.

Tony was astounded. How could he have thought that Julia had looked thoroughly loved earlier compared to the way she looked now? The blush she wore spoke volumes, as did the way she avoided looking at him.

"Julia?" Tony stepped close to her.

She shook her head, the same sad smile she'd worn before back in place on her flushed face. "We...we just got caught up in a very emotional moment." She looked up at him, her eyes begging him not to push her.

He couldn't obey. "Are you sure that's all it was?"

After a moment, she shook her head. "Maybe not, but that's all I'm willing to believe it was." She handed Rachel back and turned away. "I can't deal with this."

He expelled a breath, pushing down an uncomfortable feeling that he couldn't identify. "All right, you win. At least stay until I find someone else. Rachel needs you."

Her shoulders visibly slumped. "Okay. Maybe the Fates will find someone else to harass for a while. But you've got to keep your distance." She nodded in the direction of the refrigerator.

"On my word as a Scout." He raised his right hand and held up two fingers together, while he crossed two fingers on his left hand, safely hidden beneath Rachel's plump legs. "But I can't guarantee the Fates won't reappear and manipulate things."

"Believe me, they will, and they'll enjoy every minute of whatever situation they create."

"I see."

"Good," she said, taking Rachel from his arms and leaving the kitchen.

So she believed they were both pawns of fate, Tony thought as he spread the plates of food on the table. Perhaps they were, but did that mean they were *meant* to be together, for all eternity? Would he be bound in marriage to a woman who was determined to leave him? *Marriage* was a word that usually guaranteed he'd run screaming from the room. What amazed him the most was that although he didn't want to rush to the altar, the thought of losing Julia scared him more than the concept of a commitment with her.

But she wanted to leave.

Like…

There was that nagging feeling again.

Like your mother did to you. She loved you, said it often enough, but in the end…

It's best it's best it's best…

He squeezed excess water from a sponge, squeezing his eyes shut, too. Burying the confusion, Tony thought back to the kiss they'd shared, the warm feel of her soft lips, her firm breasts against his chest, and warmth spread through him.

Ah, hell. Heat seared him.

Keep my distance. Right.

Good thing he'd never been a Boy Scout.

"Well, thank you—" Tony glanced down at the application to see the woman's name "—Miss Garson. We'll let you know our decision soon."

Julia smiled her goodbye to the teenager and watched her exaggerated swagger as she left Tony's office.

"I almost started keeping rhythm to her snapping gum," she said, shaking her head dejectedly. She laughed briefly as Tony imitated the cowlike movement of the young woman's jaw. "I bet she had at least three pieces of gum in her mouth."

"Only three?" Tony wearily shook his head. "Are you sure you want to go on with this?"

Determined to be out of Tony's house before the end of next week, Julia nodded. "Bring in the next applicant."

Tony buzzed his new office manager, Miss Irene's youngest son, Greg, and requested the next person.

Rose was entertaining Rachel while Julia and Tony held the interviews, but so far, since Sunday, there had been nothing but duds. And there was no way Julia would leave Rachel in less-than-competent hands. So they pressed on.

She'd lost her heart to Rachel the first moment she held her, but over the past four days, Julia had found herself caring more and more for Tony. They'd spent a lot of time together, taking rides, watching late-night movies or just talking. Even though she could see desire in his chestnut eyes, he behaved like a perfect gentleman. If only she could make her hands forget the feel of his steel-hard chest, or the swell of his muscled arms, or the taste of him...

She glanced at him surreptitiously and caught him studying her intently. Her heart slammed against her ribs, as it did each time he looked at her. She forced her own desires away, and smiled at the woman who entered his office.

Would she be the one? Julia wondered sadly, then chastised herself. She had to leave. For Tony's sake. For Rachel's sake.

A woman of about twenty stood before them. Her auburn hair was neatly in a bun, and she wore a nicely tailored blue business suit.

"Ms. Templeton, won't you sit down?" Tony stood and indicated a chair in front of his desk.

She sat in the appropriate chair, smoothed down her suit jacket and smiled, tightly.

"I see by your application you're in college. May I ask what your major is?"

"It's a junior college. I'm studying cosmetology. I have aspirations to own a store immediately following my graduation."

"Oh, I see." Tony glanced sideways at Julia, and arched his eyebrows gently. She knew he could tell that her lines were well rehearsed, too.

"As a nanny, I could still go to school, and keep my night job. I work—um, am employed in food services, too." She sat up straight. "I'm paying my own way through school."

"That's admirable. But won't school and your job interfere with your duties? I'm looking for someone full-time."

"I know." She leaned forward animatedly. "My boyfriend, Joe, he said that if you need me when I'm working, he can cover for me until I'm done. He's a mechanic."

"Your boyfriend?" Julia asked, amazed by the entire concept of passing responsibility on to others. "I don't understand how you figure your boyfriend into this job."

Ms. Templeton eyed her, then directed her answer to Tony. "Me and him discussed it, and he agreed. As long as, um, Rachel is watched, what does it matter by who—uh, whom?"

Tony nodded. Julia knew what that nod meant. Ms. Templeton was no longer in the running, and Julia was sure it wasn't the fractured English that had cost her the position. It was the idea that she'd shuffle Rachel off to a stranger, someone who hadn't even come to the interview. Of all the nerve.

"Well, thank you for your time, Ms. Templeton. We'll call you with our decision," Tony said, then stood.

The young woman rose, too, once again the proper businesswoman. "I'll wait to hear from you, then." And she left.

"Tony, she was the fifth applicant," Julia blurted out, her amazement over the audacity of the applicants' bursting forth. The first woman still believed in corporal punishment, the second could barely speak English and was simply looking for a way to stay in the country. The third, a man in his fifties, wouldn't look either of them in the eyes, and had a tattoo on his hand that said Pain. "Is this what you'd faced before I came along?"

"Yes. Now do you understand why I'm reluctant to let you go?"

"Where are all the normal people?"

He shrugged his shoulders. "I don't know. Maybe we should check the basement for pods."

Julia smiled. This was ridiculous. There had to be someone out there who could... "Tony?" she asked. "I know I'm probably wrong, but you're not staging this, are you?"

Tony laughed. "Yeah, didn't you see the ad? The headline says, 'If you've graduated high school and can hold a job, *don't* apply.'"

She held up her hands. "Forget what I said. Who's next?"

"The woman Rose recommended, a Mrs. Williams."

Greg sent in Mrs. Williams, and twenty minutes later, Tony stood up and shook her hand. Julia felt the floor drop out of her stomach. Mrs. Williams was everything Tony needed in a governess. A widow, she had time on her hands. Her children were grown, all living in neighboring towns, with children of their own.

Tony agreed with Julia's assessment.

"However..." she began, wondering why she was about to say what she was about to say.

"What?"

"I'm sure it's nothing, but what about her comment that if her children needed her, she'd have to leave? It's admirable, but not necessarily reliable."

"I see what you mean. What do you suggest?"

"Well, I don't think we should dismiss her summarily, but I do think we can look a little longer. It's not like I have a job waiting for me here, right?"

"You don't have to worry about that. If you want your old job back, you'll get it."

"What about Greg?"

"He's more suited for accounting. And when Rose hired him, she explained the circumstances."

"Thanks. That means a lot to me."

Tony nodded, and Julia stared at him. How much of a fool was she? "Is there anyone else today?"

"Nope. Let's stop in town for lunch. I'm starved."

"Okay," she said, and could have kicked herself. She should be trying to avoid spending time with him, but she knew Rachel would love to be with him.

But not you, right?

"I'll get Rachel." She walked down the back stairs, and knew she was fooling herself again.

"She's on her way over, Rose," Tony said into the receiver.

"How'd it go?"

"All the applicants were terrible, except for Mabel. I thought Julia would be thrilled she could finally leave, but..."

"Julia wasn't too sure about her, especially when Mabel said how she would have to leave if her kids needed her, right?"

"Right," he said slowly. "Hey, why would you recommend Mabel, if you knew she—"

"Because I wanted proof that Julia didn't really want to leave you, and you just gave that to me. Mabel was perfect, yet Julia rejected her. What more proof do you need?"

Tony rolled his eyes. "Hell, Rose. It may not have anything to do with me at all. It could just mean she doesn't want to leave Rachel with just anyone."

"I don't think so. I know I shouldn't meddle, but...I love you guys," Rose said seriously. "And it's high time you both got what you deserved. People have been matchmaking for generations. I have no intentions of stopping."

Tony knew Julia would be furious. And he should be, too, but for reasons he didn't understand, he wasn't. Fate?

"I hear footsteps," Rose said. "Gotta go." The phone went dead.

Tony recalled Rose's words, "People deserve happiness, even if they don't think they do," and now he knew she'd *purposely* used the word *people*. She had meant Julia *and* him, too.

While Tony still wasn't too sure about their developing relationship, and what it would mean to him, he knew he wanted Julia to stay.

He had spoken with Maxine Sunday night, after their encounter at his house, and although she was still angry, Tony knew it was more from sour grapes than from love. Reluctantly they'd reached a truce. He'd explained it to Julia, but she wouldn't be convinced. She insisted leaving was best, just to make sure Rachel was safe. When she mentioned leaving, he got angry, but he tried to see things from her point of view.

Julia was a loving, caring woman who thought she knew what was best for everyone else...but didn't know what was best for her. Being occupied with her mother, and Rachel, and Tony, she could avoid thinking about what she wanted and needed. And that meant she wouldn't ever get hurt again. And she was right. She wouldn't get hurt again.

But this time, he'd be the one protecting her.

"Do you see what I mean?" Julia sat forward, whispering her comment to Tony. "Ever since we've entered the restaurant, people have been smiling at us." She fed Rachel some more yogurt, then glanced around again, frowning. "What do you think is going on?"

Tony, doing his damnedest to look as innocent as possible, merely shrugged. He picked up his sandwich and took a large bite, using the time needed to chew it to keep from laughing out loud.

Obviously, Rose had gone ahead and spread the news that he and Julia were an item. And given the reaction of the people today, who were indeed grinning and nodding in their direction, Tony knew exactly what was going on.

Their neighbors and friends were giving them their highest seal of approval.

Chapter 7

Julia packed the last of the casserole dishes in the box on the counter, then wiped down the sink and put the blue sponge by the faucet. Her Saturday was all set—she had enough food for her mother, a few books to read, and even a deck of cards.

Even if Marion complained that she was spending too much time with her, Julia knew she enjoyed the company. And it bothered Julia that her mother hadn't been feeling too well lately. Josiah felt the same as Julia, if his voice on the phone to her was any indication. She'd been at her mother's, cleaning....

I'm concerned, Julia. She's still doing too much around the house, and she's been complaining about shortness of breath.

Josiah's voice had been gruff, but more from worry than from age. Julia, glad that her mother had a protector to watch over her, had told him that she'd spoken with the doctor and that he hadn't seen anything definite to explain her mother's chest pains. But, agreeing with Josiah that her mother needed a rest, she had suggested that he try to get her to go on the cruise that Julia had been pushing for months. He'd picked up on the idea instantly, assuring her he'd do his best to get Marion to go.

With everything set to go, she went to tell Tony she was leaving. She found him, and Rachel, in the den. Tony was reading a book, and Rachel was on the floor, waving a stuffed animal around. She looked so cute in the red jumper with the pink bunny on the front placket, her feet snugly enclosed in the soft material. A warm feeling of motherhood washed over Julia, but she banished it, mentally chastising herself.

Tony looked up. "All set?" he asked, putting his book down and smiling gently at her.

Julia nodded. Tony had been completely solicitous of her needs lately, bringing her coffee before she asked, or letting her sleep late on a work morning. She knew he wanted her to stay, but his behavior lately was about more than just convincing her to stay. Something else was going on, but she hadn't been able to figure out what it was. When questioned, he'd only shrug, say that change was good, and smile the same smile everyone in town wore.

"Any interviews tomorrow?" she asked.

"Nope. Earliest one is Thursday." He approached and looked down at her. "That was when my schedule opened up. Don't worry, we'll find someone soon. I'd want the new person to take over while you're still here, so you can show her—or him—the ropes."

"I don't think there's anything here anybody else couldn't figure out."

"I was talking about Rachel's quirks. You know, how she loves being bounced in the air, but only three times. Or how you sing to her before bed—the mockingbird lulla-

by—or else she won't fall asleep. Or even how she delights
in taking a bath with us. Separately, of course,'' he added.

But it was too late. She saw the image of Tony in the
shower, the water sluicing off his body, leaving little drop-
lets clinging to his chest, his shoulders, his abdomen.

She swallowed. Hard.

"You see what I mean?'' he continued, and she looked
up sharply, but he wasn't referring to her vision. He was
talking about the baby. "There's a lot of things she—or
he—will have to learn about Rachel, things only you and
I know.'' His voice lowered even more, and instantly Julia's defenses kicked in.

"Cut it out. Any competent person will be able to figure
out a baby's needs.'' She glanced over to Rachel, who
started to pull herself up by the couch. She grabbed Tony's
arm. "Tony, look!''

Tony peered over his shoulder. Rachel stood, pumping
her body up and down, then removed her left hand and
shoved it into her mouth. With just one hand holding her
up, she teetered for a second, then fell, her big brown eyes
wide with wonder.

The two of them rushed forward and stared down at the
infant. There was silence in the room until Rachel hiccuped
and giggled, pointing at the couch.

Picking her up, Tony smiled. "That's right, sweetness.
You stood up and then, boom, you fell down.'' He bounced
her in his arms and grinned at Julia. "Thanks.''

"I know how important it is for you to see her doing
things for the first time.''

He looked at Julia intently. "She'll be walking soon.''

Julia nodded, her throat too tight to release words. Rachel
would be walking soon, and she might not be here to see
it. Suddenly her eyes filled with tears. She'd asked for this,

placing herself in this position, letting herself fall helplessly in love with this child, and this man.

You went and did it.

Her heart filled with anguish. "I have to get going," she mumbled, her face averted. She needed to escape her thoughts, as if that were possible.

"Let me help you," Tony offered, and then followed her to the kitchen. "Why don't you dress Rachel, then she can come outside with us while I load up the car."

Keep busy, Julia thought and agreed, glad for the few moments away from him. After she slipped on her coat, she picked up Rachel and dressed her in her blue jacket, concentrating on pulling herself together. Taking in some calming breaths, she reminded herself that she had always had feelings for Tony. Now, she would just have to learn to live with stronger ones. That's all.

Yeah, that's all.

Ignoring her sarcasm, she zipped up Rachel's jacket.

When they were ready, Tony, in his parka, hefted the box on his shoulder. She opened the door, the cold wind slicing through her. Pulling up Rachel's hood, she protected the baby's face from the icy air.

Tony walked out in front of her. When she turned around after closing the door, she saw that he was placing the box in his car, not hers.

"Tony, wait!" she called, but he closed the side door and opened the other side. She walked over. "What are you doing?"

"I decided we'd drive you to your mother's house. We've got nothing else to do today, have we, Rachel?" he asked the baby, smiling guilelessly at Julia. "Do you mind?"

"Well, it'll leave me stranded. I usually spend the day there. You'll have to come back later to get me—"

"No problem. By the time you're ready to come home, we'll be ready for another little jaunt." Placing Rachel in her car seat, he ushered Julia to the passenger side of the red Saab and closed her door.

They drove to her mother's house, a total of about twelve miles, in companionable silence. Julia looked out at the beautiful landscape and felt serene. When they arrived, she got out. Tony opened the door and reached in for the box of food.

"Would you grab Rachel? Your mother wanted to see her."

"How do you know that?" she asked, reaching in for Rachel.

"Know what?" he said, hoisting the box into his arms.

"That my mother wanted to see her?"

"Wouldn't she?"

"Definitely," Julia answered, knowing how much her mother adored children. "But that's not the point. You didn't say, *'She* would *love to see her,'* you said—"

"Oh, look. Josiah's here. They're waving to us from the living room window."

Julia had no more time for questions. Tony bound up the stairs, and she and Rachel followed. Josiah and her mother greeted them, ushering them into the cozy house. Her mother's face was rosy, a pretty contrast to the green paisley knit dress she wore, which she'd made herself, and Josiah, dressed in a comfortable old sweater, its dark blue color accenting his silver-white hair, smiled warmly. His blue eyes twinkled merrily, as though he were keeping a secret, and Julia had the feeling he'd made headway on the cruise issue.

After putting away the food, the men joined Marion and Julia in the parlor.

"Julia," Josiah said, "there're some things I want to tell

you. First of all, your mother has agreed to take a cruise. And secondly, it will be a honeymoon cruise, if you'll give us your blessing."

So that explained the glow in her mother's radiant face.

Julia held out her hand. Josiah clasped it. Julia looked down at his hand, leathered after so many years of working with them. They reminded her of her father's hands, so strong and sure, and of Tony's hands, so confident and steady. Swallowing back her sudden surge of emotion, she smiled as brightly as she could, but when she spoke, her voice was gravelly.

"You have it. Welcome to the family." She stood, and they hugged. Her mother joined in, bringing the baby with her.

"Come here, Tony," Marion said. "You're part of this celebration. Without you, I would have never met Josiah."

Tony moved in closer, and the four of them, with Rachel in the middle, hugged. She could feel Tony's hands on her back, his fingers gently massaging her knotted muscles.

"Hey," Tony said, in an exaggerated western drawl, "have I got a humdinger of an idea! Have the ceremony at the ranch." He looked at Julia, and winked. She kept her jaw from dropping as he continued. "We have so much room, and it's about time we broke that house in to some down-home country celebrating."

Marion and Josiah talked excitedly while Tony moved them over to the couch. Julia could hear the plans for a Christmas wedding being formulated.

Christmas. It would be here in the blink of an eye. Her mother had Josiah, Tony had Rachel, but she'd have no one to celebrate with this year. Julia reminded herself that by Christmas she would have found another job, and then she'd decide what to do with the rest of her life. By then, she might even have decided to finish her master's degree.

With that in mind, she refocused on the conversation.

"That's great, Tony! Come on," Josiah said, and headed to the front door.

Julia turned to her mother. "What's going on?"

"Oh, you know men. Tony mentioned that he saw a few things that needed to be mended, and Josiah's eyes just lit up." She bounced the baby on her lap. "They're going to work on them, together." She glanced at Julia, a smile of pleasure on her normally tired face. "That Tony's one smart cookie. He knew that Josiah needed to feel useful." Marion smiled at the baby. "Isn't that right, little one? We all want to feel important."

Julia stormed out of the living room, and ran smack into Tony, who was coming back into the house. He carried a suede handyman's tool belt.

"So, you were just going to lounge around the house today? You had no plans to do anything, did you?" She pushed Tony back into the alcove of the front door. "You and my mother cooked this up, didn't you? Well, it won't work, Tony. You won't get to me through Josiah."

Tony's eyebrows shot up. "Heavens to Betsy!"

A rush of heat warmed Julia's face. "Okay, so I over-dramatized it, but you get the point. I'm on to you, Mr. Pellegrino."

Without warning, Tony winked, kissed her fleetingly on the lips, and slid by her, whistling. He and Josiah went into the kitchen, discussing how a cabinet needed to be re-aligned.

Julia fumed. How dare he treat her so dismissively? About to march into the kitchen and confront him, she was surprised by her mother's restraining hand on her arm.

"Julia, would you deny an old man a feeling of usefulness?"

"Guilt, mother? How original."

"Effective, though, isn't it?"

Julia chuckled. "I guess. Stopped me in my tracks."

"Should have used it years ago. Now, come with me. I've something to show you."

They climbed the stairs to Julia's old bedroom, which her mother had changed into a sewing room. The only things left from her childhood were the small bed, covered in a peach-and-white comforter, and the matching lace curtains on the window above it.

In the other corner, across from the bed, stood a sewing machine and a large freestanding oval mirror. As a young girl, Julia had often daydreamed in front of it, acting out scenes from "Cinderella," or "Sleeping Beauty." She walked over to it, smiling at her reflection. "I love this mirror, Mom. Did you know that—"

"You'd stand for hours in front of it, parading around in all sorts of costumes, pretending you'd found your Prince Charming in the reflection?" Her mother smiled gently, placed Rachel in the middle of the bed, and gave her some plastic measuring cups to play with. She turned back to Julia. "Nope. I didn't know any such thing."

Julia laughed. "I knew it was your humor I'd inherited."

"Yes, but it's your father's good sense that I'm shocked to see you fighting."

"Something tells me I'm going to regret asking, but what are you talking about?"

"I'm talking about Tony. He absolutely adores you." Marion moved to the chest near the sewing machine and opened the lid. "I always thought you had more sense than to throw away something so right for you."

"How long do you really think Tony's going to be interested?" At her mother's frown, she explained. "You yourself said how he goes from woman to woman like a busy bee."

"Oh, that," she said, waving her hand. "He was just sowing wild oats. When he looks at you, I don't see that same bee." She paused thoughtfully. "He's more like a store puppy watching you from behind a glass window. Anyway, it wouldn't be so bad if it was only for a short time."

"Are you serious?"

"Yes, I think I am. Now, hold on, before you get too riled up. You know I believe in the sanctity of marriage. Your father and I were married for forty-two years. But this may be the best thing for you, something to get you out of that shell you're building. And you never know. Once he sees what a treasure you are, you may not be *able* to get rid of him. You'd be out of your mind if you tried, anyway," she added quickly.

"Mom!"

"Well, I'm not blind, you know."

They shared a quiet laugh.

"He wants a family," Julia said softly.

"So do you. There are other options." Marion smiled. "Tell him the whole story. He deserves to know the truth."

Julia wondered about her mother's advice. Would it be possible for him to accept her, knowing she couldn't have any children?

"Julia, come back to earth. Here, recognize this?"

Julia took the dress her mother held out. "It's my prom dress."

Her mother nodded, a smile of memory settling on her face. The mauve taffeta crinkled loudly as Julia placed it against her body and smoothed down the material.

"Put it on, dear. I want to see if we can salvage it. Maybe you could wear it to the Christmas social at the church."

Julia nodded, and her mother moved to her sewing box, pulling out her pincushion. Julia unbuttoned her blouse and shrugged out of it. She slid the dress over her head and only then dropped her slacks. Although her mother had seen the scar, Julia still felt uncomfortable about it.

"Stand here, where the light's better," her mother said. Julia moved, and her mother knelt down at her feet. The dress swept the floor. "If we cut it to just above the knees..." Her mother spoke to herself, so Julia just looked at her reflection in the dark-silvered glass.

The dress clung to every curve, then flared out below her hips. "I forgot how slender I was in high school. I'm not too thin, am I?"

"Huh. You almost look as good as me," her mother said.

Julia looked at her mother's slim figure, and raised an eyebrow. Her mother caught the look and blushed prettily. "Josiah doesn't complain," she said proudly, then changed the subject quickly. "Take Rose up on her offer. Go shop till you drop."

"I will. You know, you really shouldn't be doing all this—"

"Oh, stuff and nonsense. I feel fine."

"No more chest pains?"

"Oh, dear, I didn't tell you. I saw a specialist, and she says it's just a hiatal hernia. Now I eat little meals during the day and feel just fine." She spread out the material around Julia's feet. "In fact, Josiah and I are planning on taking dancing lessons on the cruise. Can you imagine me doing the waltz? Now, the tush-push would be more like it."

"I guess my services around here won't be needed for much longer."

"Don't look so sad, dear. After all, it's not healthy being so codependent."

Julia arched an eyebrow.

"Don't look so shocked dear. I watch 'Oprah,'" her

mother replied with a casual wave of her hand, then looked around. "Darn. I forgot my glasses." She lifted herself from the floor. "I'll have to go find them. Could take me a while. Don't go away." Rachel fidgeted. "Oh, you want to come with your aunt Marion? Okay." She took the baby, and left, the door still open.

Julia faced the mirror, and twirled her body from side to side, watching the yards of material sway. She ran her hands down her side, and the word *willowy* popped into her head.

Memories flooded her, of dances, being held in arms, close to bodies, moving to music. She closed her eyes to the reminiscences. She was a teenager, her whole life ahead of her. A young woman, a career in teaching chosen. A woman, a marriage, and a child on the way.

Opening her eyes, she saw her bra peeking from the low décolletage. Impulsively she unsnapped the front enclosure and worked the bra off her arms, tossing it behind her...and into Tony's outstretched hand.

Time stopped. Julia watched in the mirror as he locked the door behind him, and dropped the bra on a chair. Then he approached, as if in slow motion. The tool belt lay low on his slender hips. There was a sheen of perspiration on his forehead, and his faded blue-and-red-checked shirt was snapped open to the middle of his chest.

"You're beautiful," he whispered.

"It's all done with mirrors," Julia said lamely.

Tony didn't acknowledge her halfhearted attempt at humor. He stopped behind her and stared at her reflection in the oval glass. Watching her face, he reached out a hand and tentatively placed it on her right hip. His fingers flexed and squeezed her. She could smell his scent, released by the work he'd been doing. It mingled with wood shavings, and stirred her insides.

She had to stop this insanity, had to warn Tony that he was letting himself in for disappointment, but she couldn't. She stood, mesmerized by his eyes, burning dark with desire for her.

His other hand removed her glasses and tossed them on the bed, then caressed her neck. "Like a swan," he murmured, sliding his fingers down over her shoulder, and stopping on the upward slope of her left breast.

Instantly, her nipples hardened, pushing against material that hid nothing. She moaned as a pool of desire, the kind she'd never felt before, rushed from her midsection and heated up her limbs. "My...my mother—" she began, but gasped when his left hand pressed against her aching breast.

"I can feel your heart beating." His voice thundered in her ears. Slowly, deliberately, he captured her gaze again, and let his hand slide down over her beaded nipple, cupping her. His other hand, still on her hip, pulled her backward, then slid down her thigh, gathering material in his fist.

"Julia," he whispered, his left hand caressing her through the dress, slowly moving up and sliding in the front opening. His callused hand touched her skin and she almost collapsed, but he held her to his body with his other hand.

Moving aside the neckline, he exposed her left breast and touched her as she stared in the mirror.

In the mirror. Her Prince Charming.

Julia clung to the fantasy and let herself feel, let herself burn with desire.

He kissed her neck. She moaned. He pinched her nipple. She groaned, biting her lower lip to keep from sounding out her need too loudly.

Spreading his legs, he pulled her back. While his left hand caressed her under the right side of her dress, his other hand slowly lifted the hemline higher. She watched, her mouth dry, her knees locked.

Slowly, like a man unwrapping a present he'd so long wanted, Tony watched the satiny material glide up Julia's smooth thighs. His arousal pushed against the zipper of his jeans.

Her face glowed with passion, and his heart filled with love for the woman who'd slipped into his life. He couldn't stay away, no matter that she wanted him to. He'd hold her, and show her she mattered to him. He would erase her doubts.

Tony pushed aside the rest of the bodice, and exposed her to his eyes. He feasted on her beauty for a moment. Moving his hand around both breasts in a figure eight, he occasionally spent more time at one, feeling its softness, molding it, pressing it into the palm of his hand.

Meanwhile, his right hand had raised the hem of her skirt. Her thighs came into view, and he clasped his hand on the right one, squeezing her flesh, feeling the muscle contract. The creaminess of her breasts, the hardness of her excited nipples and the quivering of her thighs was his undoing. Slowly, watching her pupils dilate in the reflective glass, he slid his hand farther up, and cupped her intimately, pushing aside her panties.

Her knees buckled, and he pulled her to him more securely. His fingers parted her, and *his* knees almost buckled when he felt how wet she was.

"Oh, yes," he groaned, so hard he hurt.

"Oh, yes," she whispered simultaneously, and her head fell back onto his shoulder.

She gyrated her hips, her moaning reaching his soul. He slid a finger into her and moved his thumb against her sensitive nub.

"Tony!" she cried, then gasped as she climaxed.

Wave after wave of pleasure washed over Julia. Her legs gave out, and only Tony's strong grip held her up. After long moments when all she could do was lean back against him, he removed his hand from her panties, then straightened the bodice of her dress. He lifted her still-shuddering body and brought her over to the bed, laying her on it. Removing his tool belt, he joined her.

Julia looked at him.

No, not love. Please don't love me.

But she saw the love in his eyes. She felt remorse fill hers, then spill over onto her cheeks.

"Honey...sweetheart...." Tony's voice crooned tender sounds, which only served to heighten Julia's feeling of guilt and betrayal. "Jules, don't be embarrassed. You were beautiful."

"You don't understand, you don't understand!" she cried, shame washing over her, replacing the waves of pleasure she'd experienced only seconds before.

"Then help me to, honey. Why are you crying?"

She buried her head in his chest and bit her lip. Maybe she should tell him. Oh, hell, there *was* no more maybe. He needed to know.

"All right, I'll tell you, but only if you don't say anything until I'm done. I might chicken out."

"If that's what you want, sure."

"Okay," she said, and took a steadying breath. "I had a crush on you in high school. You only spoke to me five times, but that was enough. You were so handsome, and such a rebel, so different than the boys I'd grown up with. You walked with an air of authority, and I was instantly attracted to that."

Tony's eyes glowed. "Julia, love—"

"Not yet, please. I'm almost done confessing." His brow furrowed, but he nodded. She took in another deep breath and continued. "I thought that crush was over, but working with you this closely, seeing your kindness and humor, has reawakened those feelings. I'm very attracted to you, Tony, and that scares me." She exhaled a deep breath. "There, I'm done."

"But why are you scared? You know I feel the same about you."

"Yes, I do, but..." *For how long?* She ignored that and focused on something more pressing. "I also keep hearing something that Maxine said the day you two fought at the house. She said—"

"'You're lying to yourself if you don't admit you want Julia.'"

"That's right. It obviously made an impression on you, too, if you can remember it verbatim."

"It did. At first I denied it, then thought it was just a physical thing, but as I came to know you, I realized it was more than that. So she was right. And there's nothing wrong with that." He kissed her soundly. "I do want you."

"But—"

"And not just for a week or two."

She was shocked he knew what she was thinking, but saddened that it was only the tip of the proverbial iceberg. There was a bigger issue here, and she was procrastinating.

"Sweetheart, I want us to get to know each other more. I've done a lot of thinking, and, I hope, a little growing. I'm not perfect, but I do have all my teeth, and a solid future. You want me, too. So let's go with this. I'm thrilled—"

"Well, hold on. This next piece of news won't thrill you as much." She paused. "I can't have children."

Tony's brow creased again, and he rested back on his left elbow, unconsciously caressing her hip with his right arm. "Why not?"

"I developed a high fever following the miscarriage, and they couldn't treat it with antibiotics. They finally had to do exploratory surgery, and discovered an infection, and by that time, it was too late. The damage was done.''

She watched Tony's throat muscles work as he swallowed hard.

"Only my mother, and Hank, knew about this. Not even Rose knew. Each time I talk about it…'' She shrugged.

"You're hit in the face with the finality of it.''

"Yes,'' she said quietly.

"I assume you were tested afterward, to make sure?''

"Yes. So now you know the whole picture. You're a wonderful man, Tony, and I believe it when you say you're interested in having a relationship with a woman, and wanting a family.'' She slid out of his reach. "But you want what I can't give you.'' Standing, she walked to the door and unlocked it.

He jumped off the bed, and put his hand on her shoulder. "Hold on there. I'll admit this has thrown me for a loop, and I need some time to think, but this isn't over. Not by a long shot.''

"What do you want? More pain? More disappointment?''

"No, I want more time to think this through. I don't have all the answers, but I don't want you out of my life, or out of Rachel's. She needs you, and I do, too. Can you do that? Can you give me some time, without running away?''

She looked into Tony's eyes. They were dark, sparking with intensity. How she longed to be able to exchange words of love and commitment with Tony. But she knew she just couldn't do that to him. Still, she owed it to him to let him come to this conclusion on his own. Given enough time, he'd see it her way.

"Okay. I won't run. But—''

His hand covered her mouth. "No more buts. I have enough to think about as is.'' He leaned forward and kissed her tenderly. "Now, before we leave this room, there's something I want to say."

She stiffened.

"Relax. All I want to say is how sorry I am about what happened to you. You're a natural with Rachel, and I know it must kill you to know you won't ever be able to give birth." He hugged her tight.

Tears filled her eyes, but she blinked them back. "Thank you." She sniffled. "We should get downstairs. My mother went looking for her glasses and may need my help finding them." She stopped talking at the guilty look on Tony's face. "What have you done?"

"Nothing. They just told me they had some errands to run, and wanted to take Rachel with them, so I told them to go ahead."

"Errands? She didn't say anything about...any..." Thoughts coalesced. "So she *did* know you were bringing me here today. You had this whole thing planned," she said angrily.

"Guilty." He shrugged. "I wanted some time alone with you, and I figured the less forewarning you had, the better my chances would be."

"You manipulative little—"

"Hardly little," he drawled. "Although at the rate we're going, you won't have anything more than an old memory to base that on."

"You, who hates to have things decided for you, *in your best interest,* would do this to me?"

He rubbed his chin. "Hearing you say it like that, well, I'm sorry." He grasped her upper arms. "But I'm pretty sure I'm falling in love with you, and I guess I'm not thinking too clearly. I want us to be together. Hell, I even like the way you boss me around. You have some weird notions about fate, honey, but I don't believe them. I think fate's brought us together for a reason—*other* than entertainment purposes." He kissed her hard. "So get ready."

"What for?"

Grinning, he spoke. "To see what a catch I am, and then to catch me."

Tony watched Julia speed off on his mare Crystal Cove's back. The sun was just beginning to descend over the mountains in the distance, and the black clouds over her head were moving in quickly. Still, Tony knew she'd be safe—for a while, anyway.

And besides, he knew she needed time alone.

She'd actually come out and asked him.

After her mother and Josiah came back with Rachel, Julia had changed, grabbed her coat and insisted that they leave. Their drive home had been silent, but nowhere near as comfortable as the one going out. She was angry he'd manipulated her, and he couldn't blame her, but hell, she had a blind spot where he was concerned, and he was determined to open her eyes to some truths.

Even if he wasn't sure what all those truths were. And even if he couldn't figure out why she wanted to leave him.

The doorbell brought him back to the present. As he walked to the front door, it opened, and Rose peeked in.

"Anyone home?"

"Sure, come on in and make yourselves to home," he said in his best cowboy accent, ushering in Rose and her husband, Tom.

"Where's Rachel?" Rose asked, glancing around.

"She's sleeping. We were gone all morning," Tony replied. "And Julia's out for a ride. What brings you here tonight?"

Rose smiled at Tom, and Tony thought she shone. Glittered, actually. "Tell him, Tom," she said excitedly.

The three of them sat at the kitchen table, and while Tony served coffee, Tom filled him in.

"After Rose's miscarriages, we got afraid and...well, you know we filed the adoption papers right away, 'cause of the long waiting list."

"But the list shouldn't be too long for you. You still decided on the hard-to-place kids?" Tony asked.

Rose nodded. "And we can't thank you enough. Seeing you with Rachel, and how much you love her—not that she's a hard kid, but, oh..." She blushed and touched Tom's arm. "Go on, honey."

Tony was amused. In all the years he'd known Rose, he'd never seen her blush. "You got a kid already?"

"In a manner of speaking," Tom said, his ears turning red too. "Rose is pregnant."

"Pregnant? Fantastic!" Tony shouted and hugged Rose, slapping Tom on the back, then embracing him in a bear hug. "When'd you find out?"

"It's only been a week, and we're not telling everyone," Rose said hurriedly. "We're still scared. If anything goes wrong this time, we don't want... You know."

Tony nodded. They talked for a few more minutes, and Tony had to strain to keep his mind from wandering to Julia. She'd be so thrilled for Rose, but it would pain her.

"Listen, Tony," Tom said, his voice somber. "There's another reason we came out tonight." He paused, his lean face serious. "Did you know Mitch Brown hit town? He checked into the Silver Creek Inn, and has been asking around about you. He's made mention, more than once, how you cheated him, and about how it's time he got what was rightfully his. I think he means Rachel."

Tony's muscles tensed. "Yeah, I've already seen him. He contacted John. He thinks if he sticks around long enough, and causes a big enough stir, I'll cave in and pay him off." Taking in a deep breath, he forced himself to relax. "But I won't, and if he gets anywhere near Rachel or Julia, I'll—" He felt his jaw clench.

"I'll help. Damn, the whole town will," Tom said. "He was hanging with some of the local lowlife at Charlie's the other night. He got loaded, and they kicked his ass out. He was screaming in the street about how it's all your fault that he's down on his luck."

Rose nodded. "We were coming out of Cicero's and heard the ruckus. We figured it was just another Saturday night, but when we heard your name, we walked over."

"So did Jack Hanley, Mike Cross and Steve Billows," Tom added. "The steam ran right out of him when he saw us. We, uh, explained the way things are around here. He wandered away, tail between his legs."

Tony expelled a deep breath. "Thanks. It's just as I thought. He's all talk." Tony still decided to take a more active look at this, and soon. He'd take no chances as far as Rachel was concerned.

Or Julia. Hell, this couldn't have come at a worse time.

"Listen, I'd appreciate it if you don't mention this to Julia. She's got a lot on her mind lately, and I don't think she needs to worry about Rachel right now." He looked at his two friends. "I've got a plan, anyway, that I'll let you in on soon enough. After I make a few phone calls."

They both agreed.

"Speaking of Julia, anything new with you two?" Rose asked.

Tony chuckled ruefully. "You could say that. I told her I was going to keep her, and she got a little angry." He told them what had happened, leaving out the more intimate details.

"Tony, you really are serious about her, aren't you?" Rose asked.

"I'm never going to live down my past, am I?" he asked, shaking his head in mock resignation.

"It's not that, Tony...." Rose started quickly, and darted a look at her husband.

"Uh-uh, you're on your own with this," Tom said. "I'm on Tony's side."

"This isn't about taking sides. It's about—"

"Taking care of a special person," Tony finished for Rose.

Rose stared at him, and a smile transformed her face. "You *do* care about her." He nodded seriously. "Then, sugar, go after her," Rose said, heading him to the door, and plopping his hat on his head. "We'll watch Rachel."

"She doesn't want to see me."

"Tony, as antifeminist as it sounds, whenever a woman tells the man she loves to leave her alone, that's when she wants to be held the most."

Tom agreed. "It's the doggone craziest thing, but Rose is right. You know where Julia's gone?"

Tony did, and, grabbing his coat, he went after her.

Red Ray Mountain.

He knew she'd be drawn to the red colors that spread as the setting sun touched the mountain. Crystal Cove was tethered to a nearby tree, sheltered by some wild bushes. Tony was impressed she'd chosen such an intelligent place for the horse.

But then again, there was a lot that impressed him about Julia. He tied up Shadow near Crystal and surveyed the area.

Julia stood at the side of the mountain, silhouetted in the sun's rays. Her hair was pinned up, but with the wind whipping around the hills, most of the warm-colored strands had torn free of its restraints—the many pins, the ribbon.

He approached slowly, but wasn't surprised that she knew he was here. She turned slowly, and in the last of the rays' light, he could see that she'd been crying.

He felt immense guilt that he could be the reason for her tears. Gathering her into his arms, he waited out her token resistance, and held her.

"It won't work," she muttered against his chest. "You just think you love me, but you can't. It's...not real. You'll see, it won't work."

Tony captured her face and stared into her eyes. He could tell her that when he realized he loved her, he'd been scared, too, but she didn't need to hear that from him, now. "Okay, it won't work."

She seemed momentarily nonplussed. "I'm not joking."

"I know."

"What are you up to?"

"Nothing."

"Right."

He held up two fingers again, and smiled. "Promise."

"Huh. You were probably never even a Boy Scout," she said, hugging him. "Tony, you only think you've straightened it out with Maxine, but I have a feeling something bad's going to happen, and it'll be because of me. I couldn't live with that, knowing you or Rachel were in trouble." She leaned into his arms. "I know you wanted me to stay, but I'm too confused, and I need time, and... Tell me you understand."

His muscles tensed. "I understand. You want to leave. Don't let me stop you." He tamped down his annoyance; it wouldn't help in the wake of what he was about to tell her.

"You *don't* understand. I don't mean I'm leaving right now, although I *am* going back to the house. I meant after we find someone. Then, I'm packing and leaving."

"Oh, is that what you meant. I see." She stopped and looked at him. Although it was too dark to be sure, he'd have bet the ranch she had one of her eyebrows arched high. "Sorry to disillusion you, honey, but you're not leaving when we get back to the ranch." He hoisted her up on her horse, handing her the reins. "I am."

Chapter 8

Tony had not been joking.

When they returned to the house after their ride, he informed her that he had to go out of town on a business trip that night, and wouldn't return until Wednesday night.

"Where are you going?" Julia marched up the front stairs.

"Canada. I've got to check out a stallion for sale."

"Why didn't you tell me sooner?" Julia demanded, storming into the house.

"It must have slipped my mind. After all, we had more important things to talk about lately."

"Is this why we don't have any interviews until Thursday?"

"Yeah." He removed his hat, ran a hand through his hair and walked into the kitchen. "Hey, Tom, Rose. How's everything?"

Julia swallowed back her fighting words at the sight of

Rose and her husband. Rachel sat in her high chair, squishing and munching sliced apples.

"All's fine, *here*," Tom answered. "How was the ride?"

"Bumpy," Tony murmured, and cast a quick glance in Julia's direction. "Rose and Tom stopped in earlier and graciously volunteered to watch Rachel while I joined you."

Julia grimaced inwardly, realizing that she'd been so wrapped up in her own pain, she hadn't even thought to ask him who was with Rachel, and, from the way Rose and Tom were exchanging looks, it appeared she'd been talked about in this kitchen tonight.

"Hello, guys." She nodded at the two and then walked over to Rachel. "Hi, sweetness," she cooed, attempting to ease the tension in her shoulders.

Rose sprang to her feet. "Tony, did you tell her?"

"Nope, she's all yours," he said.

Julia looked between them. "What's going on now?" she asked suspiciously. Rose looked too happy, and Tom looked...delighted.

"Jules," Rose said, putting her hands on Julia's shoulders. "We're pregnant."

"We are? I mean—" She looked at Tom and back at Rose. "You are? Oh, Rose!" Julia hugged her friend and allowed herself to be maneuvered into the living room.

Once they were alone, Rose filled her in on all the details, and Julia felt dumbfounded. "You're pregnant, *and* Tom still wants to adopt?"

"Yes." Rose glowed. "I told you, he's got a lot of love, and so do I. We can't wait to fill the house with kids."

"Rose, you're amazing."

"Sugar, it's natural." Rose sat on the couch and dragged Julia down, too. "I want a family. The risk is worth it."

She touched Julia's arm. "It can be that way for you with Tony."

Julia shook her head. "There are…things here that are stopping me. It's not that easy."

"Who ever said love was easy? But *things* can be resolved. Every time we talked, you said how you were healing. Doesn't that include moving forward?" She paused briefly. "Didn't the interview with Mabel tell you anything about yourself?"

"Mabel?"

Rose filled her in on what she'd done. "I'll apologize for setting you up, but that's the only thing I'll apologize for. Not for trying to open your eyes. Tony really cares about you."

Julia was initially angry, but as she listened beyond her friend's words, and felt the love Rose had for Tony and her, her anger dissipated. But not her concerns. Long after Rose and Tom left, long after Rachel fell asleep, and long after Tony left for the airport on his three-day trip, Julia was still mulling over Rose's words.

She hardly had a moment alone to sit and think, though, since a steady progression of Tony's friends stopped by throughout the evening. No sooner had one left than, within half an hour, another showed up. They all wanted to linger, but after giving them a piece of cake and a hot cup of coffee, she shooed them out, wanting to be alone.

But that wasn't to happen. Chris showed up at midnight, and checked the house, locking all the doors, regardless of how many times she told him she could do it. "Can't let anything happen to you. Tony'd kill me," he'd teased. Finally, after he showed her the intercom and how to work it, he left.

By one in the morning, Julia, still wound up from her talk with Tony and Rose, sat in the living room. She poked the fire, and added a log to feed it. The flames jumped, heating her face, crackling and occasionally shooting sparks. Replacing the screen, Julia gave way to her thoughts. Was Rose right? And her mother? And Tony himself? Could she find happiness with Tony?

Of course I could.

That wasn't the issue. Tony would believe himself in love with her, but how long would that love last once he decided that he didn't want another man's children?

After all, Hank had said he'd adopt....

I don't understand, Hank. You said—

Well, forget it. A man wants his own children.

But, in the hospital—

For God's sake, Julia! You'd just come out of surgery. What'd you expect me to say...?

Tears burned in her eyes. She hadn't normally believed Hank, but he'd told her that when their marriage was over. He'd had nothing to gain by lying to her. Julia then thought about how Tony loved Rachel. He'd talked about having a family, brothers and sisters for her, but he'd never said anything about them needing to be of his own flesh and blood. Could he be happy with only adopted children?

No man wants adoption, even if he tells you he does.

Hank's words, and the facts in front of her eyes, warred within her. Julia sat on the plush salmon carpet in front of the fire. She thought about her losses, from her child to her marriage. After a while, she realized that being here had helped her see things clearly. She loved children, and although the pain would be there intermittently throughout her life, she had to embrace the future. As soon as the new semester started, she would complete her master's. In the meantime, she could get her local certification and try to find a job teaching in the area. She was ready to move on with her life.

But she also knew, with a certainty, that in moving on she'd have to let Tony go. And her reasoning, although painful, made sense. She and Hank hadn't seen eye-to-eye on many things after her miscarriage, but she knew that in the case of adoption, he was right. A healthy, virile man like Tony would eventually want his own children, and he would come to resent her. Therefore, loving Tony as she did, she knew that she would have to walk away. Not in anger, nor with doubt or hesitation, but with her head held high, knowing that in the long run, she was doing what was best for him.

Even if it killed her.

The storm that had threatened to erupt on Sunday finally did on Monday. It snowed fiercely for a few hours, depositing about six inches. The men had come and eaten breakfast, then stopped by several times during the morning, "Just to warm up."

By noon, the downfall had lightened, and Julia saw Jeeps and cars on the road in the distance. One blue car turned up the drive and parked next to the house.

Another visitor. This was getting to be ridiculous, but when Julia opened the door and saw that it was Miss Irene and her husband, George, she smiled warmly. "Hi, there, you two. Come on in." She ushered them in and closed the door. "What brings you here, today? And how's your back, George?"

"Gettin' better," he answered. "We were on our way to market, and just thought we'd stop in to say hello." He pulled out a chair for his wife, and watched her sit. His rugged face, showing years of hard work during the hot summer months and harsh winters, glowed with love for this woman.

Miss Irene sat down. "And I had a dandy idea. Why

don't you and Rachel come over and spend the next two days with us? You must be lonely in this big house all by yourself.''

"Hardly," Julia drawled, and told them about her many visitors. "Tonight, I'm looking forward to some quiet."

They smiled, but she thought she saw a worried frown appear briefly on Miss Irene's forehead. It was gone so quickly, Julia dismissed it as her overactive imagination looking for trouble.

"You've been baking?" Miss Irene asked, sniffing the air.

"You bet. I made a cake yesterday, but between all the people dropping in, it's gone. So, I baked another one. Death-by-Chocolate. Ever hear of it?"

Miss Irene nodded. "It's Tony's favorite."

Julia looked away, busying herself with the dish towel. "Really? That's interesting." She turned and faced Miss Irene's skeptical look.

"So, the rumors are true. Tony's trying to lasso you, and you're fighting it like a wild-born filly." She smiled fondly at George. "Remind you of anyone?"

He chuckled, and Julia knew they were sharing an age-less joke, the kind married couples kept alive. She could see Miss Irene as a young woman, driving George mad, rejecting him until he won her over. Julia longed for that kind of romancing, too, but that was rare. And she was fated for the common life.

Chris came into the kitchen. He greeted the visitors, then turned to Julia. "If you still want to run into town, we need to go now. The storm's taking a break, but there's more clouds gathering in the distance."

"Oh, I can't," Julia said. "Rachel's just gone down for a nap." She looked at Miss Irene. "She's going through a growth spurt and is so unpredictable. Sometimes she'll still take a nap, but other times, she's too awake."

Miss Irene looked at her watch, then at George. He nodded, and she removed the red scarf from around her neck. "Go on. We'll stay. I may even wake the young'n up on purpose, just to play with her," she added, smiling.

"I'll take you up on your offer. We're out of some important items. We'll be back soon," she said, then bundled up.

Chris and she drove into town. When they arrived, they parked by the grocery store.

"I'll just be a minute," Julia said. "Then we can get home again. I really appreciate this."

"No problem, Julia. I didn't want you to drive your little car into town, and I know Tony would kill me—"

"Yeah, yeah. If anything happened to me. I know the drill."

Julia jumped out of the truck, slamming the door behind her, leaving a grinning Chris behind the wheel. She wasn't sure who she was more angry with, everyone else for assuming she belonged to Tony, or herself for wanting that fantasy to last.

The store was more crowded than normal. Julia guessed that others had had the same thought—stock up in case the next storm was a big one. Pushing her cart through the packed aisles, Julia was stopped often. People, some she recognized, others she didn't, talked to her, offering her advice on raising Rachel, commenting on how pleased they were that she was watching over her now.

Several people had said they'd be stopping in later, just to say hello and see the "young'n." No matter how hard Julia tried to dissuade them, they just patted her hand, claiming only a raging snowstorm would keep them away.

Julia rooted for the storm.

Which, of course, meant there would be clear skies. While fate hadn't been breathing over her shoulder lately—she pitied the soul who had its attention—she had a feeling she was due for something soon.

Finally shaking off most of the neighbors, she picked a few vegetables and started making her way to the checkout counters. At the front of the store, she reached for a box of cookies and banged her cart into something.

"Well, if it isn't Miss Suzy Homemaker."

Lord, not an impending storm and *Maxine in the same day.*

Julia swallowed back a ripe curse at fate, and tossed the box of vanilla wafers into the cart. She heard the cookies bounce around, and wondered how many calories were in crumbs. "Hello, Maxine. What's new?"

Maxine smiled, her teeth pearly-white. "I signed a contract with a buyer in Casper. Soon I'll be making a name for myself."

Soon?

Julia smiled appropriately. "How exciting for you." She looked around. Maxine's bags had been packed and were waiting for her at the checkout counter behind her, but she didn't look as though she were in any rush. People were slowing down, obviously listening to their exchange.

Julia looked at her watch. "Well, I have—"

"What? What do you have? Oh, yes," she said, snapping her fingers, watching the neighbors come closer, enjoying her fifteen minutes of fame. "You have Tony."

She'd been right. Maxine wasn't through being angry.

"Tony will grow tired of you, too." Maxine pointed to the people around them. "Ask them how long he's been with any one woman. He'll show his true colors, in time. Behind his smooth veneer, he's just a city kid playing at being a success."

"So he's a lowlife, someone not worthy of your time? And you're too smart to get tied up with a man like him, right?"

"That's right," Maxine answered, smiling condescendingly.

"Then why were you dating him?"

Maxine's jaw dropped. She'd walked arrogantly into admitting her own stupidity. Clamping her mouth shut, she glared angrily at the townspeople. They stood around, murmuring their agreement with Julia.

Suddenly Maxine grabbed her arm. Julia tensed, ready to fight if necessary, but Maxine wasn't looking at her. She was looking over Julia's shoulder. Maxine's grip tightened.

"Julia, Mitch Brown just walked in. Where's Rachel?"

"She's home, with Miss Irene and George." She looked over her shoulder, and spotted the man, more like a boy, all dirty, with long, unkempt brown hair. He entered the store, flipping cards on the bulletin board near the door. "When did he get to town?"

"A few days ago. He's been mouthing off. Maybe you ought to wander to the back of the store so he doesn't see you."

Conversation stopped slowly, like a giant wave, starting at the front of the store and passing over her head.

"I don't understand. He's been here a few days, you all knew, but I didn't?" She glanced at Maxine and the townsfolk who shuffled about, looking suddenly guilty. "I suppose Tony knew, too?"

"Of course, but now's not the time to discuss this. Go to the back of the store," Maxine urged.

"I can see why Tony and I would be worried about Mitch being here, but why do you care?"

Maxine's lips stretched. "Listen, I may not like you, but

I like his kind even less." Maxine stepped in front of her. "And if he sees you, he may decide to cause trouble."

The people who'd been spectators in their conversation minutes ago rallied around Maxine agreeing with her, urging Julia to the back of the store. Julia didn't understand their concern. Unless something was happening she didn't know about.

"I don't know why Mr. Brown is in town, or why I'm the only one who didn't know about it, but Rachel is safe at home and he's not going to get near her." She cast a glance in Mitch Brown's direction, feeling like a mother lion protecting her cub. "Besides that, he probably doesn't even know who I am."

Maxine's eyebrows rose. "Of course he knows you. This is a small town, and since we don't know what he's capable of doing, it's stupid for you to stand here. Now, git," she said, her natural drawl pronounced.

At that moment, Mitch spotted her. He started to walk back, stumbling over a display of Christmas decorations near the first of the three cashiers. Before Julia could make up her mind what to do, Chris came into the store. He followed Mitch and, when he was close enough, tapped him on the shoulder. Mitch swayed back, and eyed him up and down.

Mitch was gaunt, and gave the illusion that he was tall, but he shrank considerably when Chris showed up at his side.

"I was just gonna ask how my little girl was," Mitch slurred. He looked at Julia. "You take care of my baby. How is she? How's uh…Rachel?"

Chris stepped forward, but Julia shook her head. "She's fine."

"I don't see her. Where is she?"

"She's in good hands, Mr. Brown. I'll tell Mr. Pellegrino you asked about her."

Mitch seemed to think for a second. "Yeah, you do that. And you can also tell him…" Glancing around at the angry faces, he obviously had a change of heart since he didn't continue. He just shrugged and headed out.

Julia felt the collective sigh of relief expelled from the entire store population. Within minutes, normal activity resumed.

She turned to Maxine. "Thanks—"

"Hold your thanks. We're not friends yet," Maxine said, her ruffled feathers back in place. "I still don't like you."

"But you protected her," drawled an amused male voice. "I always thought you had more western hospitality than you let on."

Chris pushed his brown cowboy hat high on his forehead, his dark brown hair poking from under the rim. He walked over and stood directly in front of Maxine.

Maxine's lips compressed. "Not again. Don't you have someone else to harass?"

"No one whose eyes shoot fire like yours. Spitfire, I'm mighty proud of the way you protected Julia." Chris winked at her, then smiled at the chuckles from the people that still lingered around them. "And I'd certainly think twice before going up against you."

Julia could see Maxine's jaw muscles working furiously. "You remember that, Christopher Chambers, and my name isn't Spitfire." She ground out the words, her voice low. Staring up at his face—he was a good head taller than her—she straightened her shoulders, and poked him in the chest. "Now, Julia and I were talking—"

"Well, my mama always told me never to interrupt, especially when two gorgeous women were fighting over a man, but seeing as how I'm not the man in question…"

Chris shrugged, then took another step forward. "Why don't I help you carry your things to your car?"

Not waiting for her approval, he lifted Maxine's bags from the conveyor belt and, putting his hand on the small of her back, propelled her forward. Maxine took one more look behind her before obviously deciding not to challenge Chris. At least not in front of all her neighbors.

What does he have over her?

Julia didn't have time to ponder that. The neighbors in question all said goodbye to Maxine, and praised her for her deed. Julia smiled, glad to see that, despite Maxine's outrageous attitude, people around here recognized her as one of them.

Her audience then patted Julia's back and told her she'd done okay, too. Held her ground, made Tony proud of her.

Julia made noncommittal remarks, then maneuvered her way to the cashier. While the woman checked out her groceries, she glanced out the front window, and almost dropped her checkbook.

Chris had just deposited Maxine's packages on the front seat of her black sports car, and closed the door. Then, without warning, he grabbed her around the waist with his right arm and, bending her back, plastered his lips to hers.

Maxine's arms waved in the air, and she tried kicking his legs, but she kept slipping in the slush and finally had to grab his jacket to keep herself balanced. Julia closed her mouth, but her jaw dropped open again a second later.

When Chris pulled back and set Maxine on her feet, Julia expected her to claw his eyes out, or at the very least punch him in his conceitedly stuck-out jaw. But she did neither. Instead, she stared up at him, her lips opening and closing, over and over, as if she were a fish taking in water.

Julia could almost see the steam coming from her ears as Chris swaggered away, back to the store.

"Sixty-three forty-five."

Julia's head snapped around, and she hastily wrote a check. Pushing her cart with the bagged items to the front door, she watched Chris approach, grinning from ear to ear, like a kid getting the puppy he'd wanted all his life. Maxine stood in the light snowfall, staring at him with narrowed eyes.

"Ready?"

She nodded mutely, and helped him carry out the bags. As they passed Maxine, Chris tipped his hat. Maxine muttered something, then jumped into her car and skidded away.

Settled once again in the truck, he glanced up at the sky. "Looks like the storm's about to hit."

"I'd say it already did, and passed quietly, wouldn't you?" Julia chuckled, took a tissue from her pocket and wiped the red lipstick from his lips.

He looked at her. "Damn straight." Slipping the gears into drive, he hit his thigh and laughed loudly. "Damn straight!"

On the drive home, Chris allayed Julia's concerns about Mitch. "He's just mouthing off, came to town to see if he could cause some trouble. He'd made some remarks about snatching his kid...." He shrugged.

"So Tony was afraid. That's why his friends 'dropped by' nonstop last night." Julia sighed. "He must have been very worried about her to go to all that trouble."

"Not just her. You, too. If Mitch's high enough, and you got in his way, which Tony knew you'd do, then you'd get hurt." Chris explained. "He was worried, his being gone and all."

Julia understood Tony's concern, so when they arrived

home, and Chris made sure the house was secure before he went to the bunkhouse, she didn't hassle him.

"Remember," Chris warned, "if there's trouble, you use that intercom."

She agreed, but decided she wasn't going to be bothered by anyone tonight. Turning off the lights throughout the house, Julia went to her bedroom, lay on the bed and spent a leisurely evening reading. With the house sealed up tight, she couldn't hear any approaching vehicles, and since her room was toward the back, she also couldn't see any headlights. That suited her just fine. This way, she didn't have to fight the urge to be hospitable, and since the doorbell remained silent, apparently her message had been received by any would-be visitors.

Around ten-thirty, after she checked on Rachel, the phone rang. Tony hadn't had any need for an extension in Julia's room—which had formerly been the guest room— so she walked to the living room and picked up the receiver. "Hello?"

"Hi. Can I speak with Tony?"

The male voice sounded familiar, and it took Julia a moment to realize it had the same accent as Tony. "I'm sorry, but he's not available. Is this Nick or Matt?" She'd seen them only briefly at Anne's funeral, and couldn't tell who this was.

He chuckled. "This is Nick, Tony's younger, and *much* handsomer, brother. Do I have the pleasure of speaking to Mary Poppins?"

Julia laughed. "In person. I take it Tony's filled you in on me, right down to the umbrella?"

"Yup. Let's see, you have Rachel eating from the palm of your hand, you sing the sweetest lullabies this side of Valhalla," he continued, talking so fast she couldn't get a word in edgewise. "And you can fly, come down through chimneys, and make medicine taste good, right? What I don't understand is how come you're still with Tony? I mean, after hearing about me, which I'm sure you have, why aren't you beating down my door?''

"I can't get away. I usually have a rambunctious child using my leg as a post to hoist herself up." She decided she liked this friendly, outgoing man.

"Rachel can stand?" He asked her dozens of questions about Rachel, answering half of them himself. Finally he got around to telling her about Tony's call last week, and brought up the reason he'd called tonight. "I wanted to tell Tony that we made contact with our mother. Hey, I guess I should thank you."

"Me? Why?"

"Well, *you* were *his* impetus, and *he* was *our* good-luck charm. Matt and I have been searching for years with no success. Tony calls, and zap, we find her. I call that luck, don't you?" He took in a breath, and continued. "I wanted to see if he'd want us to come up for a visit. Our mother is very excited about the prospect. She's brokenhearted about Annie's death, and wants to see Tony, before something else happens. You see, she and Tony had been very close before she left."

"Really?"

"Absolutely. I was young, but I remember them laughing a lot together, before my father died, and after dinner every night, Tony would sit with us and work on our numbers. Our mother would stand behind him, her hands on his shoulders, watching."

So that was why Tony had been so hurt by her abandonment, and why he as still angry at the mere mention of her.

"Is she a nice woman?" Julia asked, and crossed her fingers.

"I think so. She's been through a lot herself. She's nervous, chain-smokes like a chimney. But I think she's okay." He paused. "Matt and I had each other, so we were better able to deal with the whole thing. And we met with her together, too. It might be harder for Tony, but with you there…"

Julia heard the unspoken implication in his voice. "I'll certainly tell him about this, and I'm sure you'll hear from him soon." They talked a few more minutes, then she hung up.

She couldn't believe Tony had acted on what they'd talked about. Part of her was delighted that she could have influenced him in a way that Rachel would benefit from, but the other part of her worried about how attached they were becoming. And how hard it would be for her to leave Rachel.

And Tony.

She sighed. Yes, and Tony, she finally admitted to herself. She could no longer kid herself about it. It was there in bold and bright light. She *was* in love with the man, and would live to regret it for the rest of her life.

"Hope you're satisfied," she muttered to the Fates.

Checking up on Rachel before retiring for the evening, Julia rubbed the baby's back gently. "So, Rachel, it looks as though you're going to meet your grandmother," she whispered. "You'll have a full family, you lucky little girl."

And I'll have my chance to leave.

Damn. Damn. Damn.

Tony dropped his suitcase on the front porch and fumbled around in the snow, looking for his keys.

For the second time.

Yawning loudly again, he forced his eyes open. The

wind pushed at him as it whipped around the house. The porch light hardly helped, as his body shielded the area from the light. Finally, his numbing fingers latched on to the ring, and he shook the snow from them before he tried one more time to insert the proper key in the lock.

Opening the door at last, he dragged his suitcase into the front hall, shut the door and left the bag right where he dropped it. His clothes would have to wait before being unpacked. Exhausted from two days of almost nonstop meetings, including late-night negotiations to outbid others and buy the fine ribbon-winning stud—which he finally did—Tony staggered down the hallway, straight for Rachel's room.

Despite his incredible fatigue, he had to see his daughter before collapsing on his bed and sleeping for a week. At Rachel's bedroom, he paused and checked his watch. Two-fifteen.

Wednesday morning.

Pushing open Rachel's door as quietly as possible, Tony walked over to the crib. Contentment settled in him at the sight of his baby lying so peacefully. Her breathing was low and steady, and Tony stood in awe of how much he loved her.

So much so, he'd cut short his business trip by one day to return to her—and to the other vixen who'd stolen his heart. Gently he stroked Rachel's hair, the soft dark brown tresses that were beginning to thicken. Kissing her cheek, he turned to leave and check up on his other woman. A white piece of paper caught his eye. It was attached with tape to the outer rails of the crib.

He took it off and, walking to the hall, angled it downward. The night light from the hallway was dim, but he could make out what it said.

Tony,
Got the message that you're coming home earlier than
anticipated. Rachel missed you. I have to talk to you.
Please wake me, no matter what time you arrive.

                                                    Julia

Only slightly amused that she'd think to put the note here,
knowing this was the first place he'd go, Tony raked a
weary hand through his hair. She'd written that Rachel had
missed him, but what about her?

He folded the note, glancing at Julia's closed door. After
everything he'd pulled on her, she probably wanted to tell
him she was leaving. Hell, she was probably just waiting
for him to wake her, so that she could leave immediately.

Tony had no more fight left in him tonight, and he'd be
damned if he'd let her go without one, so he walked past
her room and into his own. Her leaving could wait until
tomorrow.

Removing his coat and scarf, he tossed them on a chair
and kicked off his shoes. He sat on the bed and began
unbuttoning his shirt. Thankfully, he hadn't worn a suit
jacket; it was one less thing to remove now. Shirt off, he
fell back on the bed and closed his eyes, his hands automatically reaching for the button on his pants and opening
it. A vision of Julia waiting in his bed, all tempting and
sweet, popped into his head, and he chuckled. Even if he
rolled over and actually saw her, he was too damned tired
to do anything about it tonight.

But tomorrow.

His depleted mind vaguely recalled her threat to leave.

No way could she be replaced. Not now, not ever.

She'd marry him, if he had to carry her hog-tied, kicking
and screaming, to the altar. He smiled wearily at the picture
of Julia gagged. Her remarkable blue eyes would spit fire

at him, but only until he got her to admit *he* knew what was best for *him*.

Or until their wedding night.

After that, convincing her would be a piece of cake...sweet, sweet cake....

The last thing Tony thought before sleep finally claimed him was, would he taste the arsenic in that cake?

Julia's eyes snapped open at the creaking outside her bedroom door. She glanced at the clock. It read 3:10.

Her heart thundered. Sitting upright, Julia cocked her head and listened to the loud silence. The faint moonlight that entered her windows was enough to help her eyes adjust to the dark.

There.

Another creak.

Footsteps.

Sliding off the bed, she walked quickly, her only thought—to get to the baby before Mitch did.

If he lays a hand on her...

Julia grabbed a book off the dresser to use as a weapon, and opened the door, stepping out to confront the man.

She saw Tony walking into the kitchen.

Collapsing against the door jamb, she felt the adrenaline-infused fear swiftly leaving. She tossed the book back onto the dresser and proceeded down the hall. She walked to Rachel's room and saw that she slept quietly.

She also saw the note she'd left Tony was missing.

Why didn't he wake me when he first arrived?

She dismissed the thought. Tony had obviously been home long enough to check on Rachel, get comfortable and decide to get something to eat. He must be exhausted. She certainly was, she thought as she yawned.

She glanced in the direction of the kitchen and heard

noises. Curiosity pushed her to see what he was doing. Tony was drinking milk from the container, the light from the open refrigerator door illuminating the descending motion of his throat muscles as he gulped the milk. Her gaze traveled along his wide shoulders, down his broad back. She leaned against the door jamb, continuing her perusal of his rear end, and his long legs.

The fact that he was half-nude reminded her of her state of dishabille, and she blamed her need to see if he was okay as the reason she didn't return to her room.

Right.

Well, he'd already seen most of what she had to show.

Just seen it?

Memories flooded her. She slowly entered the kitchen. The floor creaked, and Tony turned.

"Hi," he said, wiping the milk from his mouth with the back of his hand.

"Hi." She paused and looked at his big brown eyes. "When did you get home?"

He held out the milk. "Want some?"

"No, thanks. How was your trip?"

"Fine. Gotta find someone new."

Someone new?

He spotted the cake. "Oh, great. I love cake." Lifting the dome on the cake plate, he reached for a piece. "I love chocolate."

"So you've said. It's called Death-by-Chocolate."

Suddenly he looked at the cake in his hand, gingerly put it back on the plate and covered it with the dome.

"You don't want any?" she asked, confused by his actions.

He blinked in her direction, looking bewildered for a moment, then smiled. "I've gotta find a replacement."

A red flag went up. "For what?"

Tony put the milk back and closed the door, then walked past her and into his office. Julia followed. Sitting behind his large oak desk, he clicked on the table lamp and began sorting through papers. She sat in the maroon leather chair opposite him. He looked up and smiled again, guilelessly.

"Hi," he said and resumed leafing through the sheaf of papers in his hand.

"Hi, again." The red flag waved back and forth and Julia suspected that he was asleep. "You're looking for someone new?"

"Of course." He put the papers down and leaned forward, talking to her earnestly, confidentially. "She's irreplaceable, but try telling it to her."

"Her?"

"Yeah. I don't know what else to do. I have to find someone for my baby. But, she can't be replaced. She's a stay-at-home, rent-a-movie-on-Saturday-night woman, and I love her."

He loves me!

Her heart filled with joy, but then Julia pierced the bubble.

Tony is asleep and you're being ridiculous.

The hopefullness inside her died. She didn't have time to waste on fanciful thoughts, anyway, what with Tony asleep.

Just then, Tony picked up a pen and began writing on the legal pad. "One, find someone new. Impossible. Two, marry her. Three, no cake."

Just what was wrong with her cake?

"Four..." He frowned, his eyes darting about as if he were trying to recapture a thought.

His disjointed list convinced Julia that he was indeed asleep, and searching for her replacement. Feeling guilty that her quest to leave had driven him to resume his sleep-walking, she tried to figure out what to do.

Tony looked at her. "Four? Do you remember four?"

Her tired mind scrambled. "Four, go to bed?" She crossed her fingers, hoping he'd take the bait.

His face brightened. "That's right." Writing, he mumbled the words "Four, go to bed." Then he put the pen down and sat back in his chair. He looked content.

"Well, it's time for number four," Julia ventured.

He looked at her seriously. "Have I done one and two?"

"Yes."

He leaned forward, his eyes wide. "I didn't eat the cake, did I?"

Exasperated, Julia shook her head. "No, you didn't. Come on now, time for number four." She rose and held out her hand.

Coming around the desk, he took her hand and followed her down the hall and into his bedroom. She folded back the covers and sat him down, lifting his feet. Expelling a deep breath, she looked at the top button on his pants. It was undone. She clenched her fists.

No way.

He'd have to bear sleeping in them for one night.

"Good night, Tony." She'd started to walk to the door when the sound of him leaving the bed caught her attention. Sure enough, he'd thrown back the covers and walked to the door behind her. "Where are you going?"

"One, gotta find someone new." Tony smiled down at her.

Her heart flip-flopped. He looked so dark and rebellious, with his beard and mustache growing in, and his eyes half-closed, his muscled chest only inches from her itching fingers. What a contrast to the boyish grin he wore, and the air of trust he projected.

Down, girl.

"You already did, Tony. It's time for number four."

"Four, go to bed." Taking her hand, he pulled her with him.

Her heart slammed against her ribs, but Julia forced herself to remain calm. He was sleeping and didn't know what he was doing. Or did he?

At the bed, Tony lay down and yanked Julia to him. She sat on the side of the bed and studied him. His expression hadn't changed, but that didn't mean a thing. After that incident at her mother's house, she'd begun to believe he was a very good actor. Still, that didn't stop her from weaving a fantasy of lying next to him, touching him and being loved by him.

And bearing children for him?

Reality washed over her, effectively banishing her dream. "Go to sleep, Tony," she said, grateful that he didn't hear the sorrow in her voice.

"Two, marry her."

"Th-that's right," she said, her voice cracking. "Now go to sleep."

He nodded and closed his eyes. His breathing slowed, and she gently soothed his brow. After a minute, she rose, but his arm shot out and grasped her hand.

"Sing to me," he murmured. "A lullaby...mockingbirds."

"No, Tony," she said, and moved off the bed again, but as soon as she did, he threw back the covers. "Okay, okay." She pushed him down and covered him. Then, while he watched, she walked around the bed and sat down on the other side. Leaning back against the headboard, she began singing, softly, about mockingbirds and diamond rings....

* * *

"Julia?"

A voice floated into her mind, urging her to awaken. She heard it several more times. Finally, she stretched and yawned and slowly opened her eyes. "Oh, hi, Tony. Did I oversleep?"

"Nope. It's only four-thirty in the morning."

"Then what're you doing in here?"

"*I sleep in here,* usually alone, but I'm not complaining." Tony, lying on his left side, smiled. The crinkles around his eyes warmed her seconds before his words sank in.

Julia sat up and took a mental inventory. She was in Tony's bedroom. She'd fallen asleep singing to him. She looked back down at him. A smattering of hair ran across his bare chest and sloped down his flat abdomen, disappearing under his closed zipper. The soft light from the bedside lamp cast his angular face in shadows, giving him a rakish look she found terribly exciting. As she watched, his right hand played with the hem of her nightgown. His thumb brushed the soft material back and forth.

A whorl of desire pooled between her legs. How she wished he was doing that to her body instead.

"I dreamt I came home," he said, "and found you waiting for me, stretched out on my bed, your hair undone and spread on the pillow beneath you." He inhaled deeply. "Just like you were a few minutes ago. Care to resume that position and make my dream come true?"

Goose bumps broke out over her body at the sound of his deep early-morning voice. The spiral of desire gathered intensity—a minihurricane brewing. He watched her, his dashing grin spreading. Julia wanted so much to put aside her fears and spend the night making love to Tony, but the feeling that she'd be toying with his affections intruded on her fantasy.

She started to speak, but Tony slid his right hand beneath her gown, up her leg, and stopped on her upper thigh. She clutched the bedspread, her breath coming in short pants. The hurricane inside her grew in intensity.

He sat up, at eye level with her, and spoke. "I'm a grown man. I make my own decisions." He squeezed her thigh. "I love you. I want you." Tony moved forward, forcing her to lean backward. "Now." When her head hit the head-board, he kissed her jaw, then nipped her earlobe. "Are you okay?" His breath stirred the fine hairs near her ear.

Julia nodded, too turned on to speak.

He kissed her neck. "Want me to kiss the boo-boo to make it better?" Lying on her, he kept most of his weight on his elbows. The shadows on his face danced as he spoke. "Want me to kiss anything else to make it better?" he muttered wickedly.

The hurricane spiraled out of control.

"Yes," Julia whispered, and slid her hands up and over his shoulders. She wound her fingers into his hair. "My chin."

He kissed her chin.

"The corners of my mouth."

He kissed the corners of her mouth. "What else?" Tony lay down completely upon her.

She spread her legs to accommodate him and felt the hard ridge press into her. Her hips jerked upward.

Framing her face with his hands, and staring straight into her eyes, he whispered, "What else do you want me to kiss?"

Lost in her love, and feeling the passion for him stronger than she'd ever felt it before, Julia knew there was only one answer. And, pulling his head down, she said it.

"Me."

Chapter 9

Tony had waited so long to hear any words of encouragement from Julia, he actually froze when she said them.

But *only* for a moment.

Julia tugged his head down and kissed him. She opened her mouth, mating her tongue with his. Her soft mewing sounds spurred him on, making him so aroused, he was afraid he'd explode before getting inside her.

He didn't have to worry for too much longer.

Julia became insistent, and within minutes, his pants were off, and she closed her hand around his manhood. "Julia," he murmured harshly, "keep that up and... and..." His words faded into a groan.

She trailed kisses down his chest and abdomen while her hand moved rhythmically up and down. He couldn't stop moaning, but the moment he felt her mouth on him, he knew he'd have to do something, or this morning would end quickly. He hauled her up and onto her back, then loomed over her.

"Turnabout's fair play," he said, then peeled her gown off her body. She placed her hands on her abdomen, but Tony moved them away, staring into her eyes. "I won't look, I promise." She smiled gratefully. "Not now, anyway."

Her smile faded a bit. "Okay."

Tony felt the trust she placed in him. And he wasn't about to let her down. "Good. Right now, though, I've got a hot woman who's demanding my attention, and I always believed in giving a woman what she wants."

"This woman wants you," Julia whispered.

Tony insinuated a knee between her legs, and, feeling her wetness with his hand, he got even harder. "I can tell."

"Then stop talking, and do something about it," she demanded.

"Soon, love. Soon." He wanted her lost in the passion, as she'd been a few moments ago. Kissing her deeply, he parted her, and slid his fingers around gently, teasingly.

Julia couldn't believe how hungry she was for Tony's touch—and how close she was to climaxing, now that he was touching her. Just like the first time. But it wasn't enough. This time she wanted him in her. "Tony, please," she said, her body twisting on the bed. "I want to feel you in me. Please…"

"As you wish." He kissed her neck down to her breasts, then licked her nipples. She gasped and arched her back. His fingers moved faster, making small circles, and he sucked harder on her aching breasts. Just when she thought she'd lose consciousness, he slid into her.

He filled her. She wrapped her legs around his waist, and he sank even deeper. She felt complete, whole.

There was a throbbing that screamed to be released, but he didn't move. Hooking his fingers with hers, he laid her hands on the pillow. He held her head between his fore-arms.

"Julia, there's no turning back after this."

"As long as you know *this* is all it *can* be."

Slowly, a grin the likes of which she'd never seen before spread across his face. He pulled his hips back, leaving just the tip of his engorged shaft in her. "You're wrong," he warned, his breathing labored. "I love you, Julia, and *this* is just the *start* of what we can have together."

He plunged into her, covering her mouth, swallowing her moan. Then he pulled out and thrust in, faster, harder, trig-gering her climax. "Tony!" she cried as her body spasmed again and again.

He held her captive, in body and soul, and Julia didn't want to be freed. She wanted to be his, wanted to be part of him for as long as she could. She wrapped her arms and legs tight around him and held on.

Tony felt her contractions, and as they built into a cres-cendo, his control snapped. Thrusting into her, he cata-pulted into ecstasy.

She cried out. He grabbed her hips and pulled her up, pounding into her, rocking his body on hers as she reached her second pinnacle. She called out his name again, and his heart swelled even more than before.

Simultaneously, they collapsed on the bed, panting. Long moments passed. Tony could vaguely hear the ticking of his watch, which lay on the night stand near him. It re-minded him that he'd been lying with his full weight on Julia. He tried to ease off her, but he could do no more than prop himself on his elbows before she spoke.

"Don't move," she whispered. "I love the feel of you on me." She brushed a strand of hair from his forehead and looked him in the eyes. "And in me."

Her words ignited him—and certain parts of his anatomy—into renewed action. Tony pushed deeper into her.

A delighted gasp burst from her lips. "You're joking."

He chuckled. "If I am, then this joke's on you."

Julia groaned at his pun, but lifted her hips to meet his. Then she placed her hands on his shoulders and pulled him down so he rested on her again. "*Now,* the joke's on me," she whispered.

They kissed, and he began moving. Before long, the sounds of their passion began filling the air again. They made love slowly, lusciously, but their second climax rocked them just as turbulently as their first.

Breathing returned to normal, and cool air hit their sweat-soaked bodies. Tony lay on his side next to her, threaded his fingers through her hair and caressed her scalp. For long moments, he stroked her gently, wanting to tell her in actions just how moved he'd been.

Julia's languid breathing told him that she'd fallen asleep. He grinned, telling himself to remind her that men were supposed to do that, not women.

Still, it gave him an opportunity he chose to take advantage of. He kissed her chin, then the tip of each breast, then her upper abdomen, and finally he reached her scar. He could only imagine what she'd felt hearing the news. How he wished he could have been there for her at the time. He leaned down and kissed the scar, too, knowing now that it didn't matter to him.

Julia stirred. A tiny smile played on her rosy lips. She opened her eyes, and saw where he was looking. Immediately she pulled away from him.

"It's too late, honey." He dragged her to him, and covered her body with his, beginning to feel himself stir again. Only the look of horror on her face tempered his desire. "I've seen it."

"It's ugly, isn't it?"

He saw the fear in her eyes. Damn Hank! Taking in a deep breath, he lay on his back and pointed to a faded scar low on his abdomen. "I got this one from a hernia operation when I was fourteen." Rolling onto his left, he indicated his right upper thigh. "And this one is where the neighbor's dog bit me. See the teeth marks?" He poked the three spots. "Ugly?"

She shook her head.

"Neither is yours." He traced her scar, then kissed her.

Her eyes misted, and she averted her head. "Why didn't you want to eat my cake last night?"

Baffled, he asked, "What cake?"

She explained what she'd observed. Tony swallowed his laughter, recalling his last thought before falling asleep. "I have no idea." He decided to save the story for their fiftieth wedding anniversary. Now it was time to chase away some ghosts. "No more diversions. Let's talk."

"About what?" she hedged. "As a woman I'm not complete."

Tony had heard that some women felt this way after a mastectomy, or a hysterectomy. And even if Julia hadn't had either, this was just as traumatizing for her. And that was all that mattered to him.

He weighed his words carefully. "Julia, you've got everything a woman needs—intelligence, humor, kindness, and based on how I feel now, you know how to use what you have to make me feel like one hell of a lucky man. And as an added bonus, you're beautiful."

"Thank you, Tony. But you're still deluding yourself—"

"Julia, there is one more thing. It drives me crazy and you'll have to learn to stop it."

Her eyebrow arched. "What?"

"Telling me what I should be thinking. I think you're

only doing it because you don't feel you're worth anything, but that's wrong.'' He placed a finger across her lips. "Let me finish. You suffered a loss, but that doesn't make you any less of a woman. See?'' He pressed his hips against her and let her feel his arousal. "One of the dangers of believing you know what's best for me is you trying to do something for me without my knowledge, and you know how I'd feel about that. I can decide what's best for me, and that's you.''

"Hank told me some things about men and their feelings on adoption. We had already split, so he had no reason to lie about them. And you told Maxine you want more children. Every man wants a child of his own running around the house.''

"I *do* want a child, but it doesn't have to be my biological child for me to love it.'' He turned her face to his. "At least that's what the books say, and from what the woman at the adoption agency told me, she agrees with that, too.''

"You've read books? You spoke with someone?''

"Of course. I told you I needed some time. Well, I did some thinking and investigating, and for the last two days, between meetings, I placed a few phone calls, and got some answers.'' His thumb rubbed her lower lip. "I can live with adopting children, if you can.''

Julia's eyes filled with tears. "I don't know what to say.''

"How about 'That's great, Tony'? I'd have no problem with that answer.''

Julia tried to smile, but it didn't work. Tony wanted to marry her. Something she would have loved at any other time in her life now made her more sad than she could ever have imagined. She couldn't do that to him. Once the haze of romance wore off, he would resent her.

"Tony, think about it. Are you sure you don't just want a mother for Rachel?"

"Julia," he said, exasperation in his voice. "Of course I want a mother for Rachel, but I wouldn't marry someone just for that reason. Ask Miss Irene. She tried to convince me to settle down with a nice young girl from town, but it didn't work. I love you." He captured her gaze. "And I want to hear it from you. I want to hear those words."

She swallowed. "I do love you, Tony, but—"

He silenced her with his mouth, kissing her until she lost her train of thought. Almost.

"Tony, you love Rachel because she's family. Of course you have no problem adopting her. But first, it's not easy qualifying for adoption, and second, we're talking about taking in strange kids, with questionable backgrounds—"

"Like I'd been?"

"Oh, I didn't mean…"

He chuckled. "We'd be great with them."

"What if we pursue this relationship and, down the road a ways, you find out you're *not* happy?"

"Okay. What *if* we pursue this relationship and, down the road a ways, *you* find out *you're* not happy?" he asked. "Isn't that a risk inherent in any relationship? And don't we have to weigh all the other factors, like our similar values?"

"I do like being with you," she admitted grudgingly.

"Me too. When something happens, either at work or with Rachel, I think, 'I can't wait to tell Julia.' Hell, how many times have I called you in the middle of the day just to tell you something that just happened? I've never felt that way with any of the thousands of women I used to keep in my harem."

She giggled, then sobered when she recalled her marriage. Hank had done all the talking. It had always been about him, his triumphs, his accomplishments. He'd never wanted to hear about her day teaching.

Maybe Tony was right.

Maybe he was wrong.

And maybe she was just too confused to think any longer. Cupping his cheek, she felt his morning stubble. "I'm too emotionally worn out to argue with you right now."

"Good," he said, and kissed her. "Just love me. Everything else will take care of itself."

"Only if—" she leaned back and spoke seriously "—you give me some time to think. I don't know if I agree with everything you've said, but even if I do, I want time to look at it, without undue influence."

He yawned. "Take all the time you want. You can even keep your bedroom for your own space."

"No, you don't understand. Tony, what we just did was—"

"Wildly fantastic? Incredibly earth-shattering? Am I getting close? No? How about cosmically humorous?"

"You're being ridiculous. Of course it was wonderful, but you're suffering from the aftereffects of our lovemaking, and—"

"Right now the only thing I'm suffering from is the need to shake some sense into you, and then ravish you again." He kissed her. "Hank was a jackass. He lied to you— probably frequently—only telling you the truth when he needed to manipulate you, brow-beat you, and now you're afraid I'll do the same thing. I won't, but you're going to have to believe me." He expelled a lungful of air. "I want to make love to you again, but I hear the baby."

Sliding from the bed, her back to him, Julia quickly put on her nightgown. "Go to sleep. I'll take care of her."

Grabbing a pillow, he shoved it under his head. "Great

idea." Tony yawned. "I'm so tired I could sleep for a week."

"You see? Sometimes I do know what's best for you," she said in self-defense.

He dragged the blanket up and covered himself. "Good. Then in about an hour or so, why don't you crawl back into bed and read my mind some more?" His breathing started to even out.

Julia watched him for a second, then smoothed back his hair and kissed his forehead.

Muttering, Tony said, "I'll get the rope...."

"Rope?" Tony didn't answer, so she shook him and repeated, "What's this about rope?"

Half-asleep, he mumbled, "Tie you up and drag you to the altar." Yawning, he added, "So be warned. I won't fight fair."

Julia looked at the handsome man now breathing steadily, and she sighed. No, Tony won't fight fair, but leave it to him to warn her about it.

A hangover.

That was what it felt like to Tony. His head weighed fifty pounds, drums hammered an out-of-sync rhythm from within, and his mouth was dry. Rubbing his eyes, an action he immediately regretted, he rolled out of bed and placed his wobbly feet on the floor.

"Oh, Lord," he moaned, and stood. It was past noon, and he wasn't sure if he was groggy because he'd slept too much, because he hadn't slept enough, or because of the night he'd spent making love to Julia. Of the three choices, he'd have bet on the last one.

He'd never expected it to be the way it had.

Stumbling half-blind to the bathroom, he groaned at the sight that greeted him in the mirror. He looked like a vagabond. It was a good thing Julia had a sense of humor, he thought. She must have counted on it last night, if this was how he'd looked while seducing her.

While showering, he thought about how he'd never experienced the kind of emotions with another woman as he'd had with Julia. It had been more than just great sex—it had been soul-shattering. He shampooed his hair and inhaled the fragrance, instantly recalling the sweet smell of Julia's hair, and the sensual scent she exuded while in the throes of loving him.

Drying off, he decided he'd get her into the shower and, once and for all, find out how her body felt wet and sliding against his. He wrapped a towel around him, but it wouldn't cover the part of him that wanted her now.

Damn.

Her hands, her sweet mouth, her breasts, her legs wrapped around him. He shaved, and when he saw her in the mirror instead of his face, he nicked himself— "Ouch!" —two times.

Double damn.

Finally dressed, two pieces of toilet paper on his face, he controlled his raging hormones and went to see Rachel. And Julia. He would convince her that he could make his own decisions, and then she *would* marry him.

Marriage. If a month ago someone had told him he'd entertain the notion of marriage, he would have laughed aloud. And then he'd met Julia, and the thought of losing her...

Walking purposefully toward the kitchen, he heard voices coming from the living room, and went there instead.

Julia sat on the couch dressed in green slacks and matching silk blouse. He shot her a look and was pleased to see a crimson blush settle on her cheeks. Across from her sat a woman, in her mid-forties, he'd guess. She wore a blue business suit. Her blond hair was pulled back in a bun, and she had a pencil stuck behind her right ear. A briefcase was perched on her lap.

She also had the largest piece of chocolate cake he'd ever seen on a plate that rested on the briefcase. Tony contained his laughter.

"Ah, Tony," Julia said, rising and walking over to greet him. "This is Ms. Sutherland, from the department of social services, on a surprise visit." She reached up and plucked the toilet paper off his face. "Mitch called her," she whispered.

Ms. Sutherland's glance volleyed between them, resting on the small pieces of paper in Julia's left hand. Her left eyebrow arched, and she met Tony's eyes.

"Julia and I have been friends since high school," he said coolly, and extended his hand.

"Oh," Ms. Sutherland replied, and clasped his hand, pumping it in a hearty handshake. "I was telling Julia that this call was necessary because of a report filed by the baby's father."

"Dadadadadada!" Rachel screeched, as if on cue. Then, crawling quickly, she wiggled her way over to him.

He picked her up and kissed her soundly, a sense of well-being enveloping him, despite the woman's announcement. "Hello, sweetness. Daddy's missed you." He turned back to the visitor. "Sorry I wasn't awake earlier. I got in late last night—"

Ms. Sutherland beamed. "There's no need for you to explain. Julia told me how you'd cut your trip short to be home early, and how tired you were." She cut a piece of cake and chewed it slowly. "I was just having the most enlightening talk with Julia, and may I say that I couldn't be more pleased with your choice of a nanny? Mr. Brown's report indicated that he didn't believe his daughter was getting the best possible care while in your home." Cutting another piece, she added, "But that's not what I see. It's a good thing Julia was here." She took a sip of coffee from the cup on the end table to her right.

"Why do you say that?" Tony asked.

"I guess I should say it's good you have such competent help, not just that it's Julia. If there had been any signs that Rachel wasn't being looked after, I might've had to place her in another home while I checked into Mr. Brown's complaint more thoroughly."

Tony and Julia shared a look. Ms. Sutherland spoke again. "You should know that Mr. Brown also alleged there was improper conduct between the two of you." She looked at them seriously. "Our department has no right to dictate whether the parent and the hired help want to see each other socially, but if I'd seen any sign of impropriety visible…"

Tony nodded. "I understand what you're saying. You need to understand that nothing will harm Rachel, so long as I'm alive. That includes any potential relationship with this woman, or even Rachel's father himself."

"Tony…" Julia said quietly.

"It's okay, Julia. Ms. Sutherland has to know that. Rachel's welfare is the first and foremost priority for me—and for Julia," he added, looking back at the social worker.

Ms. Sutherland smiled. "I had that impression. I've been doing this for over twenty years, and I can tell when someone's giving me lip service. Now, the baby can stay. Not only does Rachel look very good, and respond well to Julia—" she relaxed back in her chair "—but Julia bakes a mean chocolate cake."

Tony cast a meaningful look at Julia. "Yeah, she does a lot of things real well." Julia turned even redder, and sent him a scathing look. "Is my suitcase still in the hall?" Julia nodded. "I bought Rachel a present. Excuse me."

Tony made his way to the foyer. He opened his suitcase and removed a small package, which he pocketed, and a larger one, which he brought into the living room. Sitting Rachel down, he handed her the bundle. She looked at it, then tore through some of it, giving the paper to Tony. When she looked at him and held out the still-wrapped present, he took it, and heard Julia speaking.

"We encourage her to do things on her own, and she feels confident to try, knowing if she can't do it, one of us will."

The case worker nodded vigorously. Julia had her eating from the palm of her hand—or her plate, in this case—and not on purpose. Hell, she probably didn't even know it.

The social worker made notes on her pad and ate the rest of the cake. "She seems very well-adjusted, and I love her room. So colorful, but not overdone."

Tony glanced at Julia's I-told-you-so expression and smiled, then handed Rachel the unwrapped stuffed penguin. She tasted it. He gently removed it from her mouth and tickled her nose with its soft black fur. Rachel giggled, grabbed it, and tossed it over his head, laughing when he returned it to her.

"Mr. Pellegrino," Ms. Sutherland said, "are these business trips of yours common?"

"On the average, about one every two months, and not for more than four or five days," he answered. "Is that a problem?"

"Since the trips are infrequent, and since you have such qualified help, I don't think so." Ms. Sutherland replaced her papers in the briefcase, and drank the rest of her coffee. "Well, as much as I'd like to stay and discuss more of Julia's ideas on child rearing, I've seen everything I need to." She walked to the hall and wrapped a blue scarf around her neck. "There'll be a few more surprise visits, but things appear good. I don't think you'll have anything more to worry about."

"Can Mitch take her?" Tony asked.

"Not without court permission. And not unless he fulfills the requirements of the court. So far, he hasn't, but we had to look into this." She took her coat from the chair near the door, and slipped into it. "You have a lot of fans rooting for you."

He looked at Julia, who shrugged her shoulders. "I know most of my neighbors are rooting for me, but fans?" Tony said.

"We've gotten several phone calls talking about you in general, but one person called me earlier today, and spoke specifically about your abilities as a parent."

"Could you tell us who that was?"

Her hand on the doorknob, Ms. Sutherland paused, then looked Tony straight in the eyes. "Normally, I wouldn't, but I have a good sense about you, Mr. Pellegrino, and my senses are always right." She opened the door and said, "It was a Ms. Mallone." Then she waved goodbye and left.

Tony and Julia stared at each other. Finally, Tony spoke. "Looks like fate is working overtime."

Julia leaned against the wall opposite Tony's office and watched him pace, the phone clenched tightly in his hand.

She hadn't had a chance last night to tell him the reason for her note, and when she finally told him, this morning, he hadn't looked too happy. He'd said he had a funny feeling her relationship with fate was rubbing off on him. Then he'd gone and returned the call. And now she was waiting outside his office so that he could talk to her if he wanted.

"You're kidding," he practically screamed into the phone. "I don't believe it. Married? Oh. An apartment?" He perched on the edge of his desk. "I don't care how small it is. She's had a good life." Standing abruptly, he paced again.

Julia could almost feel the resentment oozing from him. But she knew what really mattered—family. Rachel needed to know her grandmother, to have a sense of completion, and as much as Tony balked, he, too, needed to make peace with his mother.

"I don't know, Nick," Tony said, his voice full of angst and confusion. "I wanted to know if she was alive or dead, but I don't think I'm ready for more." He listened. "I thought I could let the anger go, too, but hearing about her life just makes it worse."

Tony's sigh could be heard in the hallway. Julia entered his office, curling her fists to keep from reaching for him. He didn't turn his head.

"It's no good, Nick," he said. "You and Matt can keep in touch with her." Another pause. "I *know* what Julia said. Don't throw her words back at me." He listened. "I *am* thinking about Rachel." Tony raked a hand through his hair. "I don't care how long she's looked for us. She abandoned us in the first place."

Like he thought I was doing.

"Sorry, Nick," he continued. "I gotta go. Yeah, I'll speak to you soon." Tony hung up and forcefully expelled his breath.

"Wasn't it you who said some changes were good, or was that your evil twin?" she joked.

He snapped his head in her direction. "Great, now *you're* throwing *my* words back at me." He slammed his hand on the desk. Julia jumped. "I won't let her hurt Rachel. You only heard part of the conversation." He strode toward her, grabbed her upper arm and pulled her to his chair. "Sit down and listen."

Julia sat and crossed her legs, outwardly controlling her nerves. She'd never seen Tony so agitated.

"Seems my mother went home—to *her* family—after she left us. It was her father who waited for her in the car. According to Nick, she says he's the one who convinced her that we'd be better off in foster placements." The muscles in Tony's jaw tightened.

"She lived with her parents—*my* grandparents—for about three years. Then she found another man, married him and lived in Manhattan for the last eleven years. Her husband died about four years ago."

"And you hate her for having had a decent life."

"Yes, damn it!" He strode away. "What kind of woman leaves her children alone even for a minute? If things were too rough for her to handle, she could have brought us to her family with her. Why didn't she?"

"I don't have the answer to that, Tony. But neither will you, unless you—"

"Don't tell me what—" Tony stopped abruptly and took in a shuddering breath. "I'm not in the mood to be dictated to."

"I'm sorry. And you're right. I don't mean to tell you what to do, I was only going to suggest—" She caught herself.

He threw his hands up. "Go on. What's your suggestion?"

"That unless you talk to her, you're going to be haunted with unanswered questions for the rest of your life." She touched his arm. Quietly, she added, "She did a terrible thing to you, leaving you alone as she did. You have every right to be angry and hurt, but haven't you spent enough of your life obsessing on why she left you? Do you want it controlling the rest of your life? Tony, you can meet with her and learn her story.'' She paused. ''Did Nick tell you anything about her? Has she been happy? Did she have an easy life?''

He stalked away. ''Who cares?'' Abruptly he took in a deep breath. ''Nick says no, but he doesn't want to tell me any more. He thinks if I hear her story in person, it'll make a difference.'' He gave out a harsh laugh.

''And you don't think it will.''

He stared at her. ''No, frankly, I don't.''

''Because you don't want it to.''

''Julia—''

''Hear me out.'' When he nodded tersely, Julia approached carefully. ''What she did was horrible. It altered your life in ways that no child should have to face. But you're a parent now. Think about Rachel. She has you, uncles, and now, if you allow it, a grandmother. And don't forget, through your mother, you may even learn about your father's parents and relatives. If they're alive, that's more family for Rachel.''

''Don't you think you're glossing over things just to preserve the family image? Isn't it possible that because you can't have children, you're clinging to the concept of family at all costs?''

''Maybe. Or maybe because I can't have children, I've learned to appreciate what I do have. Either way, I know if I were given a second chance, I would take it.''

Tony leaned back against the door and cocked his head. His shoulders slumped.

Julia plowed ahead, only vaguely aware of the change in his demeanor. ''Tony, don't let your own fears and stubbornness stop you from enriching Rachel's life. Try to get past it.''

''How?''

"With time. And love, and acceptance. Talk with her, learn the whole story, listen to her point of view."

Tony looked at the floor. "What if she's not the woman you believe she is, this...*loving* woman who thought she was doing the best for us? God, I hate this!"

"I know you do, but what will you lose by meeting her? Eventually her true colors will come out."

"Yeah, but by that time, what damage can she do to my Rachel? Suppose Rachel comes to love her, and then we discover my mother isn't what you've painted her to be? I can handle it, but what about the baby?"

"Tony, you're being unrealistic. She won't be able to do that much damage before we find out what she's really like. And suppose she's exactly like I've said? She gave you up, and you carry the scars of that, but what scars does she carry? Especially when she learns how you suffered?"

Tony stared at her.

"What is it?" she asked.

At first, he looked as though he wasn't going to speak, but then he grudgingly said, "Nick said the same thing. He talked to her, so did Matt. According to Nick, she was real upset when he told her what happened to us. Especially to Annie." He shook his head. "I don't get it. How'd you guess? You don't know her. Hell, I don't even know her."

"You're right, I don't know her, and in my experiences I've met a lot of women who weren't fit to be near children, let alone be called mothers. On the other hand, I also recall how many there were that lived in horrible situations, but truly loved their children." She looked directly at him. "Sometimes their need to survive overshadowed their ability to give love properly, and sometimes they just didn't know how to, but..." She hesitated. "I can only relate this to myself. I know what it would take for *me* to give up my children. I'd *have* to believe I was doing the best thing for them. Nothing less could force me away from them." She blinked back the sudden appearance of tears. He took a step forward, but she held up her hand. "I'm all right."

"Of course you are, but indulge me anyway." He hugged her. "I'm sorry. This must really be hard on you."

"I'll survive."

"I know. You're one of the strongest women I know." He sighed. "I admire that about you. But what if I'm not the man you think I am? I'm not very forgiving."

"One step at a time. Don't worry about forgiving her until after you've at least met her." She fit herself against him, relishing the momentary comfort, then stepped back. "You took in your niece, and love her as your own. You accepted the changes I made in her room. You've come to embrace marriage as something you want. Even this—" she indicated the office "—is a sign of your ability to change. There aren't many successful Manhattan cowboys living in Wyoming."

"You *really* think it's good for Rachel?"

"Yes, I do."

Tony stared at her for a minute. "Rachel's settled, getting along fine, discovering new things every day. She's happy. The books all say that sudden changes, especially at her age, can be damaging. Too many changes aren't good for a little kid."

"That's right, but this isn't too many. Rachel is a well-adjusted baby—even Ms. Sutherland said so. There should be no problems, and if there are, we'll deal with them."

"And what if she can't adjust, if she can't handle it?"

Julia felt his resolve weaken, and pressed on. "She will if we maintain her life-style as close as possible to what it is now. It will be a little noisy, with everyone visiting, but many children have handled more."

"But...what if she starts to have nightmares? What should we do then?"

"We'll put her to sleep each night the same way. We won't vary the ritual. We'll make sure that she has quiet time each day to unwind, and we'll make sure that her normal daily activities are followed."

"And you're sure we can do this?"

"Absolutely."

"Fine." He spoke firmly. "I'm against it, but I'll think about it. But *if* I decide to go ahead with it—and that's a big if—it'll only be because of your offer."

"What offer?"

"Your offer to stay during my mother's visit."

"What?" At the sudden twinkle in his eyes, Julia exhaled fiercely. "You set me up." He shrugged. "You're not even going to deny it, are you?"

"Would it do me any good if I did?"

"No." She paced. "This isn't fair."

"I warned you...." He crossed his arms in front of his chest. "Besides, Ms. Sutherland said if you hadn't been here, she'd have no choice but to take Rachel away."

Julia had boxed herself into a corner. She rolled her eyes up to the ceiling.

"Yup, the Fates strike again," he said. "And it's about time you knew they were on *my* side." Tony backed her up to the door.

"But—"

"But nothing. *You* said that to make sure Rachel's okay, *we'll* need to keep her life-style the way it is now, and *you're* a big part of her life. I don't want that woman here, but I'm willing to consider it, all because of you. So, here's your chance." Tony cupped her chin and, leaning down, gave her a searing kiss.

She pushed him backward. With her anger grudgingly

yielding to his cleverness, Julia's curiosity egged her on. "My chance to do what?"

As she watched, his lips stretched into a sloe-gin grin, and he said, "To practice what you preach."

The rest of the week went by uneventfully. On Thursday, Tony and Julia interviewed three more possible nannies, but they, too, weren't right for the job. Julia wouldn't leave Rachel with anyone less than competent, so she remained.

Julia, Tony and Rachel spent a lot of time together. He was truly a wonderful man, and an excellent father. He was receptive to new ideas—all the time reminding her that before he met her, he wouldn't have entertained a change at all. She even admired the way he'd stopped jumping down her throat whenever she made a suggestion to him. He seemed to be trusting her more and more.

And then there were the nights, like Thursday evening. One of the ranch hands was ill, and Tony had taken over his chores after putting in his day at the cattle ranch. Thinking he'd want to soak long and hard after working fourteen hours, she'd drawn him a bath and waited for him to enter the bathroom. But once there, he'd grabbed her, stripped them both, and carried her into the tub with him. There had been no long, hard *soak* that night.

On Friday, once Rachel was asleep, Julia and Tony watched a movie. He asked her her thoughts about different scenes, and really listened when she spoke. It sparked great conversations, and gave her lots of insight she might have missed about his thought processes— It seemed they thought alike about many things.

On Saturday night, friends dropped over and they ordered pizza and played board games. It was a delightful time, but she caught herself falling into the role of hostess too easily, and that bothered her. Tony noticed it, too, and even mentioned it to her, with a huge grin on his face.

The cocky devil. He was totally delighted with her.

On Sunday, her one day off, she spent time with her mother, but her thoughts were on the ranch, and with Tony and Rachel. Delighted as she was with her mother's company, she couldn't wait for the day to end so that she could return home.

And in this way Julia found herself believing, more and more, that things could work out for Tony and her. It was still the main thought in her mind on Monday morning, when she walked him to the door.

"I've been thinking about what you've said, Tony," Julia began, handing him his coat. "About my staying and giving us a chance."

Tony stopped in midreach from picking up his hat. "And? Come on woman, don't keep me in suspense."

"And..." she said, stepping up and hugging him. "And I think it's a wonderful idea."

Wrapping his arms around her, Tony spun around in the foyer, whooping loudly. "Hot damn! I got me a woman!" Putting her down, he kissed her soundly. "And what a woman she is." He studied her face. "A beautiful, caring, hot woman. I couldn't be happier. Tell me you are, too."

"I am, even if—"

His lips stopped her last protestation, and Julia was delighted. The kiss practically curled her toes. When they parted, Tony spoke.

"I want you, right now, in every room of the house, on every surface there is," he said, kissing her again, opening up the top three buttons of her blouse.

"Me too," she whispered, amazed at the intensity of her desire for him. "But I believe I'm being paged." She nodded in the direction of Rachel's bedroom.

"Damn." He threw his hat on his head, looped an arm around her shoulders and walked to the door. "Listen, maybe if she skips her afternoon nap, you could put her to bed earlier, and I could come home earlier, and..."

Julia playfully socked him on the arm. He chuckled.

"Okay, it was just a thought. But you'd better be ready, 'cause when we do break in this house with some heavy lovemaking—" he kissed the side of her neck "—I'm going to want all the time in the world to do it right. So wait up for me." He winked, said goodbye and left.

Julia floated as she got Rachel, dressed her and put her in the high chair for breakfast. Just then, the phone rang. "Hello?"

"Hello," said a quiet female voice. "Could I speak to Antonio Pellegrino?"

Julia's hold on the phone tightened. She recognized the accent. "I'm sorry, but he's not here. May I take a message?"

"This is...Andrea Scott." The woman hesitated. "Andrea Pellegrino-Scott. I'm...I'm Antonio's mother."

"This is Julia Rourke. What can I do for you?"

"Nicholas told me all about you. I'd like to meet you." She paused. "He also told me some...other things. Like Antonio isn't keen on seeing me."

Julia heard the distinctive sound of someone taking a drag on a cigarette. She also heard how Andrea referred to her children so formally, as if she didn't have a right to be more intimate with them.

"I called," Andrea continued, "because I was hoping to change his mind. I want to see him. Just recently I started searching for him again, and my other children. I'm too late with Annie, my baby. I need to see Antonio, to try and explain...."

The emotions traveled through the wires. Julia felt her

raw pain. "Have you discussed this with Nick and Matt?" Julia asked.

"Oh, yes. Matthew gave me Antonio's number, against Nicholas's wishes. Nicholas suggested I give Antonio time, but I couldn't wait. It's been so many years since... It's like I've been given a second chance to correct my mistake."

"I can tell Tony you called. Would you like me to do that?" Julia asked, her own insides churning.

"I...I don't know now," she said, her voice hitching. "I thought, oh, it's stupid, but I was so excited, I'd already bought a ticket to fly out before Nicholas told me Antonio's reaction." She took another puff. "The boys have listened to me. They're hurt, but they're willing to try and have a relationship with me."

Julia didn't know what to say, so she just listened.

"I—I just loved them all so much...." Andrea sobbed, and the conversation halted momentarily while she cried.

Julia's heart went out to her. Andrea had some explaining to do, but Julia felt that once Tony met her, and had answers to his questions, they'd get along fine. Andrea seemed genuinely upset.

Andrea sighed deeply. "I had the crazy notion that I'd just show up. Trust that Antonio wasn't too different now than as a child, and that he'd not turn me away. Isn't that crazy?"

"I don't think it is. Tony's a wonderful man, very generous and kind. I know he'd listen, once the two of you talked."

"Do you really think so?" Andrea asked. "I know I made terrible mistakes, but at the time they seemed to be the best for the kids." She let out a shuddery breath and spoke quickly. "Thank you, Julia. You've given me the courage to follow my heart. I *am* going to fly in. I'll be there on Friday evening.''

"No, wait—" Before Julia could get another word out, Andrea hung up. "Hello, hello? Oh, no." She replaced the receiver.

She dialed the operator, but couldn't have the number traced. Taking Rachel in her arms, she walked to Tony's office. Because Andrea had called on his private line, and not the business line, her number didn't appear on his caller-identification system.

"I'd better call your daddy and tell him what happened," she told the baby. "Maybe he knows where to reach your grandmother and stop her."

Julia dialed Tony's office. Greg answered, but told her Tony had just gone out and wouldn't be back for a while. She thanked him and hung up.

"Let's see if I can find Andrea's number in your father's phone book," she muttered aloud. It wasn't there, but Nick's was.

She dialed him, but the line was busy. She tried a few more times, but the result was always the same.

"Apparently your uncle hasn't heard of call-waiting," Julia said. Rachel gurgled and drooled. Her teeth were coming in.

She dialed again. She let out a sigh of relief when it started to ring. And ring. And ring. No one answered. When it had rung six times, his machine picked up. Nick must have finished his conversation, then flown out the door. She replaced the receiver and located Matt's number.

There was no answer at his place, either.

Didn't anyone stay at home anymore?

Walking back to the kitchen, Julia began preparing Rachel's breakfast. There was no use spending any more time spinning her wheels. She would tell Tony. He could explain to Andrea how she'd misunderstood Julia and that she shouldn't come right now.

That decided, Julia placed Rachel's bowl on her tray, sat down and spooned up some strained peaches.

"Once upon the time, there was a little engine who wanted to be a big train," she began. Rachel ate contentedly as Julia told the story of the engine who overcame obstacles to win.

"Just like me, right, Rachel?" Julia said when she finished the story. "Your father's a wonderful man, so caring and kind. And because of his blessed bullheaded belief in me," she said, wiping Rachel's chin, "I won't have to ever say goodbye to you, my little love."

Or to my big love, either.

Chapter 10

"Hi, Greg. Any messages?" Tony had entered the office after checking on his adjacent cattle ranch, and paused by Greg's desk to retrieve his mail.

"Just one. Your brother Nick called. Wants you to call him as soon as possible at this number," Greg said, and handed him a piece of paper. "Oh, and Julia called around nine-thirty, but she didn't leave a message."

"Did she sound like she needed to speak to me right away?"

"No. I told her you were out, and she just said okay, then hung up."

"Thanks." He looked at his watch. It was just about noon. If the call to his brother was short, he could make it home in time for lunch with Julia and find out in person what she'd called him about. She usually ate after Rachel went down for her nap, around twelve-forty-five. Then, if they finished lunch quickly...

Hell, if I play my cards right, we may miss lunch altogether.

"Hold all calls, Greg," he said, and entered his office.

He whistled as he dialed the number Greg gave him, and was connected immediately to his brother. "Hell, a work number, Nick? What's so urgent you'd want me to call you at work?"

"Have you spoken to Julia today?"

"Not since breakfast. Why?"

"Damn. I was hoping you already knew. Are you sitting down?"

The hair on the back of Tony's neck stood on end. Nick never hedged. "Cut to the chase, Nick. What's going on?"

"It's about our mother. You've got to hear what she's planning on doing."

"I couldn't care less what she wants to do." That wasn't entirely true. His conversations with Julia had had him thinking hard about reconsidering his mother's visit, and given Julia's declaration this morning… But he just wasn't ready to take that leap of faith yet. "Besides, what does this have to do with me talking to Julia? And why should I be sitting?"

"*Are* you sitting?"

Tony's pulse quickened. "Yes. Now what's going on, Nick?" He checked his watch. "I'm in kind of a hurry."

"Well, brother, this'll stop you in your tracks."

Tony paced the length of the living room for the ninth time.

Where was Julia?

He looked at his watch again. It read 12:58. Rachel usually napped around now, even with her growth spurt. Miss Irene wasn't here today, so he had no idea where they'd gone.

He tapped the small box in his pants pocket. Earlier it had burned a hole there, but now it lay heavy and weighted.

One o'clock. Julia not being here went against the daily schedule.

The actions of someone who's afraid of being questioned?

He tried to throw out the seeds of mistrust, but since he talked with Nick, they'd grown more, their roots finding a familiar home in his natural distrust of women.

Soon. They'd be home soon, and then he'd have his answers.

You already know the answers. She had just this morning deigned to stay with him, and already she was making decisions for him behind his back.

You're overreacting.

Hell, he'd tried to convince himself of that for the past couple of hours, but it hadn't worked. When Nick told him she'd flat-out invited his mother here, he'd lost it. She'd done something involving him, without his approval, and behind his back. Just like all the adults had done when he was a child.

But you're not a child anymore.

Tony grimaced, the anger making it hard for him to think straight. Yeah, he *was* an adult now, and that made what she'd done even worse. He cloaked himself in his protective shell, and heard the well-versed arguments in his mind.

She thought she knew what was best for you.

She went behind your back.

She had no right to decide for you.

She isn't here right now because she knows she's guilty.

The arguments hammered stakes of resentment, of mistrust, in his mind, making him angrier and angrier. His breathing came out in short puffs. His pacing grew more and more rapid.

There could be no excuse for this—

The front door opened. Tony strode to it, and watched Julia carry in Rachel and a heavy bag.

"Where've you been?" he practically barked.

Julia jumped. "Tony!" Rachel, whose head had been resting on Julia's shoulder, blinked open her eyes.

He swallowed his need to shout. "I asked where you were."

Glancing at the bag in her left arm, she said, "I had to buy some things for dinner tonight." She looked at Rachel.

She's avoiding looking at you.

Guilty guilty guilty.

"Let me have Rachel," he said gruffly. He took her and removed her purple jumpsuit. That done, he held her against his chest. Her head rested on his shoulder. "She should have been asleep already." She made little sucking motions with her mouth.

Julia nodded, removing her own coat. "I know. Traffic was bad, and she started to nap in the car." She moved toward the kitchen. "Would you put her down while I put away the food?"

She still hadn't looked him in the eye. At the kitchen, she spoke over her shoulder. "I tried calling you earlier. Greg said you'd left for the cattle ranch."

Tony couldn't believe the blasé way she was talking to him. Couldn't she sense his anger?

Yeah. That's why she hasn't looked at you.

"Why'd you call?" Tony watched her face.

She talked as she put away the food. "I needed to speak to you." She showed no sign of regret. No sign of remorse. "Something unbelievable happened this morning."

Tony managed to hold in his snort at her understatement. "I'll be right back," he said through gritted teeth, and had the satisfaction of finally seeing her lift her face and look at him with raised eyebrows.

Walking to and entering Rachel's room, he was glad Julia hadn't followed. He'd needed time to calm himself—even if only fractionally—before he talked with her. He laid Rachel in her crib and stroked her fine dark hair. The action soothed him.

Julia had looked shocked at his tone when he left the kitchen. There was no way she could have been pretending that look.

The look of an innocent person?

Rachel cooed, and sighed, and her eyes blinked closed, slowly, slowly. Tony's heart expanded to unbelievable proportions. This was what love felt like, what it should feel like.

Like he'd loved Julia. Guilty Julia.

Face it. If Julia had been truly innocent, she would have come out and told you what she'd done. Instead, she'd hedged.

Rachel made a fist, and brought it to her mouth.

And the only reason to hedge was that she knew the news was terrible. And because she knew this time she'd crossed over the line. *That made sense.* His anger grew anew, fueled by puzzle pieces that formed a picture of irrefutable evidence.

With Rachel asleep, Tony walked into the kitchen and smelled fresh brewed coffee. She turned and held out a mug. "Would you like some?" she asked softly.

She looked worried.

Guilty guilty guilty.

"Julia, sit down."

Replacing the mug on the counter, Julia walked to the table and sat. Her brow furrowed as she studied his masked expression.

"What's wrong, Tony? Did something happen to the cattle?"

"No. Something happened to me."

"What?"

His jaw clenched. "Cut it out, Julia. You know what I'm talking about."

Her mouth opened and closed, and her brow furrowed deeper.

"Damn it, Julia. Nick called and told me what you did. I know all about your conversation with my…mother."

Her eyes lit with comprehension. "Oh, that."

"Yes, *that*," he replied dryly.

She passed a hand over her hair—a nervous habit he was familiar with. "I'm sorry your mother jumped the gun. She hung up so fast, I couldn't stop her." She shook her head. "I hope she'll understand why you won't see her when she gets here."

"Oh, this is rich. *My mother jumped the gun*. You didn't do anything wrong, it was all my mother, right?"

"Right."

He sucked in a breath of air. "This is unbelievable. Not only do you go behind my back, but then you have the audacity to pass the buck."

"What exactly do you think I've done, Tony?"

"Exactly what you were too afraid to tell me, and that's why you weren't here when I showed up."

"And what is that?"

"That you invited that woman to my house, without my permission, behind…my…back," he said between gritted teeth.

"Is that what Nick told you?"

"What else? It's what my mother told him."

"I see. So it's not that your mother is coming that's

making you angry, it's that I supposedly did something behind your back."

He looked like a wild horse fenced in, seeing the restraining rope coming closer.

"Tony, I don't know what your mother told Nick or what he told you, but I do know what happened here this morning, and I didn't invite your mother here behind your back."

"Are you telling me my brother lied to me?"

"I have no way of knowing that until I speak with your brother. But it seems to me that it's a series of misunderstandings that I can clear up, if you're willing to listen to me." She reached out a hand, but he jerked back. Her hand curled into a fist.

"How convenient. *A series of misunderstandings.*" He raked a hand through his hair. "And on the very morning you tell me you're willing to stay. I can't believe this. How could you have done this?" He stood and stormed away from her, banging his hands on the counter.

"I didn't do anything but sympathize with a distraught woman."

He laughed bitterly. "You did a hell of a lot more than that. She's on her way here, thanks to you."

"I knew she would be. After she'd twisted my words—"

He pivoted. "Cut it out. Why don't you just tell the truth?"

"I am." She stood. "I'll tell you the story, but right now, can't you call her and—"

"No. She hung up from you and went to stay with some friends. She left a message at Nick's. She said she didn't want anyone to talk her out of coming, so she would meet my brothers at the airport right before the flight." He dropped his voice. "You two worked it out good. I should have known you would get along with her so well. You're two of a kind.''

Julia knew he was referring to the time he'd compared her leaving to his mother's abandonment, but something about the way he said it now set off alarms in her head. She had to give him time to calm down, to look at things more rationally.

"Tony, why don't we talk after you've had a chance to—''

"Calm down? How do I calm down from a betrayal like this?''

"Tony, you're not thinking clearly. I didn't betray you.'' She put her hands on her hips and plowed ahead. "When your mother called, she told me she had a crazy idea of wanting to show up—''

"And you, knowing what was *best* for me, told her to do it,'' he said triumphantly.

"No. All I said was it wasn't a crazy idea. Out of context, it sounds like I gave her permission, but I didn't. I never said she should come.''

"That's splitting hairs, and you know it. She was looking for tacit approval, and you gave it to her.'' He hissed air through his teeth. "I trusted you. Hell, you're the one woman I gave my heart to, the one woman I wanted to spend the rest of my life with, and you ruined it.''

"Tony, stop it.'' This time she did touch his arm, but he pushed her hand off. "If you'd have heard how upset she was, you'd understand how this could've happened. Things got very emotional—''

"Great. So you have an excuse to ease your conscience, something I can deal with after you pack your bags and leave me.''

She closed her eyes, needing time to regroup her thoughts. "Let me go check on Rachel—''

"Leave her alone. If she needs checking on, *I'll* do it. She's *my* responsibility." Tony looked down at her. "You may love her, but I make the decisions that concern her, not you. After all, once you leave, it'll just be her and me."

"That's twice you've said that. I'm not leaving."

"Yes, you are. By going behind my back, and by not admitting it, but defending it instead, you made your decision."

"*You* want me to leave?"

He turned and stared at her. "Ironic, isn't it? Now you won't need to find an excuse to run away."

"An excuse to..." Awareness slipped through her confusion. "Ah, now I get it. This isn't about what happened with your mother. This is about us."

"There is no us. There never really was." He pointed at her. "You always had one foot out the door, anyway."

"Not after this morning," she said softly. "Tony—"

"There's nothing more to say."

"There's plenty more to say, but you're too stubborn to listen."

"Too smart to listen, you mean. I hope you haven't unpacked all your bags."

"Well, this will be one for the books. Shortest commitment on record." She put her hands on her hips. "You've managed to create a conflict, where none exists, just because you're scared."

"Ah, yes, that old theory of yours, Love-'Em-and-Leave-'Em Tony."

"Make fun if you want, but at least face it squarely. You're following your pattern to a T."

A muscle in his jaw twitched.

"This situation with your mother triggered something in you, and now you're punishing me by sending me away first, so I don't abandon you."

He clenched his fists. "I have nothing more to say to you. It's best if you leave now."

"It's best?" He looked away, and she saw his shoulders stiffen. "All right, have it your way. I hope you and your fear of abandonment will be very happy together." Julia moved to the kitchen door. "If you need help with Rachel, you can reach me—"

"Don't wait for my call."

"Oh, I won't. You know, Tony, I owe you a debt of gratitude. Because of you, I've come out of hiding, and I've learned I have a life to live. I was just hoping it would have been with you, but you know what they say about the hand of fate…"

Watching the proud tilt of his jaw, Julia cradled her wounded heart and moved to the door. "Take care of yourself," she said.

"I just did."

"So you think," she said, and left the room.

On Friday morning, feeling apprehensive about the night to come, and having been moody all week, since Julia left, Tony answered the door.

His nerves coiled.

Standing in the cold was a woman with large brown eyes that zeroed in on him; Annie's eyes, in the face of a woman not much older than he. A once lovely woman, with stress lines on her forehead, and around her eyes—indications of a hard life.

"H-hello, Antonio."

Andrea Pellegrino-Scott held out a black-leather-gloved hand. After a second, Tony mechanically shook it. It felt as small and fragile as she looked. She wore a simple black coat, and a black scarf-slash-head-wrap that slipped down to reveal a haircut that was stylishly short.

"May I...may I come in?"

"Oh...yes." He stepped aside and let his mother into the house. Closing the door behind her, he helped her off with her coat and gloves.

A dark green suit seemed to overwhelm her slight frame. The only jewelry she wore were small pearl earrings and a matching one-string necklace.

Had she always been so small, so...petite?

They stood quietly in the hallway for a moment, then Tony numbed his ricocheting emotions and pulled on his business persona. He escorted her into the living room and indicated that she should sit. "I hadn't expected you until tonight."

"I know." She looked around. "This is lovely, Antonio."

He didn't answer, and after a moment he noticed her hands were worrying themselves in her lap. She was scared of him. A small sliver of emotion slipped through his wall of protection, making him more vulnerable than he wanted to be.

"I took an earlier flight," she finally said. "I was afraid if I waited for Matthew or Nicholas at the airport, they'd talk me out of coming." Her brow furrowed. "I know it was impulsive, but I was always that way, and some habits just don't stop." She leaned forward. "*And I had to see you...*"

Tony paced to the mantel. The large room felt cramped, and he was overheated, despite the small fire burning in the fireplace. He didn't know what to say.

She fidgeted on the sofa and fingered the delicate necklace she wore.

He frightened her. She was afraid of him.

And there was something about that that bothered him, but he couldn't figure out what it was.

"You look good," he said.

"Do I look like you remember?" she asked hesitantly.

"Better," he answered honestly. "I recall you being taller than me. But then again, I was only twelve—" He stopped himself, and they both looked around the room awkwardly.

"Is Rachel sleeping?" she finally asked.

"Finally. She's had a hard week...." She was the last woman he wanted to share with. Tony looked at his watch. "She's been sleeping for a while, so she should be up soon." He cocked an ear. "In fact, I think I hear her now."

Thank God. A diversion.

"That's wonderful." She lowered her eyes when Tony glanced at her. "I'd...I'd like to meet her."

He nodded. "I'll be right back." He walked to the doorway. Pausing, he looked behind him at his mother. "Make yourself comfortable, if that's possible."

She smiled, and her shoulders slumped in relief.

Tony walked into Rachel's room, and gathered the cooing child to him, garnering strength from her. With her in his arms, there was nothing he couldn't face.

Tony changed her diaper. He dressed her in a soft blue-and-white-checked flannel sleeper, then brought her to the woman he had loved more than anything as a young boy. Tony sat down next to her. "This is Rachel Anne."

Tony worried about Rachel's reaction, but it proved groundless. Rachel leaned forward excitedly.

Andrea looked at him expectantly, her arms out in front of her. "May I...may I hold her?"

Hesitantly Tony nodded. Andrea took her and sat her on her lap. Rachel grasped the pearls and yanked, sending little white beads across the floor.

Andrea stared at her granddaughter and laughed delightedly. "So, you like to play with necklaces too, just like..."

"Her dead mother?" The anger came upon him suddenly. He saw pain fill Andrea's eyes. "I'm sorry. I didn't mean it to—"

"Yes, you did." She looked back at Rachel. "And, yes, she looks exactly like Annie did. I'll bet she's bright, too, isn't she? How old is she?"

"She'll be seven months old in three days," Tony answered.

Andrea's face lit up. "Oh! I can celebrate with her."

Tony stood and shoved his hands into his pants pockets. Her smile vanished, and a haunted, defeated look appeared in her eyes.

"I shouldn't have assumed..." Her cheeks were stained red.

"This is very hard," he said. "There are a lot of things I want to know."

"I came ready to answer your questions."

"Why did you leave us?" he blurted out.

She blinked, but, to her credit, she steeled herself and spoke. "To give you a chance at a better life."

"Oh, come on. Leaving us? A better life?"

"Yes. Do you want to hear it all now?"

Tony nodded curtly.

"Okay, I met your father when I was thirteen. My parents threw me out of the house, so I dropped out of school and your father and I lived together. I had you when I was fifteen. From where I came from, that's how things went," she said with characteristic New York speed, her accent growing thick. "We set up house, and I had Matthew and Nicholas, then Annie.

"My whole life was for you kids," she continued, "and that's what caused my downfall. Your father got ill, then died, and his hospital bills were enormous. I had no money.

We had no food. I didn't know what to do, so I broke down and called my parents.''

After a moment's hesitation, she went on. ''My father acted delighted to hear from me. My mother had died the year before. He offered to help. I was so desperate, I actually thanked him. God, I was a fool. He used my weakness—my love for you all. He twisted things, told me I couldn't let you live like I'd *selfishly* allowed for so long. I—I've never been a strong woman, and he knew that. He chipped away at my self-confidence, convinced me to turn you over to his care.''

Andrea stood and looked torn between holding the baby and needing to pace. Finally she handed Rachel to Tony. Holding her, Tony could keep his anger at bay, could calm his hurt.

She spoke. ''He told me he had found a pastor who would take care of you—no questions asked. His wife couldn't have kids. At first I refused, vehemently, but he convinced me I was being selfish again. He told me the pastor had a large house, with plenty of rooms, and lived in a good neighborhood. There was nothing you wouldn't have.''

Tears that had been gathering splashed unheeded down her face. ''After I got on my feet, I could get you back again. At least that's what he told me.'' Her eyes closed. ''I...I finally agreed. We—we parked down the block. A woman, the pastor's wife, I thought, came in a lime green Dodge van and took you.'' She broke down.

Tony's insides tightened, but he didn't stand, didn't walk over; he couldn't offer her any comfort. He sat, holding his baby. ''Why didn't you just tell us? Why didn't you wait with us until the so-called pastor arrived?''

''Oh, my father had an answer for it all. He was an expert at manipulating things.'' Her tears flowed freely. ''He told me it had to be done discreetly. The pastor's wife was a delicate woman who wouldn't be able to handle an emotional scene. I'd blow the whole deal for you children if I stayed." She retrieved a handkerchief from her purse. "He always brought the conversation back to the best thing for you children. And I so desperately wanted what was best for you."

It's best it's best it's best...

Tony heard Julia's voice as he replayed the words she'd often said in the past. Andrea glanced at him, then away quickly. He saw the fear again, and in that instant, everything crystallized. He understood why seeing her fear disturbed him; her fright mimicked his.

Holy cow!

Julia.

As if a gust of wind had blown away a dense fog, Tony suddenly realized Julia had been right!

He'd been so racked with fear about meeting Andrea that he'd let that fear control him. He'd been pushed into facing something he didn't feel ready to, and protected himself. But in doing so, he'd broken his promise to protect Julia. He'd hurt her.

He looked down at Rachel.

It's a good thing you're too young to know what a colossal jerk your father was. Maybe by the time you're old enough to use it against me, I'll have lived this down.

Rachel babbled happily and grabbed his nose.

Andrea's voice brought him around. "For a year I believed you were living a good life. He told me news about all of you that he said he was getting from the preacher. Meanwhile, my life was miserable—he hadn't changed, still manipulated everything to suit his needs. I started getting suspicious when I wanted to write you—for a picture—and he kept putting me off. One day I searched the phone book for your address.''

Now Tony stood and approached. ''And you found out the pastor didn't exist.'' Andrea nodded. ''The woman who came was from social services,'' Tony said. ''She told us that her office had gotten an anonymous call about four abandoned children.''

''The boys filled me in. It was my father who'd made that call. When I found out, I mustered some strength and left him immediately. I stayed at a shelter and tried to locate you, but no one would help me, and I was too...oh, damn, too *ignorant* to know what else to do.'' She looked up at Tony, her grief-stricken face lined with black mascara. ''Years later, I met Craig Scott. He knew my story, and sympathized, but convinced me to leave well enough alone—that after all those years... I'm so very sorry. When I think of how I made you suffer... I wish I could do it over, make it right, but I can't.'' She sobbed into her hands.

Tony looked at her. From somewhere inside, he found the strength to put his hand on Andrea's shoulder.

''I don't know what'll happen now,'' Tony said. ''Sometimes there's too much water under the bridge. But it took guts coming out here, facing me, knowing how I felt.''

He hoped he'd have the guts to face whatever Julia felt for him—even if it was hatred, and boy, did she have a right to hate him, after the way he'd treated her.

''I had to see you,'' Andrea said. ''I couldn't take the risk that something might happen to me, or you, before I had a chance to tell you the whole story.'' She dried her eyes, leaving behind black lines slashed down her cheeks. ''Where's Julia? Is she here? I owe her an explanation, and an apology, too.''

''She's already forgiven you.''

Would she forgive him, too?

"Was she very angry with me?" she asked.

"No."

She was too busy being hurt by me.

Stupid stupid stupid.

He had to call her. Looking at Andrea's weary face, he said, "I'm sure you want to rest before the others arrive."

She readily agreed, and Tony showed her to the guest bedroom. Leaving Rachel with Andrea, at her request, Tony raced to his bedroom and picked up the phone. He had to call Julia. The line rang and rang, unanswered. He tried her mother's number, but there was no answer there, either. He replaced the receiver and stared out the window at the endless wave of white fields before him.

Would his life be just as colorless?

The sky was midnight blue above Julia's head as she drove to Tony's home. Closer to the horizon, it was a reddish-purple, and just on the horizon, it was a brilliant orange-red. As the ranch came into view, she drove faster. Pulling into the driveway, she wondered again what Tony would say when he saw her.

She'd gotten the messages from her mother that he wanted to see her. Had he come to his senses?

Grabbing hold of her courage, she walked to the steps. Tethered to the railing was Brewster's Alley, Chris's stallion. Removing her glove, she patted his neck, then jerked her hand back when Chris stormed from the house, muttering expletives. He took the five stairs down in one step, grabbed the reins and put his foot into the stirrup. Loping his right leg over the horse's back, he narrowly missed kicking Julia's head, then galloped off.

Tony stood in the doorway, coat open. When he saw Julia, he jumped down the steps, stopping in front of her. "You're here," he said, white puffs coming from his mouth. "I mean, why are you here? I mean, I'm glad you're here. Come in, please," he said. There were purple smudges under his eyes.

She wondered if her makeup hid hers. "All right."

"I was just on my way to your house. You didn't return my calls, not that I had a right to expect you to, but when you didn't, I knew I had to see you. How are you?" He closed the door behind her.

She sighed inwardly at the sound of his voice. "Okay."

He threw his coat on the table. He was dressed in a green flannel shirt that did nothing to hide his muscles, and jeans that...well... She looked up at him and was pulled into his stare. She leaned forward. Her heart sped up. Trailing a hand over her hair, she felt that, for the most part, it hadn't come lose from its elaborate coiffure, thanks to Maxine, of all people.

"You look great," he added, reaching out and twisting a tendril, near her temple, around his finger.

"Thanks. I met Maxine in town and she made some suggestions I decided to follow."

"You and Maxine?" Tony said incredulously. "I can't believe it. She's got Chris hopping mad. Refuses to see him."

Julia knew Maxine was baiting Chris purposely. She'd told Julia how attracted she was to him, but how scared she was about that. She'd asked Julia for some advice. That was when Julia had realized how lonely and insecure Maxine really was.

"I see. Actually, Maxine turned out to be very helpful. I went with her to her dress salon...." She unbuttoned her coat.

"Holy cow!"

Julia revealed a body-hugging silk dress in deep burgundy, with a plunging neckline. "What's wrong?" she asked coquettishly, following Maxine's advice to the letter.

Tony's nostrils flared, and he took a step forward. His eyes darkened. Her heart almost leaped from her chest. Her nipples hardened, and his eyes zeroed in on them. Swallowing, a painful thing to do with a dry mouth, Julia handed her coat to him. "Would you hang this up for me?" She flashed him a smile.

Tony took her coat, and was treated to a tantalizing whiff of her spicy perfume. She was potent and, in that dress, downright dangerous. Was she here to tease him, to show him what he'd blown?

Hanging up her coat, Tony controlled his desire to rip off her dress and take her on the hallway floor. He'd spent most of last week dreaming of her, walking around in a constant state of arousal.

"Where's Rachel?" she asked.

"She's out with Miss Irene...and my mother." Tony explained about his mother coming early. "She talked. I listened." He moved closer. "And Rachel liked her, too." He studied her flushed face. Was she excited because of him? He wasted no more time. "Julia, I've been an ass. Will you accept my apology?"

Her pupils dilated. Tony's blood churned. "Aw, hell. This is too damned civilized." He scooped her up into his arms.

"What are you doing?"

"Taking what's mine."

"Oh," she said when he put her on her feet in his room.

He turned around and locked the door. "I'm going to apologize, and you're going to listen. I was a jackass. I hurt you. I'm sorry. But now you're here." He grasped her upper arms. "Dressed like that... You look really great. Did you come here looking like that to punish me? Not that I don't deserve it. Just tell me. Do I have a chance with you?''

She smiled up at him. "Is Rachel really okay? Has she been adjusting well?" Her heart was beating out the "Minute Waltz"—in thirty seconds. Maxine had said not to accept—or turn down—his apology too fast.

Tony leaned down. "She misses you. *I* miss you. I'm sorry. I promise I won't ever hurt you again. Am I too late? Tell me." His voice dropped. "I love you." Lowering his head, he stopped at her mouth. "Tell me you forgive me. Tell me I'm not too late," he breathed on her lips.

Her heart pounded in her throat, making her voice raspy. "Do you really like my dress?"

Tony's weeklong arousal just got worse. He nodded.

She looked down, then slowly raised her eyelids. "It's so...so..."

"Tight," he said tensely. "You're not wearing a bra."

"I didn't know you could tell." She fluttered her eyelashes.

Tony's heart slammed against his ribs at the same moment he slammed his lips against hers. He pressed her back against the nearest wall. They both tore at his slacks, and finally heard the snizzle of the zipper as they succeeded in releasing him. Tony pulled up her dress and almost fell to his knees.

She wore only thigh-high stockings.

No panties.

He stared at her face. A smile of Eve's notoriety spread like melted butter across her lips.

Lifting her, he wrapped her legs around him and plunged into her. He continued thrusting into her, his arms banding around her while her legs and arms held on tight. He pushed aside the bodice of the dress and latched on to her beaded nipple. Drawing her into his mouth, he sucked on her.

She panted. She cried out. She begged.

He pounded into her, hard, against the wall.

They exploded together. Endlessly. Mindlessly.

Leaning his forehead against hers, Tony listened to her rapid breathing. It matched his. Slowly his senses returned. "I love you, Julia. I'm a jerk, and a barbarian, and I probably ruined your dress. I'm sorry. I was scared, I wasn't rational, I—"

She placed her fingers over his lips. "I forgive you for being a jerk."

"I'll take it. Anything. Just let me make it up to you." He brought her to his bed, and sat her on the edge. "Don't move."

He straightened his pants and walked to the bathroom. She was baffled, but she didn't move. When he came back, she would tell him that she forgave him, and still loved him.

To hell with Maxine's rules.

He returned with a damp washcloth and stood between her legs. "Since I'm the one who did this to you..." He gently pushed her onto her back and knelt between her legs. "I might as well start making it up to you now." Parting her, he used the cool, wet cloth to clean her.

Julia moaned. Her hips surged upward. When she thought she couldn't stand it any longer, he stopped. Her body slumped on the bed, and she pushed herself up on her elbows. Tony draped her legs over his shoulders. Before she could utter more than "Oh, my," he spread her and dipped his head.

His lips were on her, and the tip of his tongue flicked over her sensitive nub. Her second climax came in seconds, leaving her limp and panting.

He slowly stood. Leaning over her, Tony stared into her eyes. "I love you, Julia. I can't live without you. You are Rachel's mother. Stay with me. Most men say they won't beg, but I'm not stupid. You belong with me. Hell, you belong *to* me. Even fate agrees. Stay, Julia, and order me around for the rest of my born days."

His exaggerated western accent brought a smile to her face.

"Say you forgive me," he begged. "Tell me you love me."

He pulled out the small package from his shirt pocket and tugged the ribbon off. "I want you to fill my house with laughter and colors and children—ones we'll choose together to raise and love as our own. I want to grow old with you, and sit in our rocking chairs, on our porch, watching our grandchildren run around." Taking out a sapphire ring, he slid it onto her ring finger. "It matches your eyes." He kissed her hand. "Marry me. Your mother's getting married on the cruise. Let Christmas be *our* wedding date."

She didn't answer, but her smile slowly spread.

"Damn it, woman," he groaned. "There'll be people here in a few minutes. I mean to marry you, Julia, even if I have to stay up all night, locked with you in this room, until I convince you to marry me. So say yes, damn it!"

"Yes, damn it!—with a condition."

"What?"

"Convince me some more," she purred.

And, blessing fate, he did.

They showered quickly, Tony muttering something about "Finally feeling your body slide against mine." She let her hair down, scrunching it as it dried, making her waves more pronounced.

After Miss Irene returned with Tony's mother and Ra-

chel, she spent a half hour talking with Andrea alone. Then
Tony joined them, and Julia could see healing beginning
between him and his mother. It would be a long journey,
but at least it had a chance.

Now, as she helped Miss Irene put the finishing touches
on the food, the doorbell rang. Tony was getting Rachel,
so Julia answered the door, welcoming her mother and Josiah. Rose and Tom arrived next. Coats were hung up, and
everyone walked into the living room, where Andrea
waited.

After initial introductions, conversation flowed smoothly.
Miss Irene and George eventually joined them.

Julia knew the instant Tony showed up at the living room
archway, and she turned around. The sight of this tall man,
so dominant, so virile, holding a young baby so tenderly,
melted her heart. As if he knew he cast a spell on her, his
eyes never left her face. She felt herself growing warmer.

Rachel broke the spell. "Mamamamamama!" Her plump
legs kicked. She leaned forward, her arms stretched toward
Julia.

Julia walked toward the two them and lifted the baby
into her arms. "Hello, sweetness."

Tony draped an arm over her shoulder. "You look rav-
ishing, or—" he dropped his voice "—is that ravished?"
She jabbed an elbow into his ribs. He chuckled. "Thanks
for convincing me to invite our friends. Having them here
does help."

"You gave me the idea when you mentioned inviting
everyone here for Thanksgiving."

His eyes glowed. "But only you would make that idea
into a reality. I told you you'd turn my world topsey-
turvey."

"Is that a complaint?" she teased.

"Do I look unhappy?"

"If you looked any happier, people would think you were punch-drunk." She leaned against his side, and felt his fingers tighten on her waist.

Their friends eyed them both, those familiar smiles on their faces. Only this time Julia understood from where the smiles came.

The doorbell rang again. Tony ushered in two men who Julia recognized as Matt, taller and leaner than his twin brother Nick, who was muscularly broad, with a jovial expression. Greetings were exchanged. Andrea hurried over and kissed them both.

Tony called Julia over and pulled her closer to his side, anchoring her with an arm of steel. "Julia, it's time you formally met my brothers."

Nick bowed. "Now I see why it's been so hard to get you back east. With women like this out here, I might buy me a ranch and relocate."

Matt rolled his eyes. "I can see it now, one of New York's finest lassoing an outlaw on the ten-most-wanted list."

"And," Tony said to Matt, "after he's got himself a prisoner, you, a highfalutin' lawman, can come out and hang 'em."

"You're losing your touch, Tony. Why haven't you married this woman yet?" Nick asked loudly.

The room fell quiet.

Julia chucked Rachel beneath her chin, the sapphire on her ring finger sparkling brilliantly. She looked up at Tony, love radiating from her eyes. Tony winked at her. "Funny you should mention that, Nick," he said, and squeezed Julia's waist.

Epilogue

"Whoa, Shadow!"

The descending sun blazed brightly. Julia shaded her eyes as her handsome husband dismounted his horse and strode onto the porch toward her. His jeans molded to his muscular legs, and his flannel shirt hid the rippling muscles only she knew so well. Her insides tightened in an anticipation of his touch that had not diminished one iota over nearly two years of married life. If anything, it had been enhanced measurably.

He raked his eyes over her, his face dark with desire. "It was a mistake to ever let you buy a new wardrobe."

Julia stood slowly from the chair and ran her hands down her body, over the dark blue sweater that molded to her breasts, and down her thighs, tightly encased in her jeans.

He growled and hauled her to his dust-clad body, kissing her thoroughly. "Now, this is how a man should be greeted after a hard day breaking in stallions!"

"Or signing another stud contract?"

"Well, now that you mention it..." She took a step back and placed her fists on her hips. He held his hands up, palms facing her. "Don't go getting your feathers in an uproar."

She wagged a finger at him. "Listen, *Manhattan* Bill Cody—"

Grabbing her, he ground his hips against hers. "I surrender." He kissed her. "Definitely surrender."

"Later, dear," she purred. Laughter leaked from behind the porch door. "Come on out, you little criminals," Julia called.

"Jimmy don't have coat," a small voice announced.

"Jimmy *doesn't* have his coat," Julia corrected, opening the door. "It's okay, Rachel. It's one of those wonderful Indian summers I told you about. He'll be warm enough in his jumper." Rachel walked out, dragging her new brother by the hand.

"It is warm for December," Tony agreed, and scooped up his fourteen-month-old son and twenty-nine-month-old daughter. "And you, missy—you're certainly talking up a storm."

Rachel nodded, wide-eyed, and pointed at her younger brother. "Jimmy eat dirp."

"Dirp?" Tony's eyebrows rose, and he shot a look at Julia. "Another one of your culinary experiments?"

"Dirt, Tony, dirt," she replied dryly.

He nodded, slowly. "Oh. Run out of strained peas?"

She playfully socked him in the arm and took the curly-haired boy, bouncing him on her hip. "Did you get the mail?"

"Yup." He eyed her curiously. "You got some power to send that fate of yours to toy with others?"

"Why?"

"Well, we got a letter from Chris. Seems he and Maxine

have settled their differences. They want us to be best man and matron of honor at their wedding."

Jimmy pulled off Julia's glasses and waved them in the air. "I can't believe it," she said, retrieving them.

"From what he's written, I take it Maxine can't, either. She keeps saying, 'Who'da thunk it?'" They laughed.

Rachel grabbed Tony's nose. "Daddy, Jimmy brudder?"

He glanced at Julia while rubbing his nose. "Yes, sweetness. He's your brother and you're his sister. Is that okay?"

Rachel sucked her thumb and stared at Jimmy. Originally from one of Casper's poorer neighborhoods, the honeyskinned boy had formed a deep, instant attachment to Rachel when he first arrived, three months ago. It had been just after Mitch signed the papers relinquishing guardianship over Rachel. Having Jimmy here had been a slightly hard adjustment for the outspoken girl to make, because she'd been the sole recipient of her parent's attention for so long.

"Rachel love brudder." She wiggled out of her father's embrace, and scrambled up the chair near Julia. Placing a wet, noisy kiss on her sibling's pudgy leg, she said, "Love brudder."

Jimmy squealed and tried to grabbed her.

Tony's eyes brightened. "This is the first time she's acknowledged his place in our family."

"Without wanting to send him back," Julia added beneath her breath.

"Right. Family. God, I love that word." Tony held up a second letter. "It's from my mother. She'd like to come out for another visit." He smiled gently. "It'll be her third this year, and just in time for our anniversary."

"That's great. With my mother on another honeymoon cruise with Josiah, and with Miss Irene's hands full just keeping the house from tumbling around our ears, I can use the extra help.'' She moved closer to Tony. ''Especially if we get the Valesquez baby. He's only four months old.'' Tony's eyes widened. ''They called. The paperwork is being expedited.''

''Yahoo!'' Tony shouted, and threw his hat on the ground. He grabbed Rachel and spun her around. She giggled. Jimmy's body moved excitedly, his legs jerking out.

''I'll write to Mother to come, then,'' he said when he calmed down. He looked first at Julia, then at Jimmy, and finally at Rachel. ''And to think, it was all for the love of Rachel that I have a family for Christmas.'' He brushed Julia's cheek with the back of his knuckles, then pulled her and his children into a family hug.

Thank you.

Julia mouthed the words silently up to the heavens, then leaned into her husband's embrace, the setting Wyoming sun showering them both with all the colors of life.

* * * * *

Take 4 bestselling love stories FREE

Plus get a FREE surprise gift!

Welcome to the Towers!

In January
New York Times bestselling author

NORA ROBERTS

takes us to the fabulous Maine coast mansion
haunted by a generations-old secret and introduces
us to the fascinating family that lives there.

Mechanic Catherine "C.C." Calhoun and hotel magnate
Trenton St. James mix like axle grease and mineral
water—until they kiss. Efficient Amanda Calhoun finds
easygoing Sloan O'Riley insufferable—and irresistible.
And they all must race to solve the mystery
surrounding a priceless hidden emerald necklace.

Catherine and Amanda

THE Calhoun Women

**A special 2-in-1 edition containing
COURTING CATHERINE and A MAN FOR AMANDA.**

Look for the next installment of
THE CALHOUN WOMEN with Lilah and Suzanna's
stories, coming in March 1998.

Available at your favorite retail outlet.

Silhouette®

As seen on TV!
Free Gift Offer

With a Free Gift proof-of-purchase from any Silhouette® book, you can receive a beautiful cubic zirconia pendant.

This gorgeous marquise-shaped stone is a genuine cubic zirconia—accented by an 18" gold tone necklace.

(Approximate retail value $19.95)

Send for yours today...
compliments of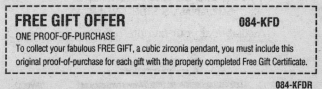

To receive your free gift, a cubic zirconia pendant, send us one original proof-of-purchase, photocopies not accepted, from the back of any Silhouette Romance™, Silhouette Desire®, Silhouette Special Edition®, Silhouette Intimate Moments® or Silhouette Yours Truly™ title available at your favorite retail outlet, together with the Free Gift Certificate, plus a check or money order for $1.65 U.S./$2.15 CAN. (do not send cash) to cover postage and handling, payable to Silhouette Free Gift Offer. We will send you the specified gift. Allow 6 to 8 weeks for delivery. Offer good until December 31, 1997, or while quantities last. Offer valid in the U.S. and Canada only.

Free Gift Certificate

Name: _____

Address: _____

City: _____ State/Province: _____ Zip/Postal Code: _____

Mail this certificate, one proof-of-purchase and a check or money order for postage and handling to: SILHOUETTE FREE GIFT OFFER 1997. In the U.S.: 3010 Walden Avenue, P.O. Box 9077, Buffalo NY 14269-9077. In Canada: P.O. Box 613, Fort Erie, Ontario L2Z 5X3.

FREE GIFT OFFER   084-KFD
ONE PROOF-OF-PURCHASE
To collect your fabulous FREE GIFT, a cubic zirconia pendant, you must include this original proof-of-purchase for each gift with the properly completed Free Gift Certificate.

084-KFDR

Return to the Towers!

In March
New York Times bestselling author

NORA ROBERTS

brings us to the Calhouns' fabulous
Maine coast mansion and reveals the
tragic secrets hidden there for generations.

For all his degrees, Professor Max Quartermain has a
lot to learn about love—and luscious Lilah Calhoun is
just the woman to teach him. Ex-cop Holt Bradford is
as prickly as a thornbush—until Suzanna Calhoun's
special touch makes love blossom in his heart.
And all of them are caught in the race to solve
the generations-old mystery of a priceless
lost necklace…and a timeless love.

Lilah and Suzanna
THE Calhoun Women

**A special 2-in-1 edition containing
FOR THE LOVE OF LILAH and
SUZANNA'S SURRENDER**

Available at your favorite retail outlet.

Silhouette®

Look us up on-line at: http://www.romance.net

CWVOL2

Available in February 1998

ANN MAJOR

CHILDREN OF DESTINY
When Passion and Fate Intertwine...

SECRET CHILD

Although everyone told Jack West that his wife,
Chantal—the woman who'd betrayed him and sent
him to prison for a crime he didn't commit—had
died, Jack knew she'd merely transformed herself
into supermodel Mischief Jones. But when he
finally captured the woman he'd been hunting,
she denied everything. Who was she really—
an angel or a cunningly brilliant counterfeit?"

"Want it all? Read Ann Major."
—Nora Roberts, *New York Times*
bestselling author

Don't miss this compelling story
available at your favorite retail outlet.
Only from Silhouette books.

▼ *Silhouette*®
™